CROSSFIRE

a J.T. Ryan Thriller

A Novel
By

Lee Gimenez

RRP

River Ridge Press

CROSSFIRE
by
Lee Gimenez

Printed in the United States of America.

Published by
River Ridge Press
P.O. Box 501173
Atlanta, Georgia 31150

First edition.

Cover photos: Copyright by Zoom Team
used under license from Shutterstock, Inc.

Cover design: Judith Gimenez

ISBN-13: 978-0-578-54037-5

ISBN-10: 0-578-54037-5

Other Novels by Lee Gimenez

Fireball

FBI Code Red

The Media Murders

Skyflash

Killing West

The Washington Ultimatum

Blacksnow Zero

The Sigma Conspiracy

The Nanotech Murders

Death on Zanath

Virtual Thoughtstream

Azul 7

Terralus 4

The Tomorrow Solution

Lee Gimenez

CROSSFIRE

a J.T. Ryan Thriller

Lee Gimenez

Chapter 1

Atlanta, Georgia

Feeling energized by the death that was about to happen, the sniper peered through his rifle's scope and adjusted the crosshairs. Although his target was in an office building a half-mile away, the custom-made scope allowed him to see clearly into the man's office on the tenth floor. The target, a tall, heavyset man was at his desk reading a report.

Using his laser finder and a small computer, the sniper made a few final adjustments to account for wind speed and direction. Then he slowed his breathing and slid his finger past the trigger guard until it rested on the trigger itself. He was using a Barrett M107, a high-precision, long-range rifle that was the weapon of choice for those in his profession.

He slowed his breathing even more, took another moment to zero in on the target, and gently pulled the trigger. The suppressed rifle coughed. A split-second later the armor-piercing round cracked the bullet-resistant window a half mile away.

The target's head exploded.

Then his lifeless body slumped forward on his desk and blood began to pool under his head.

Chapter 2

St. Croix
The U.S. Virgin Islands
the Caribbean

It was a sunny, cloudless sky, the temperature in the mid-seventies. The sky was a deep azure blue and the shoreline was crystal clear surf.

Another perfect day in paradise, John (J.T.) Ryan thought, as he exited the cottage and began walking toward the secluded beach. He noticed Rachel was already there, lounging on a chaise, sipping a drink. Ryan had booked the cottage for a week; the bungalow was part of a resort comprised of golf courses, tennis courts, several pools, restaurants, and miles-long beaches of sparkling sand.

Ryan almost reached the beach when his cell phone vibrated in his swim trunk pocket. Pulling it out, he answered the call.

"Ryan here."

"It's Erin," he heard the woman say.

"Erin," he replied with a chuckle. "My favorite ADIC." Erin was the Assistant Director in charge of the FBI's Atlanta office.

Erin sighed, used to his attempts at humor "How many ADICs do you know, J.T.?"

"Besides you? None."

"Then I guess the fact I'm your favorite isn't much of a compliment."

Ryan laughed. "You got me there. Why are you calling?"

"I'm working on a new case and I need your help."

Ryan was a former Special Forces soldier turned private investigator who did security work for law-enforcement agencies.

"My usual fee?" he asked.

There was no response and Ryan could visualize the FBI woman frowning. Finally she said, "Yes. Your usual fee. High as they are."

The PI grinned. "I'm worth it. Otherwise you wouldn't hire me."

"All right, smartass. Enough banter."

"What's the case about, Erin?"

"A high-profile murder. It happened yesterday. Here in Atlanta."

"Who's the DB?"

"The president of Face-Look. The big social media company located here in the city."

Ryan let out a low whistle. "That is high-profile. How was he killed?"

"He was assassinated. From what we've been able to piece together, he was shot by a sniper using a high-powered rifle."

"Any clues?"

"None so far, J.T. That's why I need you on this case. Your unorthodox methods are good at ferreting out information."

"Okay, I'll take the job. But I just got to St. Croix. I'm on vacation. I'll be back in Atlanta in a week."

"I need you here now," Erin said, her voice hard.

Ryan gazed toward the beach and saw Rachel waving at him. She looked delectable in her red bikini.

"No can do," he replied. "Like I said, I'm on vacation. I'll see you in a week."

"That's not good enough."

"Listen, Erin. I like working for you. And the FBI cases you've given me are some of the best work I've done as a PI. But Rachel and I have postponed this vacation too many times."

"I'm not going to change your mind, am I?," she said, a resigned tone in her voice.

"I'm afraid not. But don't worry, I'll be back next week. I'll come to your office the day I get back, okay?"

"All right, J.T."

He hung up the phone and slipped it in the pocket of his swim trunks. Then he strode the short distance to the beach, his bare feet sinking into the warm sand. He sat on a lounge chair next to Rachel's.

She rested her drink on a side table. "Who was that on the phone?"

"Erin from the FBI."

Rachel gave him a worried glance. "Does that mean ...."

"No, beautiful. I told Erin I wasn't going to cancel my vacation." He smiled. "I'll work on the case when I get back."

Her expression brightened and she returned the smile. "That's a relief." She caressed his arm and her smile turned mischievous. "We've got a lot of catching up to do, you and me."

Ryan gave her a long look, taking in her intoxicating beauty. She was a tall, lean, and curvaceous woman in her mid-thirties. With long blonde hair, sparkling blue eyes, and classic good looks, she resembled a model. Besides her looks, she also had a razor-sharp mind and a vivacious wit.

Ryan pointed toward her red bikini, which did little to conceal her curves. "Since you're a CIA operative, you must be working undercover. But looking at your swimsuit, you're barely undercover."

Rachel laughed. "You play your cards right and you may get to see a lot more."

He grinned and they held hands. Then they both looked out toward the rolling surf a few feet away. Ryan felt more at ease and content than he had in a long time.

The warm sun and light breeze lulled him into sleep.

He awoke with a start sometime later and heard the clatter of machinery in the distance. Looking around the secluded beach, he saw nothing except palm trees, rolling surf, and the white sandy beach.

As the sound grew louder, he got up from the lounge chair and shielded his eyes from the bright sun to get a better look.

"What is it?" Rachel asked. "What's that noise?"

Then he spotted it, a black helicopter flying low toward their location. He pointed. "Chopper. Could be military."

Rachel stood next to him as they watched the helicopter land on the relatively flat beach. The rotor wash sprayed sand in all directions.

As the craft powered down, Ryan noticed there were no markings on the chopper, which was a Sikorsky Black Hawk. Its bay door opened and three men climbed out and began trudging towards them, their boots sinking into the sand. All three were wearing U.S. Army fatigues, with Military Police markings on their uniforms. The PI noticed they also had holstered sidearms.

When they were a few feet away, one of the men approached Ryan. "I'm Lieutenant Holder," he said. "Are you John Taylor Ryan?"

"Yes. I'm J.T. Ryan. What's this about?"

"You need to come with us, sir."

"You haven't answered my question, Lieutenant. What's this about?"

"Sir, that will all be explained later. It's a matter of national security. You just need to come with us."

"I'm not going anywhere until I get some answers."

Ryan noticed the MP's hands moved and rested on the butts of their holstered pistols.

"We can do this the easy way," the lieutenant said, "or the hard way. It's totally up to you, sir."

Ryan glared at him, then glanced at Rachel who looked bewildered.

"This is not a request," the lieutenant added. "It's an order."

Angry and confused, Ryan balled his fists.

"You better go," Rachel said in a quiet voice. "You have no choice, J.T."

The PI took a deep breath and let it out slowly. "All right, damn it."

The MPs escorted him to the helicopter and they climbed inside.

The rotor blades spooled faster and the engines whined to a loud roar. The chopper lifted off and seconds later receded into the horizon.

Chapter 3

The Pentagon
U.S. Department of Defense
Washington, D.C.

After a five hour flight from St. Croix to D.C. on a military transport jet, J.T. Ryan had been escorted to the small conference room he was in now.

The three MPs who had put him in the helicopter were still with him, posted outside the conference room. On the flight he had been given food and a change of clothes, but none of his questions had been answered.

Ten minutes later the door to the conference room opened and an Army officer wearing his Class A blue uniform stepped inside. Closing the door behind him, he extended his hand to Ryan. "I'm General Keating."

As they shook hands, Keating said, "Please have a seat, Mr. Ryan."

They sat across from each other at the conference table and Ryan said, "Am I under arrest?"

The general gave him a wry smile. "Of course not." The man was tall and wiry, with close-cropped sandy hair, and looked to be in his mid-fifties. He was a brigadier, a one-star general, and from his military ribbons Ryan knew the man had been posted to a long list of duty stations.

"I'm sorry about the abrupt flight," Keating said. "But in light of recent events, we needed to brief you as soon as possible."

Ryan nodded, relieved he wasn't under arrest, but still confused why he was there. "In that case, General, I'd appreciate an explanation. The MP said it was a matter of national security?"

"That's correct, Ryan. It is." The man leaned forward in his chair. "Everything I'm going to tell you is classified Top Secret. Is that understood?"

"Yes, General."

"All right. Yesterday the president of Face-Look was murdered. Have you heard about this?"

"Actually yes. The FBI has already hired me to work on that, when I get back to Atlanta."

Keating gave him a hard look. "Have they now? Well, our investigation takes priority over that."

Ryan waved a hand in the air as if to encompass the whole room. "What's the Pentagon's interest in this murder?"

"I'll get to that in a moment. Are you familiar with the DIA?"

The PI nodded. "The Defense Intelligence Agency? Sure. The DIA is the military's version of the CIA."

"That's correct. I'm with the DIA. In fact, I'm second in command. And I'm heading up the Face-Look investigation."

"Sir, why is the DIA so interested in this? I would think the FBI would be the best organization to handle a case involving a private company."

"Under normal circumstances you would be correct, Ryan. But we've had Face-Look on our radar for quite some time. We've been monitoring them for years. Do you know much about them?"

"I know they're a large social media company."

Keating nodded. "Not just large, but the biggest. They're larger than Twitter, or Instagram, or Facebook."

"Okay, I'm with you so far. But I still don't see the military's interest."

"Face-Look," the general continued, "has a worldwide audience of 2.2 billion people. And all of these people give up much of their privacy when they join social media networks. They share personal details, photos, posts, friends lists, family names, etc. They take polls online, read news items, find products to buy, and message friends. And all of this vast amount of information is kept in Face-Look's computer databanks for practically forever."

"Face-Look," the general added, "has become the largest intelligence gathering organization in the world."

"I didn't realize how widespread and intrusive they were," Ryan said. "I'm not into social media very much myself. I'm too busy with my PI work."

Keating steepled his hands in front of him. "Normally this intelligence gathering is benign. They store the information about people and it is kept private. But we at the DIA have become concerned that if all of this data falls into the wrong hands, the results could be catastrophic. The potential for blackmail, corruption, and criminal activity is vast."

The general paused as Ryan realized the ominous implications of what the man had just said.

"And now that Face-Look's president has been murdered," Keating continued, "we've decided to become directly involved."

"I understand, sir. But why do you need me, General? I'm sure you have military people who can carry out the investigation."

"That's true. We do. But having you investigate this case has several advantages. First, you're based in Atlanta, where Face-Look's headquarters is located. So you know the area well. Second, we need a civilian face to head this up. The DIA is a secretive organization – we don't want it known that we're interested. And the third reason is obvious – you're former military – you're familiar with our ways."

Ryan nodded. "I can appreciate that, sir. But I've already committed to working on this for the FBI. I can't walk away from that."

Keating waved that away. "You can still keep them in the loop. As long as you understand you work for the DIA. We take priority."

"I don't know about this, General. My whole business as a PI is based on the work I do for the FBI, Homeland Security, and other law-enforcement agencies. I don't want to jeopardize that."

Keating grimaced. "You have no choice, Ryan. This is not a request. I'm giving you a direct order."

"What are you talking about, sir? I left the Army years ago."

The general pointed an index finger at him. "Don't force my hand. Accept this job or you will regret it."

Ryan's blood pressure rose and his hands balled into fists. "With all due respect, sir, what the hell does that mean?"

Keating had brought with him a thick file folder, which he opened now. "This is your U.S. Army service record, Ryan. Very impressive. You served as an Airborne Ranger, then a Green Beret, then finally in Delta Force, Tier 1. The most elite of the Special Forces, even more elite than the Navy SEALS. You received numerous commendations for valor in combat including a Purple Heart and a Silver Star. You were even awarded the Medal of Honor. Impressive stuff."

The general paused, then said, "You left the Army with the rank of Captain. But if you hadn't been such a smartass in the military, I'm sure you would have been promoted to Major or even Colonel."

Keating paused again and he removed a sheaf of papers from the file and slid them across the table toward the PI. "There's a clause in your Army enlistment contract, Ryan, which you signed years ago. The clause is in small print at the every back of contract. I'm sure you never read it – most people don't."

The general gave him a tight, hard grin. "The clause stipulates that in times of a national security need, the Army can re-activate you back into the military. All it takes is a General officer, such as myself, to invoke that national security need."

Ryan had been unaware of the clause in his contract. But as he quickly scanned the document, its meaning was now crystal clear.

General Keating's hard grin remained on his face. "Welcome back to the Army, Captain Ryan."

Chapter 4

Tokyo, Japan

The Asian woman picked up the handset of her desk phone and pressed the encryption button. Then she tapped in a phone number she had committed to memory long ago.

A man answered on the second ring. "Yes?"

"It's me," she said in flawless English. She was Japanese, but spoke five different languages. "The operation has begun. We took the first step in Atlanta."

"Excellent." The man paused a moment. "Is everything else on schedule?"

"Yes."

"Very good. Keep me informed as things progress."

"Of course." She disconnected the call and hung up.

Standing, she went to a corner of her large, luxuriously appointed office. She was an avid chess player and had installed a life-size chess set in that part of the room. The intricately carved ceramic pieces all resembled Samurai warriors from 17th century Japan. She pushed one of the smaller, but still heavy figurines forward two squares. That particular game opening move was called Pawn-to-King-four. She smiled. *It'll be awhile before I can claim Checkmate. The important thing is the game's begun.*

Then she went to a teak cabinet and poured herself a large tumbler of Chivas Regal scotch. Turning around, she faced the floor-to-ceiling windows of her office.

The room, located on the top floor of the skyscraper, gave her a panoramic view of Tokyo's ultra-modern skyline. It was nighttime and the rows and rows of high-rise buildings were lit up in a riot of neon light.

The woman sipped the scotch and mulled over her next steps.

Chapter 5

FBI Field Office
Atlanta, Georgia

Erin Welch heard a knock at her door and glanced up from her laptop.

J.T. Ryan was standing at her office entrance, a worried look on his handsome face. Erin closed the lid on her laptop.

"Come in, J.T. Have a seat."

The man took one of the visitor's chairs fronting her desk.

"Didn't expect you back until next week," she said.

Ryan frowned. "My vacation was cut short."

"What happened?"

"It's a long story."

Erin studied the tall, good-looking man in his late thirties. He was 6'4" and powerfully built, with a weightlifter's physique. He had close-cropped brown hair and brown eyes. As usual he was wearing a blue blazer, slacks, and a white, buttoned-down shirt. He looked tired, as if he hadn't had much sleep.

"What, no banter? No smartass comments?" she said, amazed he hadn't already cracked one of his lame jokes.

"Not today."

"Okay, J.T. You ready to work my case?"

Ryan nodded. "I am. But I need to tell you something before I start. I've got another boss on this besides you."

"What do you mean?"

"I've been reactivated back into the Army."

"How's that possible?"

Ryan grimaced. "Some bullshit clause in my enlistment contract. Like I said, it's a long story. I'm not happy about it, but it is what it is."

"Now I understand your sour mood. What's the military's interest in this case?"

"They've been monitoring Face-Look for some time. They're concerned with the immense data gathering capability of the social media company. When their top executive was murdered, they decided to get more involved."

Erin nodded. "All right."

She opened a desk drawer and took out a file which she handed to Ryan. "In here's the information we have on the murder. The FBI and police reports, the coroner's findings, and CSI information."

Ryan opened the folder and scanned the details. "Not much here."

"You're right, J.T. It was a professional hit. They left virtually no clues behind."

The man closed the folder and stood. "In that case, I'll get to work."

"What's your first stop?"

"The morgue."

Chapter 6

Fulton County Morgue
Atlanta, Georgia

J.T. Ryan drove his Ford Explorer out of the FBI building's underground lot and headed south. A short while later he pulled into the parking lot of the morgue on Pryor Street.

He went through the building's security checkpoint and was shown into the non-descript office of the Medical Examiner. As usual, the whole building smelled of strong antiseptic, the cleaning solvent masking, but not quite erasing the pungent stench of human decomp.

Ryan shook hands with the M.E. and took a chair facing his desk. Ryan had been here many times and knew the man well.

"So, J.T., what brings you here today?" Doctor Mallory asked. The M.E. was a gaunt-looking man with oval wire-rimmed eyeglasses and a pallid complexion.

Ryan leaned forward in the chair. "I'm investigating the murder of Matthew Ross, the CEO of Face-Look."

"Of course."

"You've completed the autopsy, doc?"

"I have." Mallory opened a desk drawer, took out a file, and opened it. "My findings are very straightforward. Ross died of a massive head wound. The bullet that shattered his skull came from a high-powered weapon."

"Could you determine the caliber of the round?"

"Not exactly. But I could give you an educated guess, considering we process an average of 2,500 deaths a year in this building."

Ryan nodded. "Go ahead. You've never steered me wrong before."

"The bullet cracked a shatter-proof window and then penetrated Ross's head. As you can imagine, all we found were the bullet's fragments. But my conclusion is that it was a .50 caliber round."

The PI rubbed his jaw. "That means a very-sophisticated, high-end rifle was used. The type used by professional snipers. No question this was a well-planned assassination."

"I agree, J.T." Doctor Mallory closed the file folder. "Anything else I can tell you?"

"I want to see the body."

"You sure? I know you've got a strong stomach, but this is gruesome."

"I'm sure. I may pick up some clues."

"All right. But I have to make this quick. I've got three more cadavers to process today."

"Don't worry, doc. Those folks aren't going anywhere."

Mallory frowned at Ryan's attempt at levity. He stood and said, "Follow me and I'll take you back there."

The M.E. led Ryan down a long, white-tiled corridor and moments later they entered what the building's employees referred to as the 'meat locker'. It was the storage area where cadavers were kept after autopsies. The room was kept at a frigid 36 degrees and Ryan shivered from the cold.

Mallory strode past a long row of stainless-steel freezer lockers and stopped in front of one of them. He opened the locker door and slid out the metal shelf. Then he removed the sheet covering the corpse and stood aside so that the PI could see.

Ryan had witnessed his share of death, while in combat and later in law-enforcement, but he still swallowed hard. The M.E. had been correct in his assessment – it was a gruesome sight. The dead man's head had literally been blown off. All that remained were bloody chunks of brain matter and skin tissue and cracked skull fragments. His neck resembled raw hamburger meat.

Ryan inspected the cadaver for another minute, then turned back to the M.E. "You can close it up."

Mallory nodded, covered the body with the sheet, and slid the metal tray into the wall.

They left the frigid room and Ryan exited the building, knowing the gruesome sight would haunt his dreams for several days.

Chapter 7

Downtown
Atlanta, Georgia

After reading the FBI report Erin had given him, Ryan pulled out a paper map from his SUV's glove box and studied it carefully. The map, which was a detailed diagram of the downtown area and its nearby surroundings, showed the avenues and all of the side streets. It also identified the numerous high-rises that comprised Atlanta's skyline.

A half-hour later he folded up the map, put it away, and fired up his Explorer. Then he spent the next three hours driving through the areas south of downtown, scouting out possible locations where the sniper had taken the shot. After stopping at multiple buildings to determine a likely sight line, he spotted an abandoned structure about a half-mile from the Face-Look skyscraper.

He parked at the curb, got out, and studied the fifteen-story building, which appeared to be an office complex. It was partially finished – no windows or doors were in place, its construction most likely halted years ago due to lack of financing.

Ryan took out a rucksack from his SUV's hatch and went inside the deserted, dim interior. Using a flashlight, he made his way around the first floor, which was covered with cobwebs and dust. He found a concrete staircase at one side of the space and began climbing the stairs to the tenth floor.

When he got there, he noticed it was a wide-open area, with only support beams in place. He headed toward the north part of it, and stopped just shy of where the glass windows would normally be installed. A light breeze was blowing, swirling dust into the room. He gazed out toward downtown Atlanta.

Taking out a pair of binoculars, he focused on the Face-Look headquarters building a half-mile away. The murdered man's office had been on the tenth floor and thru his binos the PI could clearly see the plywood that now covered the shattered window of his office.

It's a perfect sight line.

Realizing this was an excellent location for the sniper to take his shot, Ryan spent the next hour scouring the large, open space, looking for disturbed areas.

He found it eventually, a spot near the edge of the floor where the windows would normally be. Footprints and other fresh marks were evident on the otherwise dust-covered floor.

He looked for shell casings but found none. *The sniper was a pro. He cleaned up his brass after taking the shot.*

The PI had brought with him a small CSI kit, which he took out of his rucksack. Erin had given him the kit years ago. Although Ryan was not a crime scene expert, he knew enough to carry out several procedures.

Opening the kit, he took out fingerprint tape and DNA tools and started collecting samples from the disturbed area of the dusty floor. That done, he took photos of the footprints. Satisfied he'd collected as much evidence as he could, he packed up the CSI kit. He'd call Erin when he got back to his vehicle to schedule her techs to come out to the scene and do a more thorough job.

Then he made his way down the stairs and headed back to his SUV.

Chapter 8

Salt Lake City, Utah

The man was driving south on Interstate 15, away from the city. The car ahead of him, a gray Lexus sedan, was doing sixty.

The man realized the Lexus was pulling away from him and he floored the accelerator of the big rig he was driving, a Mack semi truck. The truck's large diesel engine growled, it's twin smokestacks spewed a burst of black dust, and the hulking vehicle surged forward.

The man peered into the distance ahead of him, then glanced at his rearview mirrors. There was no traffic on the mostly deserted interstate.

The timing's right. Almost perfect.

He cut the rig's steering wheel left and slid into the passing lane. He kept his foot jammed on the accelerator, the semi picking up speed. The speedometer ticked up. 65 mph. 70 mph, and he was alongside the Lexus.

The man eased off the accelerator and glanced down at the gray sedan, which was dwarfed by the massive truck. He cut the wheel to the right, the big rig edging closer to the car.

For a brief moment he caught the Lexus driver's wide-eyed look of panic, as he realized what was about to happen. The truck driver felt energized by the terrified look. He cut the wheel even further right and the two vehicles collided.

The scraping metal howled, the car's windshield exploded, and its tires shredded. The 5,000 pound Lexus was no match for the 80,000 pound truck and the car was thrown off the interstate, it spun 360 degrees, and crashed head-on into a rocky formation by the road, one of the many rock-strewn buttes that covered large parts of the mountainous state of Utah.

The semi, barely scathed from the collision, kept driving south.

The driver slowed the vehicle and glanced into the rearview just as the gas tank of the Lexus exploded, a ball of fire engulfing the crushed remains of the car.

He sped up again, wanting to quickly put distance between himself and the crash scene.

Half an hour later he pulled off the interstate, slowed the big rig, and stopped. Climbing out of the stolen truck, he started jogging away from it toward his own vehicle, which he'd hidden behind a butte. Ten minutes later he got in his Jeep. He took a swig of water from his canteen and pulled out his SAT cell phone. Turning it on, he pressed the encryption button and tapped in an international phone number.

When the woman answered, he said, "It's done."

"You've taken care of our Utah problem?" she asked in flawless English.

"Yes."

"Excellent."

"When can I expect payment?"

"I'll wire you the money today," she said.

"Good. Will you have other work for me?"

There was no answer for a moment, then the woman said, "I'm sure I will. I'll text you the details."

He heard a click on the line and realized she had hung up.

Chapter 9

Tokyo, Japan

The Asian woman hung up the call and placed the handset on the cradle of her desk phone. She smiled, pleased at the news she'd just heard. The operation was on track.

Standing, she went around her desk and strode to the life-size chess set in a corner of her massive, luxurious office. Going behind one of the intricately-carved ceramic pieces, she pushed it forward two spaces and then one space to the left. Each of the chess pieces resembled 17th century Japanese warriors. The one she had moved now, a white Knight, was her favorite chess piece because of its ability to penetrate deep into enemy lines.

Satisfied the board resembled the operation's current progress, she turned around and faced the far wall of the room. Attached to the wall was a huge flat-screen television. Picking up a remote, she turned on the TV and selected channel 13. On this channel she could monitor the activity at the businesses she owned.

Clicking the remote, she scrolled through multiple live images of industrial operations, finally settling on one. Displayed on the screen was a large room with hundreds of employees diligently working at their computer workstations.

The Asian woman zoomed in for a closer look at several of the employees. She finally stopped when she spotted one of her favorites. He was a strapping young man in his mid-twenties. He was good, very good in fact, at following directions and had given her much pleasure in bed. The operation was going so well that she had decided to give herself a special treat.

She zoomed in closer with the TV remote so she could read his employee ID number, which was stenciled below his name on his badge. Turning off the TV, she went to her desk and picked up the phone.

"Yes?" her young assistant answered on the first ring.

"Bring me employee number 38726," the Asian woman said in Japanese.

"Of course. When do you want me to do that?"

"Now!" the Asian woman snapped. "Now, you idiot. What did you think?"

"Yes, ma'am."

She slammed down the phone, irritated be her assistant's incompetence. Then she went to her teak cabinet and poured herself a large tumbler of scotch. Taking a sip of the liquor, her thoughts turned to the strapping young man from her factory.

Yes, she thought, a smile forming on her lips. *He will be a welcome diversion.* She had been putting in eighty hour weeks preparing for the operation and was looking forward to a few hours or relaxation.

Chapter 10

FBI Field Office
Atlanta, Georgia

"Good job on finding where the sniper took the shot," Erin Welch said. "My agents and Atlanta PD had been looking for that spot for days and came up empty."

J.T. Ryan grinned. "I told you I was good."

Erin rolled her eyes. "Don't let it go to your head. It's already too big as it is."

Ryan laughed. He had just come into her office and he approached her desk and placed a large manila envelope on top of it. "The evidence I collected at that building is in here."

"All right. I'll have my lab guys process it, along with anything else my CSI unit finds at the scene."

Ryan sat at one of the chairs fronting her desk. "So. Do I get a bonus?"

Erin frowned. "For what?"

He pointed to the envelope. "For getting that."

"Keep dreaming," the FBI woman said with a frown. "Your rates are too high as it is."

Ryan chuckled. "Just kidding."

She gave him a long, stern look, then her expression softened. "I should know you by now. You never stop joking around, do you?"

Ryan grinned again. "I do when there's a gun pointed at my face."

She moved aside the jacket she was wearing, revealing the Glock pistol holstered at her hip. She grinned back. "Don't tempt me, buster."

They both laughed and Ryan studied the attractive brunette, who as usual was dressed impeccably. She was wearing an expensive Ralph Lauren business suit, a dove-gray silk blouse, and Louboutin four inch heels.

The PI leaned forward in his chair and in a serious tone said, "So, what's next?"

"A few days ago I interviewed the man who's now in charge of Face-Look. He's the Executive Vice-President of the company. He seemed perplexed as to why the CEO was murdered. I didn't get anything of value from him. But I'd like you to take a run at him. Maybe you'll have better luck."

"Okay, Erin. Do you think he had any involvement in the killing?"

She shook her head. "I don't think so. But some people seem beyond reproach at first and turn out to be con-men or worse."

Ryan nodded.

She reached into a desk drawer, took out a sheaf of papers, and handed them to him. "Here are my notes and other info about this guy."

He took the sheets, scanned them, and rose. "I'll get going then."

"Okay. But a word of caution, J.T. This guy is a powerful man in the business world. He has a lot of contacts. Some, I'm sure, are high-up in government circles. Don't go in there and pull one of your Rambo stunts." She gave him an icy stare. "Don't rough him up. And don't pull your gun on him."

Ryan grinned. "Who me? When have I done something like that?"

"Go on, get out of here," she said with a sigh. "But remember. You've been warned."

The PI laughed, gave her a half-salute, and left her office.

He took the elevator down to the building's underground lot, got in his Ford Explorer and drove to Face-Look's headquarters, an ultra-modern, glass-and-steel structure that was one of downtown Atlanta's tallest buildings.

Ten minutes later he was shown into the large office of Tim Horvath, the Executive Vice-President of the company.

After introducing himself and showing the man his cred pack, Ryan took a seat in front of the executive's imposing desk.

"I already met with Ms Welch of the FBI," Horvath said, "and told her everything I know." He shrugged. "I'm not sure what more I can add."

Ryan nodded. "She told me you had been very cooperative. But, you never know, there may have been something you left out."

The man frowned. "I doubt it."

The PI studied the other man, who he knew was thirty-two, but looked much younger. He had a boyish look, with a slim build and a pale complexion. He was dressed casually in a black T-shirt and black jeans. Ryan knew the high-tech business world was run by very smart, very young people and Tim Horvath definitely fit the mold.

"You don't seem too broken up over Ross's murder," Ryan said.

"We were business partners. We were not close friends."

"Still. The killing of your CEO must have shaken you up."

Horvath shrugged. "Of course. But I saw it as more of a blow to our business plan. But now that I've had some time to process his death, I feel the company can move on."

"You're in charge of the firm now?"

"I am. Ross was the largest shareholder and my holdings were almost as large as his. That's why I'm now in control of the business."

"I see," the PI said.

"So, are we done here? I have a busy day today."

"No, we're not done here," Ryan said. "Let's start at the beginning. Tell me everything relevant about your business that happened in, say the last six months. Anything out of the ordinary. Anything that may have caused someone to want Matthew Ross dead."

Horvath glanced at his watch. "I'm a busy man. Is this really necessary? I told Erin Welch all this before."

Ryan smiled. "We can do this here. Or we can do this at the FBI office. Between driving over and back in Atlanta's heavy traffic, it might take a whole day."

Horvath let out a long breath. In an exasperated tone he said, "Fine. Where would you like me to start?"

"Tell me about Face-Look, your competitors, your overall business plan, anything that might shed light on your CEO's murder."

The executive nodded, and then spent the next forty minutes telling Ryan things he already knew from Erin's interview. Horvath began by describing how Face-Look had been able to surpass Facebook, its major competitor, and become the world's largest social media company. Then he proceeded to tell him about the rest of the industry. When Horvath was done, he said, "That's it. There's not much else I can add."

Ryan had learned nothing new, but sensed the company executive was holding something back. "Could I have some coffee?" the PI said, stalling for time. "I take it black."

Horvath glanced at his watch again. "I have a meeting soon."

Ryan grinned. "I'll drink it fast. Then I'll be on my way."

The executive scowled, but sensing the PI wasn't leaving, pressed a button on the intercom on his desk. "Mary," he said into the device, "could you bring a cup of black coffee for my visitor."

A woman's voice replied, "Of course, Mr. Horvath."

Five minutes later the door to the office opened and a woman came in holding a steaming mug, which she handed to Ryan. The woman was young and was wearing a tight, low-cut dress. Before leaving the office she flashed a warm smile at Horvath. Ryan glanced at the company executive and noticed the man blushed slightly.

After the secretary left, the PI slowly sipped the savory coffee while he gazed around the large office. On a credenza near the desk were a series of framed photographs. One of the photos was a family portrait. Horvath and a woman were in the picture, along with two young children. All of them were smiling brightly.

"You have a beautiful family," Ryan stated.

Horvath stared at the photo. "Thank you. My wife and I are blessed. We have two great kids."

Ryan took a shot in the dark. "I'm guessing your wife doesn't know you're screwing your secretary."

Horvath's face, which was pale to begin with, blanched. "I don't know ... what you're ... talking about ...." he stammered.

Ryan leaned forward. "You can deny it all you want, Horvath. But I know you're fucking her. Not that I blame you, she's a fine-looking woman."

The executive stood abruptly. "Get out of my office! I won't be insulted like this."

"Sit down," Ryan ordered. "I'm sure your secretary doesn't mind putting out to get a promotion, but I don't think she's willing to perjure herself with the FBI. What do you think?"

Horvath sank into his executive chair, a deflated look on his face. "What is this? Are you trying to blackmail me?"

Ryan shook his head. "No. Nothing like that. I'm trying to jar your memory. There's something you're holding back. Something pertinent to my investigation."

"All right." Horvath let out a long breath. "I guess there is something."

The PI drank more of the coffee and set the mug on the desk. "I'm listening."

"Three months ago, Matthew Ross had a visitor. An Asian woman. They met privately. I don't know what it was about. I asked Matt but he wouldn't talk about it. I sensed something was wrong."

"Okay. What else?"

"Last month," Horvath continued, "this woman came back and met with Matt again in private. From what I could gather, they disagreed about something. When I questioned him about it, he told me to stay out of it. He told me this woman was extremely well informed. Matt told me she could make trouble for me. She knew my secretary and I were, you know ...."

"And that's why you didn't say anything about this Asian woman before?"

"Yes, that's right. To protect my marriage."

"Okay. I understand now," Ryan said. "Who was the Asian woman? What's her name?"

Horvath shook his head. "Don't know."

"Was she alone?"

"No. She was always accompanied by a big Asian man. I assumed he was her bodyguard."

"Describe the woman."

"Striking looking – beautiful, but in a cold, hard way. Matt referred to her as the Ice Queen, probably because of her cold personality."

"How old was she?"

"Hard to say. She could have been in her thirties or older. She had a porcelain, doll-like face that many Asian women have – it makes them appear younger than they really are."

"Can you tell me anything else about her, Horvath?"

"She had long black hair and black eyes."

"Anything else?"

The man shook his head. "No."

"All right."

The company executive gave him a pleading look. "I've told you everything. Can you please keep quiet about me and Mary?"

"I won't tell anybody," Ryan said. Then he glanced at the framed photo of Horvath with his family. "But if you really are serious about protecting your marriage, I suggest you keep it in your pants from now on."

Horvath nodded, a dejected look on his face.

Ryan stood up and left the office.

Chapter 11

Grand Cayman
The Cayman Islands
the Caribbean

The Asian woman entered the bank, her hulking bodyguard trailing behind.

She glanced around the large, luxuriously-appointed lobby and spotted the bank manager sitting in his office at his desk.

She strode over, entered the room and sat regally in one of the visitor's chairs.

The banker, a thin, wiry man in his sixties, stood immediately, beaming. As usual the man was wearing an impeccably-tailored, three-piece gray business suit, something she had always thought was odd in the Caribbean. Still, the man was discreet and discretion was all-important to her.

"You are right on time for our meeting," the banker said, the wide smile still on his face.

"Have you ever known me to be late?" she replied in a chilly tone.

The man's smile dimmed. "Of course not. I meant no disrespect."

"None taken. Now, let's get down to business."

"Yes, of course."

The Asian woman had brought a large briefcase with her. She opened it and took out a file folder, which she placed on the desk.

"I've set up a new company," she said. "In there are all the incorporation papers."

He opened the file and read the documents thoroughly. "It all seems in order."

She nodded. "I want to open a bank account for my new company." The Asian woman had set up many shell companies in her business career. In fact, it was one of the reasons for her success.

The banker smiled again, obviously pleased at the news. "Of course. How will you be funding your new account?"

She placed the briefcase on his desk and mentioned a very large sum of money. "I brought cash with me. It's in the case. I'll wire you the rest later this week."

"The same arrangement as last time?"

"Yes, you'll get the same commission. Off-books, as usual."

The bank manager beamed. "Excellent!" He pointed to the closed briefcase on his desk. "Would you like a receipt for the money?"

The Asian woman stood. "No. People that fuck with me tend to disappear. But you know that by now."

The banker's smile faded and he swallowed hard.

Without saying goodbye, she turned and followed her muscular bodyguard out of the office.

Chapter 12

Midtown
Atlanta, Georgia

J.T. Ryan hung up his cell phone and put it back in his pocket. He had spent the last ten minutes filling in Erin Welch on his recent visit to the Face-Look headquarters.

Ryan finished his cup of coffee then glanced around his small, sparsely-furnished office. It contained two worn metal desks, an equally worn metal file cabinet, and a few chairs. On his desk in front of him was a tall pile of file folders, half-finished investigations he was working on, investigations he needed to complete. He shook his head slowly. *That's not going to happen. Not anytime soon.* The Face-Look murder took priority.

He then glanced at the other desk in his office and let out a long breath as he counted an even taller pile of file folders there. *Those cases aren't going anywhere either.*

His only employee at his PI firm, Lisa Booth, had taken a leave of absence. The young private investigator had gone back to the University of Georgia to get her Masters in Criminology.

Suddenly there was a knock at his office door. Startled, he opened a drawer in his desk. In the drawer was his .357 Smith & Wesson revolver. Ryan had learned that in his line of work it was prudent to be prepared for the worst. He rested his hand on the butt of the pistol.

"Come in," he said.

The door opened and a woman stepped inside, closing the door behind her.

Immediately he noticed two things about her. She was wearing a U.S. Army officers dress blue uniform, and the silver eagles on her epaulets identified her as a full colonel.

Ryan let go of his gun, closed the drawer, and rose. "Can I help you?"

She approached him and extended her hand. "Captain Ryan?" she said. "I'm Colonel Kelly O'Shea."

They shook hands as he studied the young woman, who was no more than five feet tall. Since he was 6'4" he towered over her. "Please have a seat."

As they sat down, he took in the rest of her appearance. She was slender and pretty, with auburn hair pulled into a bun. He also noticed the freckles on her face, but what stood out the most were her hazel eyes, which blazed with intelligence.

"You're probably wondering who I am," she said, "and why I'm here."

"Yes, I am."

Reaching into her uniform's jacket, she took out a cred pack, flipped it open, and handed it to him.

He examined it closely and handed it back. "You're from the Defense Intelligence Agency."

"That's correct," she said. "The general sent me."

Ryan shook his head slowly. "I wrote General Keating an email, describing the progress I've made so far on the case."

"He received that."

"But that's not enough?"

"Obviously he doesn't think so, otherwise I wouldn't be here."

He let out a long breath. Then he rubbed his jaw, felt the light stubble there. "Okay. In that case, I'll fill you in, tell you everything I've learned to date, and you can be on your way."

"I'm afraid, Captain Ryan, it's not going to be that simple."

"You can call me J.T. Everybody else does."

"I prefer calling you by your rank, Captain."

He rolled his eyes. "You're one of those."

She looked puzzled. "One of what?"

"A hard-ass, by-the-book, chain-of-command Army types."

The woman frowned. "That's how we get things done in the Army. By following rules and regulations."

He almost laughed at this, then realized she wasn't making a joke. "You mentioned it wasn't going to be that easy. What did you mean by that?"

She stared at him intently, her hazel eyes sparkling. "It means I'm here for the duration."

"What do you mean, Colonel?"

"It means I'm here to stay until the case is solved."

He gritted his teeth. "So. You're my babysitter?"

"I resent that," she stated, an edge to her voice. "In case you've forgotten, Captain Ryan, you're back in the Army now. I'm no damn babysitter. I'm your commanding officer. I'm your damn boss."

Ryan rubbed his temple, sensing a headache starting to pound in his head.

"Is that understood, Captain Ryan?"

"Yes."

"Yes, what, soldier?"

"Yes, Colonel."

"That's better."

He let out another long breath. "Since we're going to be working together, I want to warn you. I'm a smart-ass sometimes."

"I've read your Army file, Ryan. I know all about that. Held you back, I'm sure. With all of your commendations for bravery in combat, you should have made Major."

He nodded, knew this was true. "That's why I got out of the military. Too many rules. I guess I'm too much of a loose cannon."

The woman frowned and he noticed something else about her. She appeared to be in her mid-thirties, which was young for a full colonel. Then he spotted the ring on her finger.

"A ring knocker," he said. "I should have known."

"I resent that, Captain."

"Resent all you want, but it's a fact that your West Point ring opened a lot of doors for you in the military. I was ROTC myself – that doesn't have nearly the same status."

She nodded. "I won't deny it – graduating from West Point helped my career. But I got my promotions because I'm damn good at my job."

"Doesn't hurt that you're cute," he said under his breath.

She blushed, the pink coloring accentuating the freckles on her face. "I heard that. And I don't like it. Not one bit. Are you trying to piss me off?"

He held his palms in front of him. "Sorry. Just joking."

She frowned again, but after a moment her expression softened. "My looks have helped me in some ways, I admit. But just so we're crystal clear, I've never used sex to get ahead in the Army."

"I didn't mean to imply you had. But the military is still a tough place for females. I'm sure you get hit on all the time."

The woman nodded. "I do," she replied in a quiet voice.

"Men can be pigs sometimes."

"Very true," she said. "Look. I think we got off on the wrong foot. Let's start over, Captain Ryan. I'm here for one reason only. And that's to help you solve this murder." She extended her hand. "Deal?"

They shook.

"Yes, ma'am. Sounds good to me. By the way, can I ask why you were assigned to this investigation?"

"Because I've been tracking Face-Look for over a year. Computer science and social media are my specialty at the DIA."

"Okay." He rose, went to his small coffee maker on top of his filing cabinet and refilled his cup. "Would you like some?" he asked her.

"Sure."

He filled a foam cup with steaming coffee, handed it to her, and sat back down behind his desk.

She took a sip and made a sour face. "God, this is awful. How can you drink this crap?"

"It's hot," he replied with a grin, "and I'm used to the taste."

The colonel placed the cup on his desk and slid it away from her.

"So, you've been tracking Face-Look for over a year," he said. "Why?"

"As General Keating probably mentioned, we at the Defense Intelligence Agency have been concerned with the data gathering capability of social media companies. On the surface, that data mining of personal information is harmless. But if it were to fall into criminal hands, or if people within social media companies such as Face-Look had corrupt intentions, the consequences could be very dangerous to the country."

Ryan nodded. "Okay. I'm with you so far."

"How much do you know about social media?"

"Not a huge amount. I'm usually busy kicking down doors and busting heads," he replied with a grin. "It doesn't give me much time to post pictures online."

"In that case," he said, "it'd be easier if I showed you how it works." She removed a laptop from a briefcase she had brought and pointed to the other desk in the office. "Can I set up over there?"

"Sure."

Standing, she went to the other desk, pushed aside the tall stack of case files and powered up her computer. She sat down and he pulled up a chair and sat also, looking over her shoulder.

After logging into the internet, the woman went to the Face-Look website and began scrolling through numerous personal profiles. With ease she was able to access photos and read private messages from a wide assortment of people on the Face-Look system.

"How can you access all this stuff?" he asked. "I thought this type of personal information can be kept secret with the privacy settings the social media companies have."

She rolled her eyes. "In theory, that's true. But anybody with enough technical skill can hack into it fairly easily."

"Okay. So a hacker could go into your Face-Look page and find your personal information, like your birth date, where you live, your relatives, and friends."

"Yes, that's right," she said. "And someone with criminal intent could use it for malicious purposes. I'll show you."

Colonel O'Shea surfed through several more personal pages on the system and finally stopped at one. She pointed to the screen. "I've tracked that person for a few weeks. It's a good example of what can go wrong."

The Face-Look page showed a teenage girl, no more than sixteen. She had a wide smile on her profile picture. Her public posts on her page were innocuous, mostly photos of her high school.

Then O'Shea clicked on the teenager's inter-system messages and Ryan was shocked at what he saw. The girl was sending semi-nude photos of herself to a young man, probably her boyfriend. O'Shea tapped on the screen. "You can see how this information could be misused."

Ryan nodded. "The potential for blackmail is huge. When this teenager becomes an adult and is looking for a job, pictures like this could ruin a promising career."

"That's right. And it's worse than you think."

"How could it be worse?"

She tapped on the screen again. "These photos, and all these posts, and comments people make on Face-Look, and other social media sites, are stored in computer server farms. Probably for eternity. Once something gets on the internet, it's almost impossible to take down."

Ryan shook his head. "Now I understand why the DIA is concerned."

"Let me show you something else. Something that has even more national security implications."

"All right."

The colonel scrolled through several more social media pages and stopped at one. This was her own, and it showed photos of her, wearing civilian clothes and not her uniform. "I set up this page under an assumed name," she said. "With it I can access what everyone else accesses on Face-Look publicly."

She pointed to the news feed that was popping up on the right side of the screen. "That's the typical news people get on their social media page. You can see there's current event stories that are breaking today: Rioting in Paris, an earthquake in Malaysia, a jet crash in Seattle. The sources vary, of course. You can see news articles by CBS News, ABC, Fox News, The New York Times, etc."

Ryan quickly read the headlines that were scrolling on the screen, and the links that took you to the full articles. "So people use social media to get their news?"

"They do."

"I like to read about it in newspapers."

She grinned. "They still have those?"

"Yes, smart-ass," he replied with a shrug. "They still have those."

"I read your military file. You haven't hit forty yet. Although you're close. But you're *so* old-school."

"I *am* old-school," he said defensively. "But I was old-school when I was twenty. I like newspapers, and flip phones, and paper maps."

"Okay, Mr. Dinosaur. It's a good thing I'm helping you out on this case then."

Ryan was about to object, then simply nodded in agreement.

She pointed to the news feed scrolling on the computer screen. "You see the implication of this?"

"Of course."

"And remember this, Ryan. Face-Look has a worldwide audience of over 2.2 billion people. This news feed is controlled by a handful of employees at that company. These employees are called 'curators', which sounds benign. But they, and the bosses who control them, have an incredible power to filter and shape the news. They, in effect, control what vast numbers of people see every day, day in and day out. More people get their news from social media sites like Face-Look, and Tweeter, and Goggles, and others like them, than they do from television, or newspapers, or magazines. Pew Research did a study recently and found that 68% of American adults get their news from social media."

Ryan stared at the computer screen as her words sank in. The executives who controlled the news feeds and selected which stories to show, and what news organizations to feature, were very powerful people.

A sinking feeling settled in the pit of his stomach. In the wrong hands, social media could be a very destructive force.

Chapter 13

Tokyo, Japan

The Asian woman awoke at precisely 5 a.m. that morning, something she did every morning without the aid of an alarm clock .

Getting up, she threw on a bathrobe and drew the curtains of her penthouse apartment. Located in the city's most exclusive condo building, the apartment overlooked the Sumida River and from her vantage point she could clearly see the area's skyscraper skyline, with a pink and gray early morning light as a backdrop. Tokyo Tower, the city's tallest structure, was also visible in the distance.

Turning from the windows, she padded barefoot to her master bath, showered, and dressed for the day. Today it was an exclusive Dolce & Gabbana black business suit with a black silk blouse, and black four-inch heels.

That done, she sat at her dressing table and began pinning up her shoulder-length, perfectly white hair. Then she pulled on her black hair wig and combed the long tresses so they fell perfectly over her shoulders.

After inspecting herself in the mirror, she opened a drawer, took out a small case and clicked it open. Taking out the eye contacts, she carefully put them on. The contacts were tinted black and they completely covered up her white pupils. She then penciled her white eyebrows, turning them a coal black color.

The Asian woman checked herself out in the mirror once again and saw that the transformation was complete. It was a transformation she repeated every time she traveled outside of Japan. She had learned long ago that the appearance of being a black haired and black eyed Asian woman, like almost every other Asian female, gave her the anonymity she had found useful as her career evolved into criminality.

She was a strikingly beautiful woman, with delicate features. Her almost porcelain-white skin made her appear doll-like. As a child and later in her teen years she had always felt cursed by her albino characteristics. Her white eyes and white hair made her unique, but also shunned by most in Japanese society, who preferred conformity in appearance, where dark hair and eyes was predominant. As an adult she had come to terms with her unique looks. And when her business career blossomed and eventually turned to crime, she realized that altering her appearance gave her an incredible edge in avoiding law-enforcement.

After applying makeup, she rose from the dressing table and began packing clothes for her upcoming trip. When she was done she picked up her cell phone and tapped in a number.

When her assistant picked up the call a moment later, she said, "This is Aki. I want my jet fueled and ready to go in an hour."

"Of course, Ms Tanaka," came the reply. "What is the destination, so I can inform the pilot?"

"Vienna."

"Yes, Ms Tanaka. I'll take care of it immediately."

Aki Tanaka hung up the call and went into her living room. Like her bedroom, this room also had a spectacular view of the Tokyo skyline. Going to her liquor cabinet, she poured herself a large tumbler of Chivas scotch. Although it was still early morning, she much preferred the liquor over coffee. Her usual breakfast consisted of scotch and peanut butter crackers.

Taking a sip of the Chivas, the Asian woman mused that having scotch in the morning was an acquired taste, and an unusual one. She smiled. *But then there's lots of things about me that are unusual.*

Chapter 14

Salt Lake City, Utah

The man slowed the Chevy Impala as he drove past the large home, which was located in a neighborhood of similar, upscale residences. Parking on the street a half-block away, he sat in the car for the next ten minutes, observing the area. It was 3 a.m. and there was no movement, nor any traffic, in the quiet residential area.

He put on his black watch cap, zipped up his black jacket, and climbed out of the car. Then he carefully made his way toward the home. In the driveway sat a silver BMW SUV. After glancing around to make sure there were no lights inside the house and that no one was outside, he crouched next to the BMW and slid underneath it.

Earlier in the day he'd studied the SUV's mechanical schematics online and knew exactly where everything was located. Pulling out a penlight and some other tools from a pocket, he removed a cover plate from the vehicle's undercarriage, which exposed the brake line.

With a small hacksaw he cut halfway through the line. Immediately brake fluid began dripping from the line and he moved aside to avoid the drops.

He turned off his penlight, put the tools back in his pocket, slid from underneath the SUV, and stood. Returning to his own car, he climbed inside.

He drove away from the area at a steady, unhurried pace, well below the speed limit. Soon he was on Interstate 80 and in another half hour he was back in his motel room.

He would spend the day there, monitoring the news. Fatal car accidents, especially ones that snarled traffic on the city's highways, always made the news.

Chapter 15

FBI Field Office
Atlanta, Georgia

"How was your meeting with Horvath?" Erin Welch asked, when J.T. Ryan entered her office.

Ryan sat in one of the visitor's chairs fronting her desk. "Good. I learned some interesting things."

Erin nodded. "Do you think he's behind the murder of Face-Look's president?"

"Don't think so. But it's still to early to say for sure. Horvath has a lot to gain by the CEO's death. As senior vice-president he's now in charge."

Erin leaned forward in her executive chair. "That's a good motive."

"It is. But my gut tells me he's not our guy."

The FBI Assistant Director pondered that a moment, then said, "Okay. I trust your instincts. That's why I hire you."

Ryan grinned. "And here I thought you hired me for my charm and wit."

She rolled her eyes and didn't reply.

Turning serious, Ryan said, "I did find out several important things during my meeting with Horvath."

"Such as?"

"First, Horvath, who's a married man, is screwing his secretary. And they've been able to keep it under the radar."

Erin frowned. "So he's been having a secret affair? How'd you find that out?"

He smiled. "I'm an ace detective, remember?"

"Okay, smart-ass. What else did you find out?"

"According to Horvath, before Ross was murdered he met with an Asian woman. Apparently these were high-level meetings – only Ross and this woman were involved. And according to Horvath, the last meeting with this Asian woman was very contentious. They disagreed about something and it got really heated. These meetings were the only events out of the ordinary that Horvath recalls happening in the last six months."

Erin shook her head. "When I interviewed Horvath, he didn't mention anything about this."

"I know. Somehow the Asian woman had learned about Horvath's affair and was using it as leverage to keep him quiet."

Erin folded her arms in front of her. "Good work on finding this out, J.T. Did you learn the identity of the Asian woman?"

"I don't have a name yet. I got a physical description. Long black hair, black eyes, delicate features."

"That pretty much describes every Asian woman. Considering there's several billion Asians in the world, and half are female, that doesn't narrow down our suspect list much."

"That's true, Erin. After we're done here, I'm heading back to the Face-Look offices. I want to check the security video tapes for the times when this woman was there. I may be able to get a photo from that footage."

"Good idea." She leaned back in her chair. "My lab guys are still working on the trace evidence you found where the sniper took the shot. The fingerprints you lifted were all smudged, so we think he used latex gloves. But we're still checking for a DNA match. Nothing's come back from NCIC," she said, referring to the National Crime Information Center. "But we'll keep running it down."

"Okay. Listen, Erin. I need a favor."

She let out a long sigh. "You always need a favor. What is it this time?"

"I need to borrow a handgun."

"What happened to your .357? You lose it in a bar fight?"

Ryan grinned and slid aside his navy blazer, revealing the Smith & Wesson .357 Magnum holstered on his hip. "No, I didn't. I need a gun for someone else."

"Who?"

"Remember I told you I'm also working on this case for the Army?"

"I remember."

"Well, it turns out the Defense Intelligence Agency is going to be a lot more hands on than I anticipated."

"How so, J.T.?"

"They sent an agent to keep tabs on me."

"Who's the guy?"

"It's a her, actually. Her name is Kelly O'Shea and she's a colonel in the DIA."

"Okay. So why do you need the gun?"

"O'Shea wasn't issued a pistol for this case. She's a computer expert and doesn't normally carry one."

"All right. I'm with you so far. But why does she need it now?"

"Because."

"Because why, J.T.?"

"Because being around me can be dangerous. Sometimes my investigations require me to deal with sleazy characters."

"That's a fact." Erin gave him an amused look. "It's been 48 hours and you haven't shot anyone, beaten up anyone, nor have I had to bail you out of jail."

Ryan grinned. "The week's not over yet."

"Okay, smart-ass. I'll lend you a handgun. But I want it back when this case is over."

He gave her a half salute. "Yes, ma'am."

"Let's go down to the armory and I'll sign one out to you."

They left her office, took the elevator to the basement level, and Erin unlocked the door to the FBI armory room. Ryan had been there several times before and always enjoyed visiting the place. The large room contained all of the weapons impounded from crimes over the years, and also contained special-issue rifles, shotguns, bullet-resistant Kevlar vests, and other weaponry utilized by the Bureau's SWAT teams.

Erin led them to a glass-front case that covered an entire wall. Handguns of all types were there, held on metal racks.

"Take your pick," she said pointing at the case.

Ryan studied the racks of pistols, which included a wide variety of Glocks, Heckler & Koch, Rugers, and SIG Sauer handguns. After scanning the whole selection, he said, "I'll take the Desert Eagle semi-automatic."

"You sure you want that one? That's more of a cannon than a pistol."

"I'm sure."

Erin unlocked the glass case, took out the handgun and its holster off the rack, and handed them to him.

He hefted the heavy gun and admired the high-quality craftsmanship. Designed originally for the Israeli military, the .50 caliber pistol was the most powerful handgun in the world. It was so powerful that in Alaska hunters used them to kill bears. This particular one was stainless steel, with walnut grips, and had a magazine capacity of seven rounds.

"You ever shot one of these, J.T.?"

"Yeah. When I was in Delta Force, one of the guys in my unit had a Desert Eagle as his private weapon. I always admired it."

"Okay. But remember, this pistol kicks like a mule. Is this O'Shea woman going to be able to handle the recoil?"

Ryan smiled. "Actually, I'm going to lend her my revolver. I'll be using the Desert Eagle."

Erin rolled her eyes. "Boys and their toys."

Ryan laughed.

She located a case for the gun and he packed it away, along with the holster and .50 caliber ammunition. That done, she signed the weapon out to him and they left the armory.

Ryan made his way out of the FBI offices, locked the gun case in his SUV, and drove to the headquarters of Face-Look.

At the reception area he asked to see Tim Horvath. He waited in the busy, luxurious open atrium for five minutes and then saw Horvath's secretary exit an elevator and approach him. As before, the woman was wearing a tight, low-cut dress.

"Mr. Horvath is in a meeting," the woman said in a haughty tone. "He can't see you today, Mr. Ryan."

The PI tried to disarm her attitude with a broad smile. "I just need a few moments of his time."

She scowled. "That won't be possible. He's in an important meeting. It could last most of the day."

Ryan shook his head slowly. "Your name's Mary, isn't it?"

The scowl remained on her face. "It is."

His voice dropped to a whisper. "Well, Mary, unless you want me to make a scene right here in your lobby, and tell all of the people here that you and Tim Horvath are fucking each other's brains out, I suggest you get him out of his important meeting."

Mary's face turned a bright shade of pink and then crimson. "I'll ... I'll go get him." She turned and ran back to the elevators.

Five minutes later Ryan was shown into the senior VP's spacious office. Tim Horvath was already there, seated behind his desk. Like last time they'd met, the youthful-looking executive was dressed casually in a T-shirt and jeans.

Horvath stood, a grimace on his face. "Was that really necessary? You really embarrassed Mary."

"I'm trying to solve a murder," the PI fumed. "I don't have time to play games."

"What do you want this time?"

"I need the dates when the Asian woman met with your company president."

"I don't remember."

Ryan leaned forward, towering over the smaller man. "You'd better. Or you'll regret it." The PI pointed to the photo in the office showing Horvath with his family. "I'm sure you haven't told your wife about your ... indiscretions."

Horvath placed his palms flat on the desk and sat back down. "All right, all right. Don't do anything rash."

The Face-Look executive began working on the laptop on his desk, scrolling through his online calendars. A few minutes later he said, "Okay. There was one day for sure, that I recall." He pointed to the screen.

"You're sure?"

"Yes. I remember because we had a board meeting later that day."

"Okay."

"Are we done here, Ryan?"

"Not yet. Call your security department. Tell them I'm coming to see them to look at the CCTV camera footage." The PI pointed to the phone on the man's desk. "Do it now."

Horvath picked up the handset and spoke for a minute.

"All right, Ryan. I've set it up. The security room is on the third floor."

Ryan glanced at his watch. "See? This only took five minutes."

The company executive nodded.

"Remember that, Horvath, next time I need to see you."

"There's going to be a next time?"

"One never knows, in my line of work."

Ryan left the man's office and located the security office on the third floor. He showed his cred pack to the guy manning the room and they sat at a workstation which fronted a bank of TV monitors showing all of the building's public areas. Like the rest of the high-tech headquarters, the security room was outfitted with the latest in electronic equipment.

The security guy was in his early sixties, with balding gray hair, nicotine-stained fingers, and a growing paunch. He looked to be a retired police officer. His ID badge showed his photo and stated his name, Frank Reynolds.

"Were you a cop before you got this gig, Frank?" Ryan asked.

"Atlanta PD. Put my twenty in. Retired last year."

"Good for you."

"Your ID says you're an FBI security contractor, Ryan. How long have you been doing work for the Bureau?"

"Several years. Right after my time in the Army."

Reynolds nodded. "Yeah. You seem the type. So – how can I help you, Mr. Ryan?"

"Call me J.T. I'm looking for an Asian woman who visited Face-Look." He mentioned the specific date. "This woman met with your deceased company president in his office. I suggest you run the surveillance tapes of the corridor that leads to his office on the 10th floor. I don't know the time, so start early in the morning."

"Got it, J.T."

The security man typed at his computer console and a few minutes later said, "I got it. I'll put it on the top left monitor."

A black and white image flickered on that TV screen, showing an empty corridor. The time stamp on the image said 5:30 a.m. The security man began fast forwarding the images. Time marched forward and the screen began showing a few people walking to and fro down the hallway. At 7 a.m. the corridor got busier as more employees arrived at work. A few minutes later Matthew Ross went into his office.

Over the next few hours several people went into and came out of the company president's office, but none of them were Asians.

The security guy stifled a yawn.

"Gets boring sometimes, doesn't it?" Ryan said.

"Yeah, it does."

"I know that all too well, Frank. Most people think being a PI is always exciting like they show in the movies. But lots of times its dull, boring stuff like this."

A half-hour later Ryan spotted a striking-looking Asian woman with long black hair and black eyes being escorted into Ross's office. A very tall and brawny Asian man had come with the woman and he took a sentry-like position by the closed office door.

"There," Ryan said, "that must be her."

"Okay, J.T."

"Let's see her come out of the office. We may get a better look at her face."

An hour later the Asian woman came out of the room and she was escorted down the corridor and off screen.

"Frank, I need to get this surveillance footage, along with any other you have of her going into and out of the lobby."

"You got it. I'll copy it on a flash drive for you."

"That's great."

The security man removed a flash drive from a drawer and began copying the CCTV footage from the corridor and lobby area. When he was done he handed it to the PI, along with his business card. "If you need anything else, J.T., my cell phone number's on there."

Ryan extended his hand and the two men shook. "You've been a big help, Frank."

Chapter 16

Midtown
Atlanta, Georgia

When J.T. Ryan got back to his PI office he found Colonel Kelly O'Shea working at her computer. As usual the attractive woman was wearing her Army dress blue officer's uniform and her auburn hair was pulled back in a tight bun.

Ryan closed the door behind him and sat on the edge of her desk.

She looked up from her screen. "Hello, Captain. Make any progress?"

"I did, as a matter of fact." He grinned. "You know, you don't have to be so formal. We can drop the whole rank thing and you can call me J.T. like everyone else."

O'Shea shook her head. "I prefer calling you Captain."

He shrugged. "Whatever floats your boat." Reaching into his pocket, he removed a flash drive and handed it to her. "This is a copy of the surveillance tapes at Face-Look. The Asian woman who met with the company president is on here. Can you run facial rec on her?"

O'Shea nodded. "Of course. The Defense Intelligence Agency has some of the most sophisticated facial recognition software. If this woman has any type of online footprint, we'll find her."

"Good. I have something else for you." Ryan slid aside his navy blazer and unclipped his holstered pistol from his belt and placed it on the desk in front of her.

"What's this for?"

"I know you don't carry a gun, Colonel. But since you're hanging around me, you may need it. Ever fired one of these?"

"I'm in the military, I know my way around guns," she replied, picking up the pistol and removing it from the holster. She inspected the weapon closely, clicked open the cylinder, checked the load, and clicked it closed.

"Smith & Wesson revolver," she said, ".357 Magnum caliber, with a six-round capacity. You're using Federal brand jacketed hollow point bullets, 158 grain weight, which have a muzzle velocity of 1,240 feet per second."

Ryan nodded, impressed with her knowledge.

"Thanks for the weapon, Captain. By the way, I have something for you."

He laughed. "This is just like Christmas. Exchanging gifts and all."

O'Shea did not appear amused. Frowning, she didn't reply, simply reaching into her briefcase. She took out a cell phone and handed it to him.

"I already have a cell phone, Colonel."

"Not like this you don't. This is a SAT phone. With this you don't need cell towers – it uses DIA satellites for transmission and you can use it anywhere in the world, no matter how remote the location."

"Nice," he said, powering up the device. He grinned. "You must be warming up to me, to give me something so expensive. I know SAT phones cost a small fortune."

The stony look remained on her face. "Actually, Captain, your smart-ass personality isn't growing on me one bit. The reason I'm giving you this is two-fold. With this phone you can call me from anywhere and give me progress reports on the case."

"And the second reason?" he asked, curious.

"The phone has a GPS location beacon – I can track exactly where you are at all times."

Ryan smiled. "So I can't play hooky anymore and skip school?"

"That's a fact," she said, not returning the smile. "And just so you know, the SAT phone was General Keating's idea. He wanted to make sure I keep you on a tight leash."

Ryan laughed. "Tight leash, huh? I never figured you for a S&M bondage type of girl." He chuckled again. "But I have to admit, it does turn me on when you talk dirty."

The woman blushed a deep shade of crimson. "That's ... that's ... not what I meant *at all.*"

"I know, I know. Just kidding."

Her lips pressed into a thin line. "I don't appreciate that kind of humor."

"Sorry, Colonel. I get carried away sometimes. Truce?" He extended his hand and after a long moment she shook it.

"Apology accepted," she said. "So while I work on the facial rec part of this, what are you going to do?'

"I implement plan A."

"What's plan A?"

"I turn over rocks and see what's underneath."

"Are you looking for something in particular?"

Ryan nodded. "A clue would be nice."

"And if plan A doesn't work?"

"Then I go to plan B, Colonel."

"What's that?"

He grinned. "What I do best. Break down doors, kick ass, and take names."

Chapter 17

Vienna, Austria

Aki Tanaka's private jet touched down at Vienna's Schwechat Airport, rolled down the runway, and taxied on the tarmac to an unmarked hanger building. The hangar door slid open and the Gulfstream jet rolled inside.

The Asian woman deplaned, and with her hulking bodyguard trailing behind, climbed into the waiting Mercedes Benz limousine. The car, which was owned by her partner, began its journey west on the A4 highway toward the city center.

Aki had made this trip many times and hardly bothered to gaze out the limo's tinted windows. The Mercedes skirted the Danube river and then went through the scenic capitol city of Austria. Vienna, with a population of 1.8 million residents, has a compact inner core of mostly historic buildings dating back to the 1800s. Many of the elaborate structures were from the Hapsburg era, when the Austrian Empire ruled much of central Europe. The Austrian Empire had been defeated in World War I and the vast area they controlled had been cut up into many separate countries.

The car drove past the famed Hofburg, the former Imperial Palace and court. The palace, now a museum with an extensive assortment of Gothic and Neo-Renaissance buildings, was the city's number one tourist attraction.

Aki watched as the limo left the city center behind and reached her final destination, a historic castle overlooking the banks of the Danube river.

Her business partner, an Austrian billionaire, had purchased the 17th century structure ten years ago after the former owner had sold it at auction, finding the drafty, multi-turreted estate too costly to maintain. Her partner had spent the next several years refurbishing the Hapsburg era castle to its former Imperial glory and updating it with the latest in 21st century technology.

The Mercedes went into the walled estate grounds and parked in the large, circular driveway that fronted the impressive stone castle. With its tall turrets, elaborate ramparts, columns, arches, and wide moat that circled the structure, the estate was one of Austria's best preserved historic monuments. Whenever Aki visited the place, she was always amazed by how much money her partner had spent updating and restoring the stone castle. Seeing it from both the outside and the inside, you felt like you were transported back centuries.

The limo's door was opened by a uniformed butler and the Asian woman was escorted inside. She was shown to her usual room, a high-ceiling bedroom outfitted with a historic four-poster bed, marble floors, and a stone fireplace. Priceless woven tapestries from the Middle Ages hung on the walls.

Her bodyguard inspected the room to make sure it was safe, then took a sentry position outside the door.

After unpacking her clothes, Aki left the bedroom and took the elevator to the first floor, closely followed by her brawny bodyguard. She entered the massive office of her business partner, Karl Strada. Finding it vacant, she headed to the large sitting area in the room, which was close to a roaring fireplace. Her bodyguard, as always, took a sentry position outside the room.

She sat on one of the brocade antique wingback armchairs and gazed at the crackling flames. She had always found the vast, high-ceiling office drafty and cold, but sitting close to the fireplace provided a comforting warmth. The chilly temperature was one defect that no amount of technology could solve. In fact, every area of the castle had the same problem.

Aki glanced toward a corner of the room, where a life-size ivory chess set was kept. Unlike the chess set in her own office in Japan, here the intricately-carved pieces resembled knights and royalty from the Middle Ages. Although Karl Strada fancied himself a master chess player, she knew he rarely played the game and had installed the priceless life-size set in his office for show only, to impress his guests. Proving her point was the fact that all of the chess pieces had a thin layer of dust covering them, indicating they hadn't been used for quite some time.

Aki heard a rustling behind her and turned, seeing Strada enter the room. The tall, distinguished-looking man approached her, a wide smile on his face.

"Aki, it is so good to see you again," he said in German-accented English. Although the Asian woman spoke fluent German, the two of them always communicated in English.

She rose from the chair. "It's good to see you also."

The man kissed her cheek and they sat across from each other. Though the man was in his early eighties, he was physically fit, giving him the vigor of a much younger man. With his graying hair, graying mustache, and exquisitely-tailored Sevile Row suit, the distinguished-looking man had the appearance of a prosperous banker. He had made his billions in hedge funds years ago and now spent his money freely to extend his power and influence. The man had bankrolled many of Aki's businesses and projects.

Strada leaned forward in his wingback chair. "Thank you for flying here on such short notice. You have been keeping me well informed, but I thought it would be good for us to meet in person. How is the operation going?"

"Overall," she replied, "it's going well on several different fronts. But as you know, we had a setback. I was hoping the Face-Look president, Matthew Ross, would have been more cooperative." She paused a moment. "When that didn't happen, I dealt with the problem. He was eliminated."

Strada nodded. "You are, as always, very efficient. By the way, why did you pick such a public way to murder him? Having a sniper kill him in his office made all the news channels."

"I wanted to send a signal to others in the social media industry that may try to oppose us in the coming months. Fall in line or die."

"Good thinking, Aki."

"Thank you."

Strada smoothed down his mustache. "What is your plan now to implement our agenda at Face-Look?"

"I'm working on that, Karl. I believe I have a solution."

"Good. That company is a key component of the Viper operation."

She nodded. "Don't worry. I'll get it done."

"I know you will. You have never disappointed me in the past."

"On another matter," the Asian woman said, "we've had good success in the Salt Lake City phase of the operation. I've eliminated two obstacles there."

Strada rubbed his hands together in satisfaction. "Excellent work."

She smiled. "And the other parts of the Viper operation are coming along nicely also. We've completed about half of our objectives." She spent the next hour detailing the progress she'd made in the global venture.

"You are to be commended, Aki." He rose from his chair, went to an antique mahogany cabinet and opened it. "Would you like some coffee?" he asked. "Or something else?"

"I'll have my usual," she replied.

Strada opened a silver carafe and poured himself a steaming cup of coffee, then filled a Waterford crystal tumbler with Chivas scotch. After handing her the glass, he sat back down.

"You have flown such a long distance, Aki. It would be a shame if you returned to Japan so quickly. Stay for a few days."

"I should get back. I still have a lot to do."

Strada smiled. "At least stay one night. We can have dinner."

She had expected this request. Although the two of them had always been just business partners, deep down she knew he wanted their relationship to be more.

"All right," she said. "I'll stay until tomorrow."

"Excellent! I will have the chef prepare a special meal." He gave her a long, appraising look, taking in her long black hair and dark eyes. "Maybe tonight at dinner, you can dispense with your disguise. You know how much I admire your natural beauty."

"I prefer to conceal my identity when I'm outside of Japan. I've always found it safer that way."

"Humor me, Aki. Please."

She took a sip of scotch. "As you wish."

Strada beamed. "Excellent."

***

Tired from the twelve-hour flight from Japan, Aki went back to her bedroom, undressed, and took a long nap on the four-poster bed.

Rising, she dressed in a white, flowing, ankle-length gown for the upcoming dinner with Strada. Then she sat at the dressing table and studied her reflection on the mirror. She took off her black wig and set it aside. Unpinning her own white hair, she began brushing the long tresses. Satisfied with her hair's appearance, she removed the black contacts and applied makeup and perfume.

That done, she left the room and made her way to the castle's dining room, shadowed by her ever-present bodyguard.

Karl Strada was already there, seated at the head of the massive table, which could easily accommodate forty people. Several uniformed maids stood nearby, pouring drinks and setting down dishes. A fireplace was burning, giving off a comforting warm glow to the room. The aroma of wood and scented candles filled the air.

Strada rose from the table, went around it and approached her. "You look lovely," he said, kissing her cheek. His hand gently stroked her long white hair. "Thank you for gracing me with your natural beauty."

Aki smiled but said nothing as they sat down close to each other at the long table.

Strada clapped his hands and one of the uniformed maids approached the table and poured Aki a cut-crystal goblet of scotch, while another maid served coffee for the billionaire.

Strada took a sip of coffee and set down his cup. "I had my chef prepare a special meal. Duck a L'Orange. I hope you enjoy it."

"I'm sure I will," she replied as she drank some of the Chivas.

The meal was served, an elaborate seven-course affair that included Dom Perignon champagne and a chocolate mousse dessert.

Aki, never a heavy eater, downed scotch as she picked at her food, which was delicious as always. She had dined at her partner's mansion many times before and had always been impressed by the food served.

"The dinner was excellent, Karl."

The man beamed. "I am glad you enjoyed it. Would you like anything else?"

Aki finished off her fourth glass of Chivas and raised the goblet. "Another one of these would be nice."

Strada clapped his hands and one of the maids scurried over and quickly refilled her glass. Then he turned to the staff of servers and said, "You may leave us now."

The servers left the room, closing the massive wooden door behind them. The billionaire, who was seated across from Aki, covered her hand with one of his. "Aki, I have been meaning to talk to you about something."

The Asian woman tensed, sensing the topic he would bring up. "What is it?"

Strada stared at her. "You have the most beautiful eyes. Crystal white pupils. I find them mesmerizing. Almost hypnotic. They never cease to amaze me."

She smiled but said nothing.

"Do you know what 'aki' means in Japanese?" he asked.

"Of course. 'Aki' means 'sparkling' in the Japanese language."

He rubbed her hand sensually. "Like your eyes, 'sparkling'."

"Thank you."

"I always hoped, Aki, that we could become close."

"But we are. We've been business partners for years."

He caressed her hand again. "I am not talking about that."

"What do you mean, then?" She knew very well what he meant, but dreaded talking about the topic again. He had poured so much money into her business ventures she hated to disappoint him.

"I would like for us to be closer, Aki. In a personal way. An intimate way." He continued to sensually stroke her hand.

She shook her head slowly. "We've had this conversation before. I don't think that's a good idea."

"But why not?"

"We're not compatible, Karl."

"I do not understand. You have told me this before, that you thought we were not compatible, but you never explained what you meant."

She pulled her hand free and her eyes bore into his. "You're a domineering man. You like to give orders and have them followed. And I'm exactly the same way. So you see, Karl, we wouldn't be compatible. Especially in the bedroom. I like, in fact, I expect the men I take to bed to follow instructions and service me."

Strada's eyebrows shot up and then a frown settled on his face. He picked up his cup of coffee, drained it, and set it back down. "That is disappointing. Very disappointing."

"You have a den full of whores. I'm sure they'll do anything you want them to do."

"I pay those women. It is not the same," he replied in a sad voice.

He seemed so dispirited by the discussion that she almost felt sorry for the billionaire. *But it won't work. If I agree to have sex with him, it will turn out bad. I know it will. So bad our whole business relationship will sour.*

Attempting to cheer him up, she reached over and touched his arm. "I'm sorry, Karl. I really am." She mulled something over for a moment, then said, "I'll tell you what. From now on, whenever I visit you here at your home, I'll change out of my disguise. At least that way you can always see me as I really am."

A glimmer of a smile appeared on his face. "Thank you, Aki. That means the world to me."

Chapter 18

Atlanta, Georgia

J.T. Ryan was scrambling eggs when he heard a knock at his apartment's door.

Turning off the flame on the cook-top, he left the kitchen and headed to his foyer. He pulled his gun and peered through the spyhole.

Holstering the pistol, he opened the door. "Well, if it isn't the intrepid Kelly O'Shea," he said with a grin. "Come in, Colonel."

The young woman stepped inside and he shut the door behind her.

"How'd you know where I lived?" he asked. "I never told you."

"In case you've forgotten, I'm with the DIA. We know everything."

Ryan laughed, although from her stony expression it was clear she wasn't making a joke.

"I was cooking eggs. Would you like some?"

O'Shea glanced at her watch. "It's 8 p.m. Who has eggs for dinner?"

"I do. I'm a crappy cook. I only know how to make a few things."

The woman nodded. "I see. And no thanks on the eggs. I already ate at my hotel." As usual she was wearing her dress blue Army uniform and her auburn hair was pulled back in a bun.

"Well, I'm starved. Let's go to the kitchen and we can talk in there."

Ryan led her back and she sat at the small dinette table.

"Want some coffee, Colonel? I just brewed a fresh pot."

"It probably tastes like the coffee you make at your office. I'll pass."

Ryan opened the refrigerator door with a flourish. "In that case I can offer you a Coke or a Coors beer."

"I'll take the soft drink."

He pulled out a can, closed the fridge, and placed the drink in front of her. Then he went back to finish making his eggs and bacon and toast. When he was done a few minutes later he sat across from her, a heaping platter of food in front of him. Popping open a can of beer, he held it in the air. "Cheers!"

O'Shea nodded and took a sip of her Coke.

"So, Colonel," he said, in between bites of food, "is this a social call or business?"

She pursed her lips. "Business, obviously."

Ryan grinned. "I knew that. I'm trying to loosen you up. You're wound up pretty tight." He could tell she was about to object to this, then she simply shrugged.

"The general called me today," she said.

Ryan took a bite of toast and washed it down with some beer. "General Keating," he said under his breath. "Someone else who's wound up as tight as a drum."

"I heard that, Captain. And just to remind you, the general is your commanding officer."

He took a sip of Coors. "Don't worry. That fact is etched in my brain. So. What did Keating want?"

"He's been reading my progress reports and he ran the data through DIA software. He thinks there's a link between the murder of the Face-Look CEO and two accidental deaths at a high-tech company in Salt Lake City."

Ryan stopped eating and set down his can of beer. "That sounds like a promising lead. Tell me more."

"The company in Salt Lake is named Tekk-Sky. They're the largest server farm in the U.S. Two of their employees died recently in car accidents."

"What's a server farm?"

"Yeah, I forgot," she said. "You're a dinosaur when it comes to technology. Server farms are warehouses for data. In effect, they're giant computers that provide storage for all of the billions and billions of data streams generated every single day. Emails, text messages, instant messaging, photos, documents. People refer to this type of electronic storage as 'clouds'. There are no 'clouds'. They're simply large buildings that house countless mainframe computers that store data. Companies like Face-Look, and Tweeter, and Verizon, and AT&T, and every other tech company in the world store data in places like this Salt Lake City company."

Ryan nodded. "I understand. So two of Tekk-Sky's employees died recently?"

"That's right. In car accidents on different days and different locations. Random acts, except for the fact that Tekk-Sky is the largest server farm for social media companies like Face-Look."

The PI pushed aside his plate. "Sounds like a good lead. I need to get up to Salt Lake City right away."

"Correction. We need to get up there right away. I've booked us both on a flight first thing in the morning."

Ryan rubbed his jaw. "I'm guessing the general doesn't trust me enough to tackle this on my own."

"That's an accurate assessment."

He leaned forward in his chair. "How about you? Do you trust me?"

"The jury's still out on that," she said, and took a sip of Coke.

Chapter 19

Tokyo, Japan

Aki Tanaka's desk phone buzzed and she glanced at the info screen. The caller was a man she had on retainer in the United States. She pressed the encryption button and picked up the handset. "Yes?"

"We have a problem."

"What kind of problem?"

"I've heard from one of my sources," the man on the phone said, "that the FBI has opened an investigation into the murder at Face-Look."

Aki's grip tightened on the handset. "I see."

"And there's something else. Something even more problematic."

The Asian woman picked up her glass and drained the remaining scotch whiskey. "Tell me, damn it."

"The American DIA is working with the FBI on the investigation."

"The Defense Intelligence Agency?" she screeched. "Why are they involved?"

"I don't know, Aki."

"I fucking pay you to know."

"Yes, ma'am."

Aki poured herself another drink from the bottle of Chivas Regal on her desk. She took a sip to calm her nerves, and said, "You're right. We do have a problem. A fucking big problem."

"What do you want me to do?"

"Deal with it."

"You mean?"

"Whatever it takes, damn it!" Then she slammed down the phone.

Chapter 20

Salt Lake City

"Thank you for seeing us on such short notice," J.T. Ryan said as he shook hands with the city's police chief.

"Anything to help the FBI," Chief Hayes replied.

"This is Colonel O'Shea," Ryan said, motioning to the Army officer. "She's also working on the case."

Hayes nodded to her. "Ma'am. Please have a seat."

Ryan and Kelly sat in the chairs that fronted the chief's desk.

"On the phone," Hayes said to Ryan, "you said you were investigating the deaths of the two executives at Tekk-Sky."

"That's right, Chief. We think their deaths are connected to a murder that took place in Atlanta. The assassination of Face-Look's president."

Hayes opened a desk drawer and withdrew a file folder. "I've made copies of the incident reports. In both of the cases here in Salt Lake, the deaths were the result of auto crashes. Both were ruled accidental." He handed the file to the PI.

Ryan scanned the contents. "Okay. We'll check it out. Chief, what can you tell us about Tekk-Sky? Any problems you're aware of?"

"No. They're one of the area's largest employers. They're a fast-growing business. They do data storage for companies from the U.S. and around the world."

Ryan nodded. "All right. As I said, we'll be conducting an investigation on this. We'll keep you appraised of our progress."

They spent the next hour going over the details of the case with the chief, then Ryan and Kelly left the police station and climbed back in their rented Honda Accord.

After Ryan fired up the car, he turned to the DIA officer, who as usual was wearing her Army uniform. "I'm assuming you'll want to keep tagging along as I work here in Salt Lake City."

O'Shea nodded. "Those are my orders."

"In that case, Colonel, I suggest you lose the uniform."

She looked down at her clothes. "What's wrong with this?"

"A lot of my work as a PI is done undercover. Involving seedy places and even seedier people. An Army uniform like you're wearing is really going to stand out. You do have civilian clothes, right?"

"Of course I do, Captain."

"Then I suggest you use them."

O'Shea thought about this a moment. "All right. That makes sense."

"And one other thing. I can't keep calling you Colonel and you keep calling me Captain all the time. That's not how people talk in the civilian world." He grinned. "We usually refer to each other by our names."

The colonel frowned. She didn't reply for long moment, then said, "All right, Captain. I grudgingly agree with you."

With the frown still on her face, she added, "But I don't like it."

Chapter 21

FBI Field Office
Atlanta, Georgia

Erin Welch snapped out the empty clip of her Glock pistol, inserted a full one, and went into a shooter's two-handed stance.

Taking aim at the paper target ten yards away, she fired off all seventeen rounds, the loud blasts echoing throughout the empty indoor range.

Then she pressed the cubicle's control pad and the paper target slid toward her and stopped a foot away. Erin studied the center bulls-eye of the target, which was completely shredded. Satisfied with the results, she snapped out the empty clip of her gun, took off her plastic ear muffs and protective glasses, and packed the pistol and her shooting gear in her gun case.

Just then her cell phone buzzed and she removed it from her pocket. The info screen simply said *Washington D.C.*

"This is General Keating," the caller said. "Do you know who I am, Ms Welch?"

"I know who you are, General. Ryan told me all about you. By the way, how'd you get my phone number? The FBI keeps that info under wraps."

"I'm in the Defense Intelligence Agency. There's not much we don't know."

Erin gritted her teeth. "I can see that. Why are you calling?"

"Both the FBI and the DIA have an interest in solving the Face-Look murder. Since you're heading up the Bureau's investigation, we need to talk."

"All right, General. Go ahead then."

"Like I said, we need to talk."

"We're talking now."

"Not over the phone, Ms Welch. In person."

"Okay. When are you coming to Atlanta?"

She heard the general chuckle. "I don't leave the Washington area much. You'll have to come here."

Erin tightened her grip on the phone, aggravated by the man's superior attitude. "I'm in charge of the Atlanta office. We have a full case load, with dozens of active investigations. I don't have time to make the trip."

"You need to make the time, Ms Welch. Anyway, I've already talked it over with your boss. He's cleared it."

"You talked with the director of the FBI?"

"I have. I've known the director for years."

Erin gritted her teeth again. Then she breathed in and let it out slowly. "Okay. I'll check my schedule and see when I can book a flight out of Atlanta."

"No need for that. I've already sent a military transport plane to pick you up."

Jesus Christ. Ryan was right about the general. He's a bossy, know-it-all, son of a bitch.

"The plane will pick you up today. I'll text you the details," Keating said and hung up.

Chapter 22

Salt Lake City

J.T. Ryan pushed aside his empty plate and drained his cup of coffee. He leaned back in his seat.

"We can get going as soon as you're ready," he said to Kelly O'Shea, who was sitting across from him. They were in a booth of the Holiday Inn's in-house restaurant.

O'Shea took a bite of toast and nodded. As Ryan had suggested the attractive woman was now dressed in civilian clothes, wearing black slacks, a white blouse, sensible flats, and a gray jacket which nicely concealed the pistol holstered at her hip. Instead of her usual severe bun, today her auburn hair was pulled back into a relaxed ponytail.

"You look good in civvies," he said.

She frowned. "Don't forget, Captain. I'm still your commanding officer."

Ryan laughed. "Don't worry. I wasn't making a pass at you. I was paying you a compliment."

Her eyebrows arched and she gave him a long look as if trying to judge his veracity. After a moment her expression softened. "Sorry. I'm sensitive about my looks. From all my years in the military getting hit on by every Tom, Dick, and Harry."

"Understandable."

She finished eating her breakfast and leaned back in her seat. "I'm done. You got a plan for today?"

"Of course."

"Care to share, Captain?"

"I thought we were going to drop the whole Army rank thing."

She pursed her lips. "It's a hard habit to break."

"Yeah," he said with a grin. "I'm sure it is." He extended his hand and she shook it. "How about you call me J.T. and I call you Kelly?"

The woman withdrew her hand. "How about I call you Ryan and you call me O'Shea?"

He laughed. "That'll work."

"You never answered my question."

"Which one?"

O'Shea took a sip of coffee. "What's your plan for today?"

"The same one I have every day on an investigation. I break down doors, kick ass, and take names."

"You never stop kidding around do you, Ryan?"

He turned serious. "Sorry about that. It's a bad habit of mine. To answer your question, my plan for today is we drive over to Tekk-Sky and ask a lot of questions."

"Okay. And if we don't get answers?"

"Then we ask more questions and look under every rock we come across. That's what PIs do. Sniff around long enough and you're bound to trip over a dead body or two."

***

Ryan drove to the Tekk-Sky complex of buildings in the outskirts of the city and parked in the headquarters lot. The extensive Tekk-Sky operation consisted of at least fifteen industrial buildings, and a glass and steel office structure, all nestled in a valley with a majestic snow-covered mountain range as the backdrop.

After showing their credentials at the ultra-modern foyer, Ryan and O'Shea were escorted to a conference room on the building's top floor.

A moment later a very pregnant woman wearing a gray business pants suit entered the room and closed the door behind her. She was in her forties and had short, curly hair and a ruddy complexion.

"I'm Jan Hamilton," she said, approaching the two people. "The receptionist told me you're with the FBI?"

"That's right, ma'am," Ryan said, handing her his cred pack, which she examined and returned. "I'm J.T. Ryan and this is Kelly O'Shea."

Hamilton nodded. "I need to sit down," she said, patting her large stomach. "I'm getting close."

They all sat around the conference table and Ryan said, "We met with Police Chief Hayes and he gave us your name – said you were in charge."

"That's right," Hamilton replied. "I'm the remaining partner of the original three managing partners of Tekk-Sky. Since the deaths of my two colleagues, I'm now heading up the firm."

Ryan leaned forward in his chair. "That's why we're here. We're investigating their deaths."

Hamilton's eyebrows knitted. "They both died in car accidents. At different locations and on different days. I talked to the police about this and they said the deaths were accidental."

"We believe there's a connection to a murder that took place in Atlanta," O'Shea interjected. "Are you familiar with the killing of the Face-Look CEO?"

"Of course," Hamilton said, rubbing her forehead. "A horrible, tragic event. Face-Look is one of our largest customers. We do data storage for them."

"We know that, Mrs. Hamilton," Ryan said. "That's why we're here. You do storage for all of the social media companies, isn't that right?"

"Yes. We're the biggest in the industry. So you think the deaths of my partners were not accidental at all?"

"That's right," Ryan said. "It would be helpful if you could tell us more about your company, how it's structured, and other details."

"I'd be glad to. My two partners and I started Tekk-Sky fifteen years ago. We were equal partners." She pursed her lips. "Or at least it started out that way. Over the years the two of them began agreeing with each other more and more, and since I only owned a third of the shares, I was outvoted on many company decisions."

She patted her large stomach. "It got worse when I got pregnant. They thought I would sell my shares to them after my baby was born, but I told them I had no intention of doing that."

"I see," Ryan said. "Can you tell us anything out of the ordinary that happened at Tekk-Sky over the last six months?"

Hamilton looked pensive and she ran a hand through her short, curly hair. "They were cooking up something."

"Your partners?"

"Yes. I asked about it several times, but they would never tell me. It was something big, though. I got the feeling it involved selling the company."

Ryan leaned forward. "To who?"

The company executive shook her head. "Don't know. I do know it involved a woman."

"Did you meet this woman?" Ryan asked.

"No. They met with her offsite, not here at Tekk-Sky. I don't know her name."

Ryan glanced at O'Shea, then back at Hamilton. "Was the woman Asian?"

The executive shook her head. "Can't help you there. I don't know anything about her."

Sensing that what Hamilton was telling them could be a huge break in the case, Ryan said, "Is there anything else about the potential sale of the company that you could tell us?"

She ran her hand through her curly hair again. "I think they got cold feet about selling."

"They told you that?"

"No. It was just a feeling I got."

"I see."

Ryan and O'Shea spent the next hour talking with the executive, asking her questions about the company.

After they left the firm and got back in their rental car, Ryan turned to O'Shea. "You think Hamilton is telling the truth?"

"Yes, I do. She seems like an honest person. But you're the detective. What do you think?"

Ryan gazed out the windows of the Honda Accord, at the cluster of buildings with the scenic snow-capped mountains of Utah in the distance. "Yeah. I've been doing this a long time. And my gut tells me she's not lying."

"It's a shame she never met the woman involved in the possible sale of the company."

"I agree. That would have been a huge break in the case."

"What's next for today, Ryan?"

He fired up the sedan. "I want to go to each of the scenes where the two executives died. We may get some clues from that."

They spent the next several hours visiting the scenes, then the rest of the day interviewing the wives of the dead executives. They learned nothing pertinent to the case and headed back to their hotel.

By the time they drove into the lot of the Holiday Inn it was early evening. Florescent lighting cast a harsh glow over the mostly deserted parking lot. They climbed out of the sedan just as a black GMC Yukon screeched to a halt right behind their car. Three men brandishing guns piled out of the SUV.

Ryan, his heart racing, pulled his gun and dropped to one knee. He saw muzzle flashes and heard gunfire, one of the incoming rounds shattering his car's window as another bullet ricocheted off the pavement.

The large pistol bucked in Ryan's hands as he squeezed off three rounds. He heard a groan, then shouting, as the attackers took cover behind the SUV. With his adrenaline pumping, he fired three more shots, the Desert Eagle's .50 caliber rounds booms echoing in the night sky. His shots clanged into the SUVs bodywork and shattered a taillight.

Suddenly the attackers piled back in their vehicle and it sped away, its tires screeching as it raced out of the parking lot.

Ryan took in big gulps of air, relieved to be alive. He sprinted around to the passenger side of his car and his heart sank.

Kelly O'Shea was laying on the pavement, unmoving, a bloody gash on her temple.

Chapter 23

Headquarters Building
Defense Intelligence Agency
Washington, D.C.

"Thank you for coming, Ms Welch." General Keating rose from behind his desk and motioned to a visitor's chair fronting it.

Erin Welch sat down. "Not like I had much of a choice."

"That is a fact. No doubt you talked with the director?"

"I did, General. But just so you know, I'm not happy about being ordered around by the DIA on a case that clearly the FBI has jurisdiction."

General Keating steepled his hands on the desk. "I can understand that. That's why I wanted you to come up here. So you could see this is a much bigger case than a murder investigation." The man was wearing his Army officer's blue uniform, with his many commendation ribbons pinned on the chest of his jacket.

"Okay, I'm here now. So talk," she said in an irritated tone.

"As I said, this case is much bigger than you suspect."

Erin leaned forward in her chair. "I want to catch a killer."

"If we pool our resources, we'll catch the killer and accomplish my mission at the same time."

She glanced at her watch and then back at him. "Then tell me. I've got a truckload of cases stacking up in Atlanta."

The general stood. "Instead of me telling you, it'd be better if I show you. But just to be clear, anything you see here at the DIA is considered top secret."

"Of course. I know the drill. I've been in law-enforcement a long time."

Keating went around his desk and led the FBI Assistant Director out of his office and down a corridor. They took an elevator down to an underground floor. He used a retinal scanner to access a room and they both stepped inside.

The large space contained a group of computer workstations. Erin counted at least thirty people in the room, all wearing military uniforms, all intently studying computer screens.

The general approached one of the workstations and said, "Sergeant, pull up the social media sites on your screens. The ones we talked about this morning."

The crew-cut soldier nodded. "Yes, General." He began tapping keys and a few moments later the three computer screens at his workstation displayed the sites.

Keating pointed. "Are you familiar with these?"

"I am," Erin said. "Those are three of the most prominent social media websites – Tweeter, LikeU, and Inagram. I have accounts on all of them."

"That's helpful. When I told Ryan about these he seemed clueless about them."

Erin nodded. "He's very good at his job. But old school. Doesn't like all this high-tech stuff."

"Sergeant," the general said, "show us the news feeds on each of these sites."

"Yes, General." The soldier typed on his keyboard again and Erin watched as the screens began displaying news headlines from the U.S. and around the world.

"You notice anything unusual, Ms Welch?"

She studied the news items intently for several minutes. She then turned to the Army officer. "I didn't notice it at first, but I'm sensing a pattern here. Each of these social media sites is showing the same news stories from the exact same news sources."

Keating nodded. "That's right. It's a pattern we at the DIA picked up." He pointed to the screens. "These are just three social media companies. But there are many others, as you know. And these days, a lot of people in the U.S. and around the world get their news from these sites. That's why we're so worried. What if someone with criminal intent controlled these news feeds. What if they selected which stories were shown. And worse yet, what if these social media sites directed you to biased or even fake news sites."

Erin mulled this over a moment, the implications becoming crystal clear. A sick feeling settled in the pit of her stomach.

Chapter 24

Salt Lake City, Utah

J.T. Ryan entered the hospital room and approached the bed.

A very pale Kelly O'Shea was laying on it, a sheet over her torso. A large bandage covered her temple and she was hooked up to an IV. Her face was so blanched that even her freckles were almost invisible.

She was asleep, her only movement being the slow rise and fall of her chest. He noticed she was wearing one of those silly PJs they give you in hospitals, this one was yellow with tiny purple flowers printed on it.

Ryan gently touched her arm. "Wake up, sleepy head."

Her eyelids flickered open. She gazed at him with a vacant expression and after a moment she focused. "Captain Ryan."

He grinned. "The one and only."

O'Shea glanced around the room. "Where the heck am I? What happened?"

"You don't remember?"

She shook her head.

"We were ambushed. At the hotel."

She processed this and nodded. "I remember now. Those men ... started shooting at us. After that, I'm drawing a blank."

"You were shot." He pointed to her bandage. "Luckily it only grazed your forehead. The doctor told me you should be okay in a week or so."

Her hand felt the bandages. "What happened to the attackers?"

"I fired back, wounded one, but they fled and got away, damn it."

"We're lucky to be alive, Ryan." She looked pensive. "You saved my life. If you hadn't shot at them I'd be at the morgue right now."

"That's a morbid thought. Cheer up, will you? By the way, have you heard this joke? 'I had amnesia once. Okay, maybe twice.'"

A small smile played on her lips.

"Or how about this one," he said. "'I've often wanted to drown my troubles. But I can't get my wife to go swimming.'"

Her smile grew.

"Or this one," Ryan continued. "'I fell down a really deep, dark hole today. I couldn't see that well.'"

She chuckled.

"That's better," he said, smiling. "I got another joke for you. O'Shea, did you realize that when two people get married, they have three kinds of sex?"

The woman shook her head.

"First, there's house sex, which means they have sex in every room of the house. Over time, it turns into bedroom sex, where they only have sex with the lights off and under the covers. And the final stage is hallway sex."

"What's that?" she asked.

"That's when you pass each other in the hallway and say, 'fuck you'."

O'Shea laughed heartily. "You're incorrigible, Ryan."

He pointed at her. "Made you laugh."

"You did. But seriously, you did save my life. Thank you for that. I guess I'm in your debt now, Captain. Not a position I'm pleased about."

"I tell you what, Colonel. I know a simple way you can repay the debt."

A suspicious look crossed her face. "What?"

"I'm really not into the Army rank stuff. And I'm tired of calling you by your last name and you by mine. Sounds way too formal. How about you call me J.T. and I call you Kelly?"

She looked pensive. "I'm still going to be your commanding officer, Captain John Taylor Ryan. Are we clear on that?"

"Of course."

"In that case, J.T., I think it'll be okay."

Chapter 25

Grand Cayman
The Cayman Islands
the Caribbean

Aki Tanaka entered the bank and headed for the manager's luxuriously appointed office.

Spotting her immediately, the banker got up from behind his desk and after a slight bow, waved her to one his opulent visitor's chairs.

Aki sat, while her ever-present Asian bodyguard stood nearby. The heavily-muscled man, who was well over six and a half feet, had a shaved head, hooded black eyes, a jagged scar that ran down one cheek, and an aura of menace that shadowed his every move. He was carrying a large suitcase, which he rested next to him on the floor.

"Welcome to our lovely island," the bank manager said, addressing Aki. "How can I be of service this time?" The thin, wiry man in his sixties was wearing an impeccably tailored three-piece business suit.

"I want to buy another company," she said. "I need your help with that."

The bank manager beamed. "It would be my pleasure." His eyebrows arched. "Our usual arrangement?"

Aki nodded. "Yes."

"Excellent."

She placed a large manila envelope on his desk. "The details are all in there. I'll need to set up several shell companies to distance myself from this purchase."

The bank manager opened the envelope and read through the documents. His eyes got big and he sucked in a quick breath.

"Is everything in order?" she asked.

"The paperwork is quite clear." He tapped the documents. "I recognize the company you are buying. It's a ... very sizeable investment. Much larger than any of your previous transactions."

Aki ran a hand through the long tresses of her black wig. "My business is growing. And will continue to grow over the next year. I hope you'll be able to handle it." In a hard tone she added, "But if this deal is too big for you, I can find a dozen other bankers that would love to take it on."

The man's face turned ashen and he blinked rapidly. "No ... no ... of course not. This deal is not a problem for me ...."

"Good. I would prefer dealing with you. You've competently managed all of my projects in the past. I'd rather not change horses midstream."

The color came back to the banker's face. "Thank you, madam. You're my best customer and I'll do whatever it takes to make you happy. Do not worry, I'll be able to handle this deal and any others you have."

"Good. I recognize this company purchase is extremely large. So I want to compensate you appropriately for your efforts." She snapped her fingers and glanced at her bodyguard, who stood nearby.

"Honshu," she ordered. "Give him the case."

The bodyguard nodded, picked up the large suitcase and placed it by the banker's chair.

Aki mentioned a very large sum of money. "The cash in the case is just for you. Off-books, of course. I'll wire you the money for the purchase of the company."

The bank manager beamed. "You are very generous, madam."

"Generosity has nothing to do with it," she said, her tone icy. "I pay well because I expect, in fact, I demand positive results."

Aki stood. "That concludes our business. I'll be on my way."

"Don't you want me to count the cash in the suitcase and give you a receipt?" the banker asked.

She flashed a cold grin, which had no humor in it. "No. That won't be necessary. People who try to fuck me over have a way of disappearing." She glanced at her bodyguard. "Isn't that right, Honshu?"

The hulking giant nodded, but as usual stayed silent.

Chapter 26

FBI Field Office
Atlanta, Georgia

J.T. Ryan strode into the Bureau's cafeteria on the first floor and scanned the room for Erin Welch. He spotted her at a booth in the back, sipping coffee, an empty plate in front of her.

He approached the table and sat across from her. "Good to have you back in Atlanta," Erin said.

"Good to be back."

"How's Kelly O'Shea?"

"In her hotel room," Ryan said. "Still recuperating."

Erin took a sip of coffee. "The men who ambushed you in Utah. You think it was a robbery gone bad?"

"I doubt it. I think it's all connected to the case."

"I agree, J.T. Which means we've got more problems than we thought."

"Yeah. It means the criminals involved in the Face-Look murder have a source inside somewhere. The thugs who attacked us knew who we were and what we were up to."

Erin nodded. "Any idea where the leak is?"

"No."

"Me neither. Which bothers the hell out of me. It could anybody – even someone at the Bureau." She rested her cup on the table. "On a positive note, we did get a break on the case."

"What?"

"You remember the trace evidence you collected at the location where the sniper took his shot?"

"Sure, Erin."

"Well, we were finally able to match the killer's DNA to someone in the system. NCIC cross-referenced it to a guy who did a nickel at the state pen in Reidsville."

"Finally. Some good news. I told you my ace detective skills would solve this case."

She jabbed a finger on his chest. "Don't even think about it. I'm not giving you a bonus."

Ryan grinned. "You know me too well. Who's the guy?"

"His name is Joe Padilla, although he goes by a couple of AKAs."

"Do you have him in custody now?"

Erin shook her head. "No. We went to his last known, but the landlord in the building told my agents he hadn't lived there in over a year."

"Too bad." Ryan thought about this a moment. "This Padilla – you said he spent five years as a guest of Georgia's finest penitentiary?"

"That's right."

"I may be able to get a lead from that."

"How?"

"I know a guy, Erin."

Erin nodded. "You always know a guy. Who's the CI?"

"No way. My confidential informants stay confidential."

She shrugged.

"Do you have any particulars on Padilla?" he asked.

She filled him in on the few details the FBI had been able to uncover.

When she was done, he said, "I'll need a few things."

"What?"

"Some Kevlar, a tactical shotgun, an AR-15, some flash-bangs, and plenty of ammunition."

"You planning on starting a war, J.T.?"

Ryan shook his head. "No. But after what happened in Utah I want to be prepared for anything."

"Okay." She reached into her briefcase, took out a notebook, and scribbled on it. She tore the sheet and handed it to him. "Give this to Agent Wilson. He runs the FBI armory. He'll give you anything you need."

"Thanks."

"And J.T. One last thing. Don't get killed."

He grinned. "Because you'd miss my wit and charm?"

Erin frowned. "No. Because I need your help solving this damn case."

He laughed and stood up.

***

After drawing the Kevlar vest, a Remington tactical shotgun, a Ruger AR-15, and the other items from the FBI armory, Ryan packed his duffel in his SUV and drove over to the Marriott Hotel, located near I-75.

He took the elevator to the third floor and knocked on one of the rooms. He heard locks clicking off and the door opened.

Kelly O'Shea stood there, holding his .357 Magnum revolver at her side. The young woman was wearing a sweater and jeans, her reddish hair pulled into a ponytail. A bandage still covered part of her temple.

"Come in, J.T."

He went inside and she shut the door behind him.

"How are you feeling, Kelly?"

She gently massaged her forehead. "Damn headaches won't go away."

"Take your meds?"

"You sound like my mother. Of course I took my medicine."

Ryan nodded. "The doctor at the hospital said it'd be a week or more before you'd recover. It's only been a few days."

"I know. But I'm going stir crazy in here. There's just so much TV I can watch." The set in the room was blaring and she walked over and shut it off. Then she rested the pistol on a table and sat on the bed.

"Any progress on the case, J.T.?"

Ryan filled her in on his meeting with Erin.

"So what's next?" she asked.

"I go find this Padilla guy."

"I'll go with you."

"The hell you will, Kelly."

She glared at him. "You don't tell me what to do!"

Ryan held his palms in front of him. "I know. I just think you need to recuperate a little longer. You got shot, remember?"

Kelly gave him a hard look, then folded her arms across her chest and let out a long breath. "All right."

"Good. By the way, I think we ought to keep this between ourselves."

"What do you mean, J.T.?"

"It'd be better if you didn't tell the general that I was flying solo."

"Why not?"

"He's liable to send another DIA agent here to keep an eye on me."

"You want me to lie to my commanding officer?" she said.

"Not lie, exactly. Just don't tell him all of the details."

Her shoulders sagged. "You trying to get me court-martialed?"

Ryan shook his head. "Hell, no. When we crack this case wide open, you'll get a commendation. Maybe even a promotion. How does that sound?"

She suppressed a smile. "Sounds like a load of bullshit to me."

***

Ryan left the hotel, got back in his Ford Explorer and drove on I-75 and then on SR 400. Half an hour later he parked in front of a run-down bungalow with a sagging roof and peeling paint. There was a rusted-out Chevy pickup in the driveway so Ryan knew the man was home.

The PI checked the load in his pistol, got out of his SUV, and knocked on the bungalow's front door. There was no answer so he tried the knob and found it unlocked. He slipped inside the dimly-lit interior. The blinds in the living room were drawn and it was almost pitch black in the room.

Ryan pulled his gun and held it at his side. "Stich, you here?" he called out.

There was no answer. He found a light switch and turned it on. The place was a shit-hole. Empty beer cans, pizza boxes, and trash littered the floor and covered the dilapidated furniture. The whole place stank of spilled beer and piss.

Ryan heard a moan from one of the other rooms and he tightened his grip on his pistol. He cautiously made his way there and turned on the light in that room. He found the man stretched out on his back on the sagging bed.

"God damn it!" the guy yelled. "Turn off the fucking lights."

Ryan sighed and sat on the bed, the worn-out springs groaning in protest. "It's me, Stich."

The man's eyes snapped open. "Ryan? What the fuck you want?"

"Information."

"Go away ... I need to sleep."

Ryan knew the thin, wiry guy was fifty, but looked much older. He had sunken eyes, long greasy hair, and an unkempt beard. He was wearing soiled dungarees, a torn undershirt, and stank of body odor.

The PI grabbed one the man's skinny arms and held it up to the light. The track marks there were fresh. He then noticed the spent needles among the other trash on the floor.

"You've been shooting up again, Stich?"

"Tell me something I don't know. Go away and let me sleep, motherfucker."

Ryan slapped the man hard across his face and Stich yelped and recoiled into a corner of the bed.

"What happened, Stich? I got you into that rehab program last month."

"It didn't take."

Ryan shook his head slowly. "I can see that." He stared into the man's sunken and bloodshot eyes. "You awake now?"

Stich nodded, but looked ready to bury himself into his pillow again.

"How much money you got left?" Ryan said.

"I'm broke."

"You're going to need to shoot up again soon."

"You're a fucking rocket scientist to figure that out, Ryan."

"No. I just know a junkie when I see one. I'll pay you for the information. I'm assuming you're interested."

The man's bloodshot eyes got big. "Hell, yeah. What do you want to know?"

"You did time at Reidsville."

Stich nodded. "What of it?"

"I'm looking for a guy. His name's Joe Padilla. He served five years at the state prison. Ever heard of him?"

"Maybe I have, maybe not. How much is it worth to you?"

"Two hundred."

"That's bullshit, Ryan. Five hundred."

The PI stood and turned to go. "Three, and that's my last offer."

"Okay, okay, that's good."

"Now talk."

"You got the cash on you?"

Ryan patted his jacket.

"Okay. I knew a guy by that name when I was inside."

"Tell me about him."

"He was a criminal, like me."

Ryan grabbed Stich by his undershirt and shook him. "You better have more than that or we're done here."

"Take it easy, man! Let me think." He rubbed his bloodshot eyes.

The PI let go of the man and he sagged back on the bed.

After a long moment, Stich said, "I remember Padilla had a girl he talked about sometimes. She worked at the Starlight."

"The strip club in Sandy Springs?"

Stich nodded. "Yeah. Padilla said his girlfriend was an exotic dancer." He grinned, exposing his crooked, brown-stained teeth. "But I've been to the Starlight. They don't got no exotic dancers there. They got strippers and none of the ones I saw there were modeling material, if you get my drift."

Ryan rolled his eyes. "Glad you have such high standards. What's this stripper's name?"

"Don't know her real name. But her stage name is Ruby."

"Like the jewel?"

Stich nodded. "Yeah. Like the jewel."

"Okay." Ryan took out his wallet, counted out the cash, and handed it to the man. "If I find out you're conning me, Stich, I'll be back." He patted the man's cheek hard. "And I'll want my money back plus interest."

Stich's eyes grew wide. "It's all true. I swear."

"All right." Ryan felt a stab of sadness for his CI, a burned-out junkie who a long time ago had served in the military. Ryan knew the man was going down a dark tunnel, his life spiraling out of control every day. Eventually he'd end up on a slab at the county morgue.

Ryan rummaged through his wallet and found the business card he was looking for. He handed it to Stich. "The guy on this card," Ryan said, "runs a program for heroin addicts in downtown Atlanta. From what I heard, he's got a pretty good track record on getting people clean. Go see him."

"Thanks, Ryan."

The PI stood, hoping Stich would take his advice, but knowing deep down he wouldn't.

Chapter 27

Sandy Springs, Georgia

The Starlight Club was located in Sandy Springs, a suburb north of Atlanta. The club was on a side street a few miles from Route 9. It was a run-down, one-story concrete building with a garish neon sign. The sign said *The Starlight – Georgia's Premier Gentlemen's Club*. In smaller letters it said *Beautiful Girls – the Best Drink Prices in town*. The building was nestled between a seedy-looking massage parlor on one side and a dilapidated pawn shop on the other.

Ryan parked his Ford Explorer in the Starlight's half-empty lot, and after paying the cover charge at the door, strode in the place. Rock music pounded from overhead speakers and cigarette smoke hung in the air. The whole place stank of sweat, tobacco, vomit, and a few other sour odors. A stage was at the far end of the large room, illuminated by multi-color strobe lights. Two female dancers gyrated listlessly on poles as guys in work clothes gaped from nearby tables. The dancers wore tiny G-strings, hooker heels, and tired smiles.

Ryan approached the long bar and sat at a stool. When the overweight bartender came over, the PI said, "I'm looking for Ruby."

"You a cop?" the guy said.

"No," Ryan said.

"You look like a cop."

"I get that a lot."

"What do you want with Ruby?"

"That's my business."

"Beers are twenty bucks."

Ryan stared at the fat bartender. "That's a hell of an expensive beer."

The bartender gave him a crooked smile. "Beer is ten. But I get another ten to find Ruby for you."

Ryan pulled out the cash and placed it on the countertop.

The fat man scooped up the money, turned, and went into a back room. When he came back he said, "Ruby be out in a minute."

"Where's my beer?" Ryan asked.

"Take my word for it — you don't wanna drink the swill we serve here."

A few minutes later a middle-aged brunette wearing a white robe and flats walked out of the back room and sat next to Ryan at the bar. She had short curly hair, ruby-red lipstick, a haggard look, and from the way she filled out her robe she probably sported 36DDs, a slim waist, and generous hips. She wasn't pretty at all, but she exuded an animal sexuality that Ryan figured paid off in spades in her profession. She also gave off a pungent lavender scent, as if she'd bathed in the perfume.

"Heard you lookin' for me," she said, in a southern drawl, as she turned to face him.

"You Ruby?"

"The one and only." She gave him a long up and down look. "You a cop?"

"You're the second person in the last five minutes to ask me that."

"Well?"

"Well, what?" he said.

"Are you a cop or not? You gotta tell me. If you lie about it's called entrapment."

Ryan nodded. "You've been around the block a few times."

She flashed a tired grin. "Honey, I haven't been just around the block a few times. I've been around the world and I've never stepped foot outside of Georgia."

"I'm not a cop. I'm looking for information."

"You got cash?" she said. "I don't take plastic."

"Yeah."

"I got five minutes before I go back on stage. Ask fast."

"I'm looking for Joe Padilla. I've been told you know him."

"Cash first."

Ryan stared at her. "Talk first. Then I pay you."

She rose from the stool, an impatient look on her face. "You know the old saying. Money talks and bullshit walks."

"Okay." He pulled out his wallet and handed her a hundred bucks.

She flashed a tired grin. "That's better. By the way, what's your name, honey?"

"Ryan. J.T. Ryan."

Ruby placed a hand on his arm and rubbed it slowly. "Nice name. Maybe you want more than information." She leaned forward and her robe fell open, revealing her generous cleavage. She was completely nude under the garment.

He was instantly aroused and forced himself to look up from her voluptuous body and focus on her eyes. "Like I said, I'm just looking for information."

She took her hand away and cinched her robe closed. "Shame. I don't get hunky guys like you in here very often."

"I've been told you're Joe Padilla's girlfriend."

She grimaced. "I know Joe. But I'm not his girlfriend."

"But you know him, right?"

"Yeah. Joe and I go way back," she said. "He used to come here to the Starlight and watch me dance. Took a liking to me. We had some drinks, some laughs, and before long he was paying me to suck his cock every night."

Ruby flashed another tired grin. "Like I said, I wasn't his girlfriend, but I knew him as well as any woman can know a man."

Ryan nodded. "I need to know where he lives now. We checked on his previous addresses but he's long gone from there."

"How much?"

"How much what, Ruby?"

"How much you gonna pay me to tell you. I learned a long time ago not to give out freebies. In bed or anywhere else."

The PI mentioned an amount.

She counter offered.

After another minute of haggling they agreed on an amount and Ryan handed the money.

She opened her robe and seductively tucked the cash between her nude 36DDs. After closing the robe and cinching it tight, she told him where Joe Padilla lived and a few other things about the man.

"Okay, Ruby. You've been a big help." He got up from the bar stool.

"Hey, honey," she purred, "if you ever want a private lap dance, you know where to find me." She rubbed his arm and gave him a suggestive grin. "I'll give you my very best price."

"I'll pass."

"It's your loss, honey. It's your loss."

Chapter 28

Tokyo, Japan

Aki Tanaka strode to the teak cabinet in her office, poured herself a tumbler of scotch, and went back to her life-size chess set, which was in a corner of the luxuriously-appointed room.

Aki sipped liquor as she studied the placement of the ceramic chess pieces, which were as tall as she was. Going behind the black Bishop, she pushed it diagonally five spaces. Now that the FBI and DIA had begun an investigation into the murders, the chess game she had been playing had taken on a new urgency. Before the investigation the game had been a casual diversion. But now she had a real opponent not just an imaginary one.

Downing the rest of the scotch in one long gulp, she set down her glass, the buzz from the liquor energizing her. She then turned her attention to the white chess pieces, the ones that symbolized herself. She had always had an affinity for the white pieces, since it reminded her of her own natural hair and eye color.

Aki went behind the white Knight and pushed it two spaces forward and one space left, effectively blocking the black Bishop's move. Satisfied with her strategy, she refilled her glass with Chivas and sat down at her desk.

Just then Aki's desk phone buzzed. Glancing at the encrypted code on the info screen, she instantly recognized the caller.

She picked up the handset. "Karl, it's so good to hear from you. But I wasn't expecting you to call. Is everything okay?"

"I have been thinking," Karl Strada replied in his German-accented English. "About the schedule."

"What about it?"

"I am concerned, Aki. I think Viper is falling behind our target dates."

She massaged her temple, her head beginning to throb. "I don't know what you're talking about. We're on schedule."

"You are forgetting about the American election. It is coming up soon."

Her headache intensified. *Fuck. Not that shit again. Damn it.*

Forcing herself to keep calm, she said, "Everything is going to be fine, Karl. We'll be able to meet all of our objectives with time to spare."

The billionaire didn't reply for a long moment, then said, "I am not confident of that at all. You know how important the U.S. election is to me. I have bankrolled many of your ventures over the years. But this aspect of Viper, the political objective, is by far my biggest goal."

"But, Karl —"

"Do not interrupt me," he replied, his voice harsh. "I know to you this whole project is about making money. About blackmail, and theft, and money-laundering, and who knows what else. But not to me!"

Aki massaged her temple again, wishing to God her bottle of Chivas was on her desk and not in the cabinet. "I understand, Karl. I'll make it happen. You'll see."

"The American presidential election only comes up every four years. If we miss this one ...."

"We won't."

"We will miss it, Aki. With our current pace of acquisitions. You have to speed up the schedule."

"But that's dangerous. Our involvement could be exposed."

"I do not care. Make it happen."

A stab of fear shot down her spine. *Damn. The FBI. The DIA. Maybe others. And now this. Damn it all.*

"Aki, if you do not follow my instructions this will be the last project of yours I will fund."

She gripped the handset tighter, her fear intensifying as the liquor in her stomach turned sour. She was about to respond when she heard a click on the line and realized the man had hung up.

Chapter 29

Atlanta, Georgia

J.T. Ryan drove north on State Road 400, got off the highway, and took Route 9 toward Milton, a lightly-populated upscale suburb of Atlanta.

According to Ruby, Joe Padilla now lived in a large track of land in the Milton area. As Ryan wound his way through the scenic, rolling countryside, he realized Padilla had prospered in recent years, having left behind the gritty streets of central Atlanta.

Ryan continued north for three miles, passing upscale, multi-story brick homes, several with horses grazing on large, gated properties.

A few minutes later he spotted the right address on a mailbox, slowed his Ford Explorer, and stopped. The wooded property looked to be at least five acres, all ringed by ornate wood fencing. A gravel road led up to the obviously expensive two-story home. There were no cars in the driveway nor lights coming from inside the house. It was dusk and the only illumination at the home were floodlights at the front and rear.

Ryan drove past the property and pulled off the deserted road and into a sheltered, wooded area. Climbing out of his SUV, he opened the back lift-gate and rummaged through the large rucksack he'd obtained from the FBI armory.

He donned the Kevlar vest, slung the tactical shotgun over his shoulder, and stuffed a couple of flash-bangs into his pockets. Then he shut the lift-gate, checked the load on his Desert Eagle, racked the slide and set the safety. That done, he pulled the brim of his Atlanta Braves baseball cap low over his eyes and advanced into the woods in the direction of the home's backyard.

A few minutes later the woods thinned out and he crouched by a thicket of vegetation. He was facing the rear of the large home, which was set in a clearing about a hundred feet away. He spotted a barn off to one side and also a swimming pool. It was nighttime now and the area was illuminated by floodlights. He saw no people, nor dogs, and as in the front of the home, no lights shone from any of the windows.

He remained hidden in the thicket for the next ten minutes, his senses alert, trying to figure out if anyone was in the house. It was a technique he'd been taught in the Army Rangers called SLLS, which stands for *Stop. Look. Listen. Smell.*

Ryan heard no sounds, save the rustling of branches, the whisper of wind, and the chirping of birds. He smelled no cooking scents nor the aroma of a fireplace. As a last precaution he found a few pebbles on the ground and lobbed them toward the home's backyard and back wall. No dogs barked and no lights turned on.

The PI took the safety off his pistol and held the weapon at his side and cautiously approached the back entrance. Hugging the back wall, he peered into the dim interior of the home through the French doors. He spotted a tiny red light blinking inside.

From a pocket he pulled out a small device he'd drawn from the FBI armory. He tapped multiple keys on the device and the blinking red light turned green. Satisfied the house alarm was deactivated, he took out his lock-pick set and fiddled with the lock.

Ryan turned the knob and slipped inside, closing the door behind him. Using a penlight, he advanced deeper into the large house, searching all of the rooms on both floors and the garage. In the basement he found a closet stocked with a high-powered snipers rifle and other sophisticated weaponry. But as he had expected the whole house was vacant.

He retraced his steps back to one of the rooms in the first floor, an office. Using the penlight he rummaged through a roll-top desk that was in a corner of the room. But he didn't find what he was looking for, a laptop or computer tablet. He did find a small leather-bound notebook, filled with numbers and letters. The words made no sense and it was obvious Padilla was a cautious man who kept records of important things in code. He pocketed the notebook and continued searching the office. He found nothing else of value, just water, electric, and phone bills. The bills were not in Padilla's name and it was clear the man used aliases to evade the law.

Suddenly Ryan heard engine sounds and the crunching of gravel from outside the house.

His heart racing, he sprinted out of the office and went to the front of the home. Peering through a window, he spotted car headlights and heard the creaking open and close of a garage door. With his Desert Eagle trained forward he made his way toward the kitchen, the room that adjoined the garage. Crouching by the granite top counter, he waited.

A door opened and the overhead lights flicked on.

Holding his pistol with both hands, Ryan stood and pointed the weapon at the man. "Freeze! Or I shoot."

The man's eyes went wide and the grocery bag he was holding crashed on the tile floor, glass shattering and liquids spilling.

"Hands up! Do it now!" Ryan yelled.

The guy complied as the PI studied his face and features. Erin had showed him a mug shot of Padilla and this man was definitely him, a middle-aged, heavy-set guy with slicked-back hair, a crooked nose, and a pock-marked face.

"What do you want?" the guy said. "Is this a robbery?"

"Shut up, Padilla."

The man's eyes went big again. "My name's Alex Norman."

"Bullshit. You got a rap sheet a mile long. You're Joe Padilla, ex-con and now a murder suspect."

"You a cop?"

Ryan shook his head slowly. "Christ, I'm so tired of that question. Now shut up, lay on the floor face down and put your hands behind your back."

"Fuck you, whoever the hell you are."

"Do what I say, Padilla! Or you'll regret it."

"Like I said, fuck you and whatever horse you rode on."

"Wrong answer." Ryan stepped forward, and using his pistol like a club, struck the guy across his face.

Padilla's knees buckled, his eyes rolled white, and his body sagged to the floor.

Ryan holstered his gun, squatted down, and searched the man's pockets. He found a Glock pistol which he pocketed, and then used plasticuffs to bind his hands behind his back. That done, he dragged him across the kitchen and sat him up on one of the dinette chairs.

Ryan pulled another chair across from the man and sat.

A moment later Padilla regained consciousness, his eyes blinking rapidly. Blood dripped from his nose and mouth, staining his blue shirt.

"Let me tell you how this is going to work, Padilla. I ask questions. You answer them. Got it?"

"Go to hell!" the guy yelled as more blood spurted from the cuts on his face. "I'm not saying a damn word without a lawyer!"

"Wrong answer, friend."

Padilla's eyes burned with hate. "I've been in the system. Lots of times. I know my damn rights. Lawyer. Lawyer now!"

Ryan shook his head. "From my viewpoint it looks to me like you're in no position to demand anything."

"No way I'm talking."

"That your final answer?"

"Fuck you."

Ryan closed his fist and punched him hard in the gut. The guy folded and his body slipped off the chair and on the floor.

The PI grabbed him by the shoulders and hauled him to a sitting position again on the chair. "You ready to talk now?"

The guy said nothing, a scowl on his face.

"I know you murdered the Face-Look CEO, Padilla. We've got your DNA evidence at the scene where the sniper took the shot."

"Means nothing. That evidence could have been planted. My attorney will get me off if that's all you got."

Ryan leaned forward in his chair. "I found a sniper's rifle in your basement. Ballistics will show the round that killed the Face-Look guy came from that weapon."

A worried look crossed the man's face. Then he said, "If you know so much, why do you need me to talk?"

"Because I don't care a rat's ass about you. You just pulled the trigger. I need to know who hired you."

Padilla scowled. "I'm not saying a word. I know my damn rights."

"You leave me no choice." Ryan pulled his pistol and pressed the muzzle against the guy's forehead.

Padilla's eyes went wide. "You can't do this! You can't kill me!"

"Of course I can. Who's going to stop me?"

Ryan had learned long ago that the fear of death is a powerful motivator. He hoped the man would break and start talking before he had to torture him.

Padilla started sweating and his face flushed crimson. "I need ... I need my medicine ..." the man stammered, "I have a ... heart condition ... I have to ... have my pills ...."

Ryan shook his head. "You know how often I've heard a bullshit line like that? Give me a break." He pressed the muzzle of his pistol harder against his forehead.

Padilla's eyes got bigger still and sweat continued to drip down his face. "Please ... it's true ... I need my heart pills ...."

"Talk, Padilla. You got five seconds or I pull the trigger!"

Ryan smelled the stench of feces and knew the man had lost control of his bowels.

Suddenly Padilla doubled over, his body jerked, and he sagged to the floor.

The PI reached down, grabbed him by the shoulders, and hauled him back up to a sitting position on the chair. Padilla's head lolled forward on his chest and his body was inert.

Ryan slapped his face lightly. When that didn't revive him he did it again harder. The guy didn't respond. Perplexed, he felt for a pulse and found none.

Padilla was dead.

Chapter 30

Salt Lake City, Utah

Aki Tanaka belted down another scotch, her eyes fixed out the window of her private jet. The plane was making its final approach over the city's international airport, the area below coming into view. In the distance she could make out the jagged, snow-covered peaks of a mountain range.

Aki refilled her glass from the bottle of Chivas Regal and sipped the amber liquid, the strong liquor giving her that burning and comforting sensation as it went down her throat. But even the multiple drinks she'd had on the flight couldn't erase the blur of the last three days. Her partner's demand that they accelerate the Viper schedule had forced her to alter her plans drastically.

Aki gritted her teeth as she visualized Karl Strada's face. *Damn him. Damn his stupid focus on the U.S. election. Like I give a crap about that.* Every time she replayed their last conversation in her head, her face flushed and her heart raced. The grip on the glass tightened. But more than aggravation, Aki felt something much worse. *Fear.* Moving up her carefully planned schedule as Karl demanded was putting the whole operation at risk. *Putting me at risk.* The FBI and the DIA didn't hire stupid people. She was a master at covering her tracks. *But if I slip up. Even a little.* She willed herself to put that aside for now.

Aki had to. She had no choice. Without Karl's immense financial resources, half of her business ventures would collapse.

As the Gulfstream jet touched down at the airport she sipped more scotch, her thoughts turning to the day ahead.

***

The Lincoln Navigator slowed down then pulled into the driveway. The SUV drove toward the large estate, passing gardens, a fountain, and beautifully manicured lawns along the way. A moment later the Lincoln reached the circular driveway that fronted the three-story mansion and stopped.

Aki's bodyguard Honshu climbed out of the driver's side of the vehicle and after scanning the area, opened the rear door of the SUV.

The Asian woman stepped out and marched to the entrance, her giant bodyguard a discrete distance behind. Aki was wearing a black business suit and black heels which matched the color of her perfectly-coiffed wig.

She rang the buzzer and waited.

She heard muffled footsteps, locks un-clicking, and the front door opened partway.

A very pregnant woman stood at the entrance, a frown on her face. "Can I help you?"

Aki recognized Jan Hamilton immediately from the photos she'd seen of her. The woman had curly hair, a plain face, and intelligent eyes.

"Mrs. Hamilton? I'm Nikita Nashamura," Aki said, using one of the aliases she had created. "I'd like to speak with you for a few minutes."

The frown didn't leave the other woman's face. "What about?"

"About your company, Tekk-Sky."

Hamilton patted her large stomach. "Now's not a good time. Morning sickness. Call my office and make an appointment. I should be back in a few days."

Aki gave her a pleasant smile. "I'm sorry, Mrs. Hamilton, but this can't wait."

"It'll have to wait," she responded, starting to close the front door.

Aki motioned to Honshu and the big man barreled forward, pushing the door fully open and almost knocking Hamilton to the floor.

The woman cowered in the lavish foyer, her body trembling.

Aki shut the door and pointed to the adjoining living room. "Let's sit there, Mrs. Hamilton. So we can talk."

The pregnant woman was wearing casual slacks and a loose sweater and she wrapped her arms around herself protectively. "What ... do you want ...?" she said, her voice breaking.

Aki pointed to the sofas. "Move. Now!"

Hamilton complied and sat on one of the couches while Aki remained standing.

"What do you ... want ..." the woman repeated, "... money? I have ... cash ... jewelry ... upstairs ...."

The Asian woman flashed a hostile grin. "No. I don't want that."

"What ... then ...?"

"Like I said, this is about Tekk-Sky. The company you now head up."

"What ... about it?"

"I want to buy it, Mrs. Hamilton."

The pregnant woman glanced nervously at Honshu and then back at Aki. "It's ... not ... for sale ...."

"I'm here to change your mind."

Hamilton's eyes darted toward the front door. "My husband's due back any minute ... he just went to buy groceries ...."

"That's a lie," Aki spat out. "I know for a fact your husband is in France right now on business."

The woman's eyes bulged and she rubbed her pregnant stomach nervously.

"You have a choice, Mrs. Hamilton. You sell me your company. At a very fair price, I may add. Or two things are going to happen." Aki lowered her voice and in a menacing tone added, "Two very bad things."

"What? What's ... going ... to happen?"

"First off," Aki said, "your husband will never return from France. He'll die in some tragic, accidental way. If you doubt me on this you should know that I'm the one that ordered the murders of your two partners at Tekk-Sky."

Hamilton's face drained of color. She opened her mouth and attempted to speak but no words came out.

"Then there's the second bad thing that's going to happen, Mrs. Hamilton. Something much, much worse."

"Oh, God ... what?"

Aki leaned forward and gently placed her hand on the pregnant woman's large stomach. "You love that baby very much, don't you?"

The woman pulled away, cowering in a corner of the sofa. "Please ... please ... leave me alone ...." she whimpered, her voice trembling, her hands covering her belly protectively.

"I'll leave you alone, Mrs. Hamilton. You have my word on that. As long as you agree to sell me your company. If not ...." Aki turned toward her bodyguard. "Honshu, show her what's going to happen if she doesn't agree to my generous offer."

The hulking giant nodded and without saying a word, slipped a long knife from his jacket. He held the blade close to Hamilton's face, its razor-sharp edge glinting from the chandelier lights in the room.

The pregnant woman's eyes showed true terror as she tried to get off the sofa. Honshu grabbed her arm with a vice-like grip and tightened his giant hand so much that the woman gasped in pain. With his other hand he slashed the knife down, cutting off the sweater's buttons and tearing her polo shirt.

Hamilton screamed and struggled to get away but she was no match for the brutal thug.

"Show her, Honshu," Aki ordered. "Show her what's going to happen!"

The bodyguard slid the tip of long blade downward, cutting open the front of her polo shirt and her bra, exposing her nude breasts and extended stomach. The woman screamed again, her body shaking uncontrollably.

"Cut her, Honshu!," Aki yelled. "She has to know we mean business!"

The bodyguard nodded and pricked the nude stomach with the tip of the sharp blade. A trickle of blood seeped from the tiny wound.

Hamilton screamed again, tears flowing freely from her eyes.

"What's your answer?" the Asian woman snapped, her voice cold and hard. "Will you sell me your company now?"

"Yes! Yes ... yes ... I'll do it!"

"That's much better. I thought you'd see it my way." Aki sat down next to the woman and faced her. "And don't even think about calling the police or the FBI or anyone else about this. They can't protect you. Nobody can. If you breathe a word of our arrangement to anyone, I'll be back. And then I won't be so gentle."

Aki looked up at her bodyguard. "Give me the knife, Honshu."

The big man handed her the blade and Aki pressed the sharp tip to Hamilton's stomach. "If you renege on our deal, I'll come back," she growled, her voice ice cold, "and I'll cut out that baby myself and butcher it into little pieces. Then I'll force you to eat your baby, piece by bloody piece. Are we clear on that, Mrs. Hamilton?"

Chapter 31

FBI Field Office
Atlanta, Georgia

"What the hell were you thinking?" Erin Welch said, pacing her office.

J.T. Ryan raised his palms in front of him. "How was I supposed to know Padilla had a heart condition?"

Erin stopped pacing and sank into her executive chair. She rubbed her eyes with a hand. "He was our only lead, J.T. And now he's dead of a heart attack."

"I know that."

Erin pointed a finger at him. "You should have arrested him and brought him in. We could have interrogated him here. I would have made him talk."

Ryan shook his head. "That's crap, Erin. And you know it. That guy would have lawyered up immediately."

She grimaced and after a long moment her shoulders sagged. "Yeah. I know. It's just, we have nothing else on this case."

He reached into his blazer's pocket and took out a small, leather-bound notebook which he placed on her desk. "I found this at his house. I think it's a logbook Padilla kept. It's written in some type of code that I couldn't figure out."

She picked up the notebook and flipped through the pages. "Okay. This could be good. I'll give it to my tech guys and see if they can crack the code." She glanced back up at Ryan. "Sorry I snapped at you."

He waved that away and grinned. "No problem."

Erin's desk phone rang and she stared at the info screen. "Jesus," she muttered. "It's the general calling. What the heck's he want now?"

She pressed the speaker button on the phone. "Erin Welch here."

"Ms Welch," the man said, his voice filling the room. "This is General Keating."

"How can I help you?"

"Our DIA surveillance satellites picked up an interesting conversation this morning."

"About what, General?"

"The call was between two Wall Street investment bankers."

"I didn't know the Defense Intelligence Agency," she said, "was authorized to monitor phone calls of private American citizens."

The general chuckled. "There's lots of things we do here at the DIA that people aren't aware of."

"I can see that. Tell me about the call."

"The word is out, Ms Welch, that Tekk-Sky, the big data storage company in Salt Lake City, is being sold."

Erin and Ryan exchanged glances. "J.T. Ryan was there recently," Erin said. "He questioned the woman who runs that company now. According to Ryan she had no intention of selling Tekk-Sky."

"Something's changed," Keating replied. "You need to get Ryan back up there ASAP. Find out what's happening."

"Yes, sir. Ryan's with me here now, General. I have you on speaker so he's heard our conversation."

"Ryan," the general said, "I want you to catch the next flight to Salt Lake. Tekk-Sky's the largest cloud storage company in the world. I'm pretty sure the organization behind the murders is planning on buying Tekk-Sky."

"I agree, General," Ryan said. "It's too coincidental for it to be anything else. I'll leave right now."

"Good," Keating said. "And take Colonel O'Shea with you. I want her sticking to you like white on rice."

"You don't trust me?" Ryan said in an irritated tone.

"Not even one bit. You're a cowboy. A loose cannon that has to be reined in."

"But, sir –"

"No buts, Ryan. Colonel O'Shea *will* go with you. If that doesn't happen I'll bust her down to Private O'Shea and lock you up in Leavenworth. Is that understood, Captain Ryan?"

Ryan grimaced. "Yes, sir."

Chapter 32

Salt Lake City, Utah

After showing their credentials at Tekk-Sky's ultra-modern foyer, Ryan and Kelly O'Shea were escorted into a conference room on the building's top floor.

A moment later Jan Hamilton stepped into the room, her face a mask of fear. The woman was wearing a loose pants suit and held a hand protectively over her pregnant stomach.

Ryan held open his cred pack. "I'm J.T. Ryan, Mrs. Hamilton, and this is my associate Kelly O'Shea."

Hamilton glanced nervously at both of them. "I remember you from our last meeting." Her voice was whisper low.

"Mrs. Hamilton," Ryan continued, "we heard rumors that you're selling Tekk-Sky. Last time we talked, you had no intention of doing that."

The woman said nothing. Her face was ashen and her eyes red-rimmed.

"May we sit down?" the PI said, motioning to the conference table. "You look tired, Mrs. Hamilton. I'm sure you'd prefer sitting."

Hamilton shook her head. "No ... I don't have anything to say ... to you." she said, her voice breaking.

"Are you selling Tekk-Sky?"

The pregnant woman nodded. "Yes ... but ... I don't want ... to talk about it."

Ryan exchanged glances with Kelly, then he faced the company executive. "Is someone threatening you? If they are we can protect you."

Hamilton shook her head furiously. "No ... no ... please leave ...."

Kelly O'Shea placed a hand on Ryan's arm. "Maybe it's better, J.T., if I spoke with Mrs. Hamilton in private."

Ryan gave her a questioning look and then shrugged. He nodded to the company executive and left the room, closing the door behind him.

"May we please sit down?" Kelly said in a soothing tone. "This will only take a minute."

The woman looked uncertain, her eyes beginning to water. After a moment she carefully sank into one of the deeply-upholstered chairs in the conference room. She held both her hands on her extended belly.

"How soon is the baby due?" Kelly said in a gentle voice.

"The doctor told me ... a couple of weeks ...."

Kelly smiled. "Have you picked out a name for your baby yet?" she said, trying to calm the obviously frightened woman.

Hamilton shook her head slowly and suddenly her eyes welled with tears. She lowered her head and began sobbing into her hands.

Kelly reached over and gently stroked the woman's back. "It's going to be okay."

After several minutes of crying, the company executive raised her head and wiped the tears from her bloodshot eyes. "I am ... selling the company ... but ... I can't talk ... to you about it ...."

Kelly stared at the woman's terrified eyes and then glanced at her pregnant stomach. "They're threatening your baby, aren't they?"

Hamilton gasped and her body trembled.

"Now I understand," Kelly said in a soothing voice.

"You can't ... change ... my mind ... I will sell it ...."

Kelly nodded. "All right. I could promise you we'd be able to protect you and your baby, but that wouldn't be an honest thing to say. No one can be protected 24/7 from a determined killer."

Hamilton wiped away more tears and remained silent.

"Let me propose something to you, Mrs. Hamilton. We can't stop you from selling your company. But maybe you could give us a clue about the buyers. I'll mention a few things and you nod your head if they're accurate. And anything you disclose to us we'll keep strictly confidential."

Hamilton's eyes watered again and more tears ran down her face.

"I'm asking you woman to woman," Kelly said softly. "We're just trying to prevent other people from being murdered."

After a long moment, Hamilton nodded.

"Okay, that's good," Kelly said. *Maybe we're getting somewhere.* "The person that wants to buy Tekk-Sky is a woman? An Asian woman?"

Hamilton nodded.

"Good. Does this Asian woman have black eyes and long black hair?"

The company executive nodded again.

"And this woman has a bodyguard, a big Asian man?"

Hamilton's face blanched and she cowered in her chair. She said nothing and began sobbing again.

Kelly gave her a moment to compose herself and then said, "I take that as a yes?"

The other woman wiped her tears and nodded.

"Okay, that's very helpful. One last question and then, I promise you, I'll leave you alone. Is there anything else, anything at all, that could help us solve this investigation?"

Hamilton wiped away more tears and looked deep in thought. Then in a trembling voice she whispered, "The Asian woman said ... her name was ... Nikita Nashamura."

Chapter 33

Atlanta, Georgia

"Stop the car, Honshu," Aki Tanaka said. "I think I see him."

The Lincoln Navigator pulled to the curb and Aki glanced down at the picture of the five-year old boy. She gazed back out the window of the SUV and watched as the young boy played on the swing set of the exclusive day-care center. "Yeah, it's him. Stay here, Honshu."

The bodyguard nodded and Aki opened the passenger door and climbed out. She studied the playground and waited until the pre-school attendant who was watching over the children went inside the building. Then she strode into the playground and approached the boy.

The kid stopped swinging and got up from the equipment.

Aki flashed a broad smile and crouched so that she was eye-level with the young boy. He was a cute kid, with freckles and moppish hair. He was dressed in a matching Ralph Lauren jacket and pants, the kind of upscale uniforms Aki knew kids wear at exclusive preschools.

"Billy?" she said sweetly. "I'm Nikita."

"I'm not supposed to talk to strangers," the boy replied, an uncertain look on his face.

Aki smiled again. "You're a good boy, Billy. And smart too. You're right, you shouldn't talk to strangers." She grinned. "But I'm Nikki. I'm a close friend of your mother, Rebecca."

At the sound of his mother's name the young boy relaxed.

Aki took a photo of the Horvath family and showed it to Billy. "See, Billy, this is your family portrait. You and your daddy and mommy and your brother are all in the picture."

Billy nodded. "That's right."

"Do you like candy bars?"

"I *love* candy bars."

Aki put away the photo and removed a Hershey bar from a pocket. She held it up in front of him. "Would you like this?"

The boy smiled. "Yes!"

She handed him the candy bar and he unwrapped it and began munching on it happily, some of the chocolate crumbs staining his jacket.

When he was done, she tousled his moppish hair. "You're such a good boy, Billy. I have a big surprise for you. Your mommy Rebecca asked me to pick you up and bring you to your home. Do you know why she did that?"

Billy shook his head.

"Because she's at home getting ready for your birthday party!"

"My birthday party?" he said excitedly.

"That's right! Your birthday's coming up soon and she wanted to surprise you!"

The kid grinned. "Really?"

"That's right, Billy! All your friends are going to be there. And your mommy's making a chocolate cake and she's getting ice cream and cookies and candy. You like cake and ice cream, don't you?"

"I love it!" he replied, his head bobbing up and down.

"And she's bought you birthday presents! Lots of presents!"

"Wow! I can't wait!"

Aki tousled his hair again. "You're such a good boy, Billy. My car's right over there. I'll take you home to mommy now." She held out her hand and the kid took it.

Aki led them back to the Lincoln Navigator, where she opened a door to the back seat and the boy climbed inside. She followed and closed the door behind her.

She tapped her bodyguard on the shoulder. "Drive Honshu. You know where."

The SUV pulled away from the curb and drove away.

Aki pulled out another Hershey bar and gave it to the five-year old boy. "Here, Billy. Have this. We'll be home soon."

The kid happily unwrapped the candy bar and began eating it as more chocolate crumbs fell on his stylish preschool uniform.

A few minutes later Honshu pulled into a wooded park and wound his way until they reached a desolate, secluded area. Aki and her bodyguard had scouted out the park earlier in the day.

"Stop here, Honshu," she ordered. The Lincoln Navigator parked by a copse of trees and she gazed out the heavily-tinted windows of the SUV. There were no people or cars in the area and she relaxed.

"You know what to do," she said to the bodyguard. The man climbed out of the driver's seat and got in the back seat with Aki and the young boy.

Billy's eyes grew big and wide. He dropped the half-eaten chocolate bar and shrank away from the hulking bodyguard.

Aki smiled. "Relax, Billy, everything's going to be okay."

Honshu took out a roll of duck tape, tore off a piece, and slapped it over the kid's mouth. Then he roughly grabbed the boy's small arms, pulled them behind his back, and taped his hands together with more tape. The bodyguard then slid a black ski mask over his own large, shaved head.

He got behind the little boy and put one of his massive forearms around the kid's neck.

Billy squirmed, his eyes bulging, his face bright red. He tried to get loose from the man but the giant's vice-like grip easily held him in place.

"Be still, Billy," Aki ordered, her voice icy, "and we won't hurt you. If you sit still and do what I say, I'll let you go. All right?"

The kid's petrified eyes darted around the back seat of the SUV, and then he nodded and stopped struggling.

The Asian woman pulled out a cell phone and turned the camera toward the boy. "I'm just going to make a little movie, Billy. Then we'll be all done."

She pulled out a newspaper from the door's pocket and held the front page over the boy's chest. It was that day's edition of the Atlanta Journal. Turning on the phone's camera, she began video taping the scene.

Although Billy stayed still his eyes were as big as saucers and his face was beet red.

She pulled the newspaper away and dropped it to the floor. Still filming the scene, she said, "Honshu, the knife."

The bodyguard slipped the large blade from a pocket and he held the sharp edge to the kid's face.

Billy struggled to get away but he was no match for the brutish thug.

"Be still, Billy, or he'll cut you," Aki said harshly.

The kid stopped struggling as perspiration flowed freely down his face.

"That's a good boy," Aki said as she continued to film the scene. "Honshu, you know what to do."

The big man touched the tip of the blade to the kid's cheek and held it there. Billy's face drained of color but he stayed absolutely still.

"Do the last thing," the Asian woman ordered.

Honshu nodded, pulled the knife away from the boy's face, and cut off one of the locks of hair from his head.

"That's perfect," Aki said, taking the lock of hair. "That should do it." She turned off the camera and composed herself for the upcoming phone call.

A minute later she tapped in a phone number and waited.

The call was answered on the third ring.

"This is Nikita Nashamura," Aki said.

"What do you want *now*?" Tim Horvath responded in an aggravated voice.

"The same thing I wanted yesterday at our meeting."

"I told you then," Horvath yelled, "and I'm telling you now. Face-Look is not for sale!"

"Sure about that, Horvath?"

"God damn you, Nikita. I said no and I mean no!"

"I offered you a fair price. Actually a great price. A 20% premium over what your company is worth."

"I'm not selling! Can't you get that through your head? I'm hanging up now!"

"Don't do that, Horvath, or I'll kill Billy now."

"What? What are you talking about? What's my son have to do with this?"

"I'm sending you a video of Billy. I just made it."

"What? Are you crazy? Are you on drugs?"

"I'm sending you the video now," she said, pressing a button on her phone. "Watch it, Horvath, and we can talk."

The phone was quiet for a minute then Horvath got back on the line. "Oh, my God ... oh my God ... what have you done?" the man said, his voice cracking between sobs. "Please ... please don't hurt him ... please ... I beg you ...."

"I won't. You have my guarantee on that, Horvath." She paused and then whispered. "I'll let Billy go unharmed. If you agree to sell me Face-Look."

"Yes! Yes! I'll do it!"

"You sure?"

"Yes. Of course yes ... please, don't hurt him ...." The man was crying as he spoke.

"I won't. Once I hang up I want you to sign the documents I left with you. Then send them to my banker via FedEx. Is that understood, Horvath?"

"Yes! ... I'll do that right now ... what about Billy?"

"I'll let him go, like I promised. But remember this, Horvath. You renege on our deal and I'll come back and kill not just Billy, but also your other son, and your lovely wife Rebecca, and then you. Is that crystal clear?"

"Yes ... yes ...." he replied, his voice hoarse.

"Good. And one other thing. Don't even think about calling the cops or the FBI or your own security people. They can't protect you. Nobody can. If I find out you called the police or anybody else, I'll come back and not just kill you and your family, I'll torture all of you first, then kill you!"

She heard the man sobbing and she hung up the phone.

Chapter 34

Atlanta, Georgia

J.T. Ryan was about to unlock his office door when he heard muffled sounds coming from inside.

He instantly pulled his gun and placed the box he was carrying on the floor. Crouching, he turned the knob and kicked open the door. He swept the room with his pistol, surprised to find Kelly O'Shea sitting at her desk, working at her laptop.

The young woman glanced up, a startled look on her face. "Jesus, J.T. You trying to give me a heart attack?"

Ryan put away the pistol, picked up the box, and entered the office. "Sorry, Kelly. I didn't think you'd be here this early."

"I've been here since 5 a.m." With a slight smile she added, "Somebody's got work around here."

He grinned, thankful the Army colonel was developing a sense of humor. Then he placed the box he was carrying on her desk and flipped open the lid.

"I stopped at Krispy Kreme on the way over," he said. "Got a dozen doughnuts. Have one."

She wrinkled her nose. "Not big on doughnuts. Anyway, I had an early breakfast at the hotel."

"You sure you don't want any? It's the Breakfast of Champions."

Kelly rolled her eyes. "Spare me."

"All right. More for me." He picked up one of the chocolate covered pastries and happily wolfed it down. Then he snatched another and ate that one as well. After wiping his hands with a napkin, he pulled up a chair next to her desk and said, "What are you working on?"

"I'm trying to run down the name of the Asian woman we got from the Tekk-Sky CEO."

"And?"

Kelly frowned. "Nothing yet. I did find several women with the name Nikita Nashamura. But they all checked out. None had a criminal record, nor any suspicious financials. One woman was a school teacher in Kansas City and another one was a clerk in Beijing, China. There's a few more but they were squeaky clean too. I also looked up their photos and matched them with the picture we have of the woman. That didn't match either. And I've used facial recognition software on the photo we have of Nashamura but didn't find any possible suspects."

"That's too bad. What databases are you searching?"

"Pretty much all of them, J.T. I started with NCIC, and the State Department, and Interpol. I also used the NSA and the United Nations databases."

"So what's next?"

She pointed to her laptop. "I'm running a second search now on the DIA's internal system. The Defense Intelligence Agency keeps tabs on hundreds of millions of people from around the world. I'm hoping something pops from that."

"Okay." Ryan leaned back in his chair and studied the attractive woman, who today was wearing a gray polo shirt, black slacks, and a blue windbreaker. Her auburn hair was pulled back into a ponytail. A small bandage was on her left temple, the only evidence of where the bullet had grazed her head.

"You recovered from the wound?" he asked.

She gingerly touched her bandage. "Pretty much. Although the doctor told me I'll have a small scar for quite a while."

"You have knockout looks, Kelly. Nobody's going to notice."

She blushed, the bright pink coloring accentuating the freckles on her face. "Jesus, J.T., cut that out. I'm your commanding officer."

Ryan nodded. "I'm not hitting on you, if that's what you think. I'm just stating the obvious."

She frowned. "Please keep your opinions to yourself, okay?"

He grinned and gave her a half-salute. "Yes, ma'am."

Kelly gave him a long look and eventually the frown left her face. "I know you weren't hitting on me. And I know why."

His eyebrows knitted. "What do you mean?"

"You have someone."

Ryan rubbed his jaw. "How would you know that?"

"I'm DIA," she said with a smug look. "I know everything."

"Okay, smarty-pants. Spill it."

"I know her name is Rachel West," Kelly said, "and she's an operative for Central Intelligence. I know you and her have a had thing for quite some time. I looked up her picture – she's a stunner. Blonde, blue eyes, long legs, and big ti –"

He held up his hand. "Hold it right there. You've made your point." He sighed. "Rachel and I have been close. Very close. But lately her schedule, my schedule, the fact she lives in the Virginia area and I live in Atlanta ... sometimes these long-distance relationships are hell. Let's just say we're taking a break."

"Whose idea was it, J.T.?"

"What?"

"Whose idea was it to take a break from each other?"

"What does it matter, Kelly?"

"Trust me, it matters."

"You're DIA. I'm surprised you don't already know."

Kelly grinned. "Okay, we don't know *everything*."

"All right, I'll tell you," he said in a glum voice. "But only because I'm sure you'll find out on your own." He pointed to her computer. "Using one of those sophisticated programs of yours."

"Well?"

"Well what, Kelly?"

"Whose idea was it to take a break from each other?"

"Rachel's."

She nodded. "I thought so."

"Why?"

Kelly tilted her head. "I've been around you long enough to know what makes you tick."

"More of your DIA insider knowledge?"

She shook her head. "No, just a woman's intuition. You miss her, don't you?"

He rubbed his face with a hand and let out a long sigh. "Yeah. I do."

Just then her laptop chirped and Kelly turned toward her computer and tapped some keys. "Well, I'll be dammed," she said excitedly. "I got a hit."

"What is it?"

Kelly typed some more on the keyboard and read the screen. "This could be her, J.T."

She faced Ryan. "A bank in the Cayman Islands lists a Nikita Nashamura in a couple of financial transactions."

"The Cayman's?" Ryan said. "Banks there are notorious for laundering money."

Kelly pointed to the computer screen, which showed a document referring to Nashamura several times. "This very well could be our elusive Asian woman."

"You're right, Kelly. Let's check the airline schedules and find out when the next flight is to the Caymans."

Chapter 35

Tokyo, Japan

Aki Tanaka studied the life-size chess board in her opulent office. Going behind the white Rook, she pushed the heavy ceramic figure forward five squares. After resting a moment, she moved more of the chess pieces, both white and black, and considered the board again. The intricately-carved pieces, which resembled 17th century Japanese Samurai warriors, glinted from the overhead lights.

She smiled and took a sip from her tumbler of scotch. *Yes, that's it. That's it exactly.* The chess board now reflected her current progress in the Viper operation.

Turning away from the board, she walked to her desk and picked up the handset of her phone. She pressed the encryption button and tapped in a number.

The man answered on the second ring.

"It's me," she said.

"I have been looking forward to your call," Karl Strada replied, his German-accent coloring his otherwise flawless English.

"Viper is on track, Karl."

"Exactly what I wanted to hear. The Tekk-Sky purchase is complete?"

"Yes."

"And Face-Look? What about that, Aki?"

"All of the documents were signed yesterday."

"So it is ours?"

"It is."

"You are a treasure, Aki."

The Asian woman smiled. "Thank you."

"With these two purchases," Strada said, "and with the others we already have, we can move ahead aggressively on the American election part of Viper."

"Yes, Karl."

"You will start implementing that today?"

"Of course."

"That is excellent." He paused a moment. "Aki, now that things are moving along so well, I was hoping ...."

"Hoping what?"

"To see you again ... here in Vienna."

She gripped the handset tighter. "But I'm so busy with the operation. It's taking up so much of my time. I'm working 24/7 as it is."

"I know, Aki. It is just ... I want to see you again ... you make me feel ... young again ...."

She grimaced. "We've had this conversation before. You have your whores there. You don't need me for that."

"It is not the same. Anyway, I want to ask you something important."

"Ask then. We're talking now."

"No, Aki. Not over the phone. This is important. Very important."

Her mind raced, trying to figure out what the old man wanted. A queasy feeling rose up her throat as the topic dawned on her. *Could it be that? I hope the hell not.*

"Please," he said, his tone almost pleading, "I need to see you. I have to see you."

"Soon. I promise. Soon I'll come to Vienna."

She heard him exhale a long breath.

"That means the world to me," he said elatedly.

"I have to go, Karl. I need to get back to work."

"Of course. Of course."

They said goodbye and she hung up the phone.

She went to the teak cabinet in her office and refilled her tumbler to the brim with Chivas. She belted down the scotch whiskey in one long, delicious gulp, the amber liquid soothing and at the same time burning down her throat, as she tried to erase the image of Karl from her thoughts. *I know what he wants. The bastard. And I'm not giving it to him.*

Aki turned around and faced the floor-to-ceiling windows of her massive office. The room's top-floor location gave her a panoramic view of Tokyo's ultra-modern skyline of soaring skyscrapers. Although it was an overcast, gray day, she could easily make out the Tokyo Tower and the Sumida River as it wound its way on the eastern side of the city. Tokyo was a densely-packed metropolis, with a population of 38 million people. Yet from this vantage point on the top floor the choking traffic at street-level below was almost invisible. She had always found the view serene and peaceful.

Turning away from the windows, she strode to her private elevator and input a key code. The elevator descended all of the floors of the skyscraper and stopped at the basement level.

Known only to her and a handful of her employees, this area of the building was used exclusively for Operation Viper. After using a retinal scanner, she accessed the room. Ten employees were there, all of them men, all of them hard to work. They sat at computer workstations, inputting and extracting data. Unlike the luxurious trappings of her office, this room was bare of any decoration. It had gray concrete walls and harsh fluorescent lights. Industrial-grade linoleum covered the floor.

Aki gazed around the room and approached one of the workstations. The young man sitting there was the room's lead technician and also her favorite employee.

He stopped what he was doing, glanced up at her, and bowed his head slightly.

"Ms Tanaka, how may I help you?" he asked in Japanese.

"I want you to do something," she replied in the same language. She handed him a slip of paper. "These are the passcodes I told you about earlier. I want you to pull up the Tekk-Sky data stream and do a search for me."

The man bowed his head slightly. "Of course, Ms Tanaka."

He fixed his gaze back to his computer monitors and began typing on his keyboard. There were four screens at his workstation.

Aki went behind him and looked over his shoulder as the man worked. Moments later the Tekk-Sky welcome screen appeared on one of the monitors and after another minute the man said, "We're in their data stream, Ms Tanaka."

"That's good, Kobe. Now I want you to do a search of wealthy American men with assets of over twenty million U.S. dollars. And put in one other parameter — all of these men have to be married."

The young man input the parameters and said, "Here's the list."

"Good. Now pull up the social media sites — the ones we have access to."

Moments later the welcome screen of the various social media sites appeared on the multiple screens.

"Now, Kobe," she said, "I want you to cross-reference the list of wealthy, married men on these sites that have an unusual number of contacts with teenage girls. Girls under 18 years of age. Girls that are not their relatives."

Kobe's cheeks flushed and he hesitated.

She placed her hands on the man's broad shoulders. "Kobe, I know you're married and you're very committed to your wife and young child, and I know you want to provide a good life for them. So remember that I pay you well. Very well. More than you can ever hope to make at any other company. When I gave you this job I told you there were things I expected you to do. Things you may not be comfortable in doing. Isn't that right?"

"Yes, Ms Tanaka."

"Then do what I say."

The young man went back to his keyboard and continued to work as she looked over his shoulder. Fifteen minutes later another list appeared on the screen. Kobe pointed. "This is the list."

"Excellent. Now, Kobe, I want you to cross-reference this list with instant messaging of each of these social media sites. Use a few key words: sex and nudity. Also see if any nude or semi-nude photos of these teen girls and the wealthy men show up in their communications with each other."

Kobe blushed again but simply nodded and continued working.

Half an hour later he stopped and said, "This is the list, Ms Tanaka. On it are all of the wealthy men that are having inappropriate contact with teen girls on the social media sites."

"Good. Now put this list on a flash drive for me."

Kobe did as instructed and handed her the flash drive.

The drive felt almost electric in her palm. She closed her fist and closed her eyes at the same time. *This is what Viper is all about. Power. The power of blackmail. Not Karl's bullshit about the American election.* She'd do the election part only because Karl wanted her to. But to her it meant nothing.

Aki opened her eyes and pocketed the flash drive. Then she placed her hands on Kobe's broad shoulders as she looked at the screens. "You've done well, Kobe. Very well. Expect a bonus in this week's pay."

"You are most generous."

She squeezed his shoulders, felt a thrill from his hard-packed muscles. "Of all the men in this room," she said in a low voice so none of the other workers could hear, "you're my favorite. You have excellent computer skills. But that's not the reason you're my favorite, Kobe." She squeezed his muscles again. "You know why you're my favorite, don't you?"

His cheeks reddened but he said nothing, continuing to stare at his computer screen.

Aki felt herself getting wet as she visualized the strapping young man, on his back, nude on the bed, as she straddled him.

"You're my favorite," she whispered in his ear, "because you follow my instructions so, so well."

She reached over and turned off the computer screen. "You need a break, Kobe, from all of this computer work." She chuckled. "But more importantly, I need a break. Let's go to my office upstairs."

Chapter 36

Grand Cayman
The Cayman Islands
the Caribbean

"Thank you for seeing us," J.T. Ryan said, shaking hands with the bank manager.

"Not a problem," the man replied, waving Ryan and Kelly O'Shea to the deeply-upholstered chairs fronting his imposing, cherry wood desk. Caramel color deep-pile carpeting covered the floor of the sumptuous office and gilt-edged oil paintings decorated the walls. The place smelled of money.

The bank manager sat behind his desk. "On the phone you said you're with the FBI?"

"That's right, Mr. Smythe." Ryan handed the man his FBI cred pack which the banker inspected and handed back.

Ryan motioned to Kelly. "Ms O'Shea and I are conducting an investigation into several murders that have taken place in the U.S."

Smythe's eyebrows knitted but he said nothing. He was a thin, wiry man in his sixties and he was wearing an impeccably-tailored, three-piece gray business suit.

"We've identified a suspect we think is responsible for the killings," Ryan said. "And that person is a customer of your bank."

Smythe frowned and he tented his hands on his desk. "I see. Well, as you can imagine, we have many, many clients here. We are a respected financial institution, with incredibly high standards. But we're not required to pry into the backgrounds of our customers." He flashed a tight smile. "I'm sure you can understand this."

Ryan leaned forward in his chair. "The suspect's name is Nikita Nashamura. Do you know her?"

Smythe's smile faded. "No. As I said, we have many clients at our bank. I don't know them all."

"Are you sure?" Kelly asked. "She's a beautiful Asian woman with long black hair. She would be hard to forget."

The banker glanced at Kelly and then back at Ryan. "No. I'm sure I don't know her." He waved a hand in the air. "But I employ many other people here. They may know her."

Ryan shook his head. "I don't think so. The documents we looked at show that you signed the incorporation papers for several of her companies."

Smythe blinked rapidly. He took a long breath and let it out slowly. "You must be mistaken. I'm sure I don't know this woman, Nikita Nashamura. And if I did, we keep our client's dealings confidential."

"We're investigating a murder," Ryan cautioned. "I'm sure you don't want to be complicit. Might do damage to your sterling reputation."

"I'm sorry. But our bank records are confidential."

"We're with the FBI," Ryan said. "We can get a court order and have those records released."

Smythe shook his head and a smug look settled on his face. "You're not in the U.S. The Cayman Islands are a sovereign country. No local judge would grant you a search warrant."

Ryan bolted from his chair and planted his large hands flat on the man's desk. "Tell us what you know, damn it, or you'll regret it."

The banker shrank away from him and rolled his chair back, putting distance between the two men.

Kelly placed a hand on Ryan's arm. "Please, J.T., don't make a scene."

The PI glared at her, then noticed several bank employees and customers were watching the commotion through the office's glass walls. He let go of the desk.

"This meeting is over," the banker said, regaining his composure. "Or do I need to call security?"

"Let's go, Kelly," Ryan said. He turned toward the door and in a low voice said, "This isn't over, Smythe. Not by a long shot."

***

"You think he's lying?" Kelly asked as she rested her laptop on top of the hotel room's desk. They were staying in adjoining rooms at the Westin and were in her room now.

Ryan nodded. "I'm sure he's lying. He's a liar who lies." He motioned to her computer. "Boot that thing up and work some of your DIA magic. We need to find out where Smythe lives here on the island."

Kelly turned on the device and logged on to the Defense Intelligence Agency's mainframe. A few minutes later she said, "Got it. I'll plug the address on a map and see where it's located." She tapped keys and soon a detailed map of Grand Cayman island filled the screen. She zoomed in on the large property and the surrounding streets.

The PI wrote down the address and directions and pocketed the note. "Okay. That's all I need. I'll take it from here, Kelly."

She closed the lid on the laptop and turned toward him. "I'm coming with you."

"Why?"

"Because where you go, I go. Those are the general's orders."

Ryan shook his head. "I have to do this alone."

"I can help."

"Have you ever interrogated a suspect, Kelly?"

"No."

"Trust me, you don't want to start now. It could get ugly fast."

"I'm still going with you, J.T."

"With all due respect, Colonel, you'll only get in the way."

She glared at him as she fisted her hands. "You can't tell me what to do! I'm the one giving the orders, not taking them!"

He raised his hands in front of him. "Look, I'm not giving you an order. I'm just trying to show you things from a different perspective."

She folded her arms across her chest. "I'm listening."

"You've never interrogated anyone. And I'm sure you won't be comfortable watching me threaten someone. Maybe more than threaten. Maybe bloody him a little. Maybe more than a little. Maybe press the muzzle of my gun to his head and watch him squirm. Maybe even more than that —"

She held up a hand. "Okay, okay. I've heard enough."

"There's another advantage to you letting me handle this alone," he said. "If this interrogation goes sideways and I end up getting arrested in the Caymans, you won't be involved in any way."

He paused and then said, "You're an Army colonel with a squeaky-clean record and a bright future." He smiled. "My bet is one day you'll get your one star and make brigadier."

Her face lit up. "You really think I've got a shot at making general?"

He nodded. "I'd put money on it."

Kelly considered this for a long moment. "Okay. I agree you can do this alone. But on one condition only."

"What?"

"If you get in trouble, you call me. I'll rush over and give you backup."

Ryan grinned. "You got it, Kelly."

***

Ryan slowed the rented Toyota Camry as he passed the large mansion. The estate was mostly hidden by seven-foot high walls, and the back of the property overlooked a broad sandy beach. He heard the crashing of waves in the distance. I was 11 p.m. and he spotted lights coming from several of the home's windows.

He drove past the mansion and found a secluded spot under a canopy of palm trees.

Climbing out of the car, he scanned the property with his binoculars. The whole estate was surrounded by the walls, except for the large back yard fronting the beach. He saw security cameras perched on top of the walls and counted two armed guards patrolling the grounds, one in the front and one in the rear, and figured there were more inside. Floodlights lit up the estate grounds.

Putting away the binoculars, he took out a zip-lock plastic bag and placed his pistol inside. Closing the bag, he put it in his windbreaker pocket. That done he advanced toward the shoreline, using the palm trees for cover. He reached the wide, sandy beach and waded in. The Caribbean water was warm and salty, drenching his clothes and shoes.

Using a crawl stroke he swam past the wall and studied the shoreline looking for the patrolling guard. He spotted him smoking a cigarette, a rifle slung over his shoulder, trudging over the sand. Waiting until the man began heading toward the house, he crawl-stroked forward, reached the beach, and took cover behind a large palm tree. His clothes clung to him as he took off his shoes and drained them of the saltwater.

Taking out the plastic bag, he removed his pistol and tucked it in his waistband, determined to use it only as a last resort. *Gunfire brings cops.* The last thing he wanted was to get arrested in a foreign country. Even Erin at the FBI would have a tough time getting him out.

Ryan advanced slowly, skirting the large swimming pool and hiding behind a row of bushes.

A few minutes later he smelled cigarette smoke and heard the scuffle of boots over the terrazzo floor. He spotted the guard once again making a circuit of the back yard. When the man's back was visible, Ryan sprang forward and he looped his brawny arm around the guy's neck and yanked hard. The guard was big and muscular and he struggled to get free, but was no match for the PIs brute strength. The man's knees buckled and his body sagged to the ground, unconscious.

Taking out a roll of duck tape, Ryan slapped a piece over the guy's mouth, then taped his hands behind his back and bound his feet. Dragging the limp body behind a palm tree, he used more duct tape to tie him to the trunk of the tree. Reaching into the guy's pocket, he removed a loop of keys.

Ryan was breathing hard and his heart was racing. He waited a moment to catch his breath, then raced toward the home's side wall and made his way toward the front yard.

Crouching, he peered around the wall and spotted a guard as he patrolled the lushly landscaped grounds. This guard was short and squat and he was cradling an AK-47 rifle.

Ryan waited until the man turned toward the driveway then he sprang forward and hid behind a palm tree. The area under the tree was bordered with large decorative rocks. Picking up one of the stones, he raced toward the guard. When he was nearly on top of him, he swung his arm down, the rock making a crunching sound as it hit the guy's head.

The man went down fast, collapsing on the driveway, his AK crashing down a few feet away.

Ryan froze and faced the house, watching for new activity there. When no new lights came on he breathed a sigh of relief. Once again pulling out his roll of duct tape, he bound the man's hands and legs and gagged his mouth. The guy was unconscious but breathing and would have a hell of a headache when he woke up.

The PI slung the AK over his shoulder and eased his way toward the house. When he reached the front entrance, he tried the ornate, brass doorknob. As he expected it was locked, so he pulled out the loop of keys he'd taken off the other guard. He began trying each of the keys until he found the right one and unlocked the door.

Ryan stepped inside, closed the door behind him, and crouched in the dim foyer. After waiting a moment to let his eyes adjust to the dimness, he un-slung the assault rifle and held it by the barrel, planning on using the weapon as a club.

He advanced slowly into the home along a wide corridor, treading quietly over the blue and white tiled floors. He passed several dark rooms, but saw a light at the far end of the hallway. He headed in that direction, holding the AK in front of him.

Ryan stopped short of the doorway, his adrenaline pumping. He heard the muted sounds of a television, a soccer match he guessed, and smelled the distinctive odor of a cheap cigar. He peeked around the jamb and spotted the guy right away. A big black man, slouched on a couch, his feet propped up on a coffee table, his eyes glued to the TV set. He was chomping on a big fat cigar, the hazy smoke filling the room. The guy was holding a bottle of Red Stripe beer in one hand. An AK-47 was leaning on a wall nearby.

It was obvious the guy was not Smythe and by his big size and brawny build was clearly another guard. Ryan was a good twenty feet away from him, too far a distance to go without being noticed.

The PI crouched in the hallway, mulling his options, all of them bad. He had to incapacitate the man and do it quietly. Hopefully the TV sounds would mask the brawl.

After taking a few deep breaths, he jumped into the room and raced forward, brandishing the rifle like a club. When he was halfway to the sofa the big black man sprang off the couch, his beer bottle and cigar flying in the air.

Ryan swung the rifle down, but the other man blocked it with his thick forearm and rushed toward him. He tackled Ryan, knocking him off his feet.

The guard kicked him with his booted foot, the blow striking him in the gut. Ryan grunted from the pain, then rolled away and jumped to his feet.

They circled each other like angry wrestlers, both men breathing heavy, their fists up, both looking to strike a knockout blow.

The guard sprang forward, swinging a huge roundhouse punch. Ryan sidestepped it and struck him with blows of his own, a hard jab to the man's kidney and an uppercut to his chin. The guy staggered and went to one knee, but recovered quickly, lunging at the PI with his huge arms open, obviously trying to bear hug him to the ground.

Ryan front-kicked him hard in the groin and this time the guy went down and stayed down. The man howled in pain while clutching his groin with both hands.

Picking up the AK-47, Ryan swung it down on the guy's head and the man's body sagged, unconscious.

With his heart pounding and his breathing labored, the PI winced from the blows he'd received. After taking in a few lungfuls of air, he bent down by the unconscious man and gagged him and bound his hands and feet with duct tape.

Then he grabbed the assault rifle again and headed out of the room, hoping the sound of the television had masked the fight. He searched the rest of the mansion's first floor rooms and found no one else.

There was a wide staircase in the center of the house and he climbed up toward the upper floor. He saw no lights when he reached the second floor hallway so he pulled out a penlight.

Glancing both ways of the corridor, he spotted a double door at the far end to his right. He cautiously made his way toward it, treading lightly over the plush, deep-pile carpet. Kneeling by the closed door, he pressed his ear to it and heard nothing. He shut off his penlight, slowly turned the door knob, and slipped inside the room.

After waiting a moment to let his eyes adjust to the dark room he noticed two people on the king size bed. Both were snoring and wearing night clothes. He recognized the banker, Smythe, right away. He assumed the very obese woman next to him was his wife.

Seeing no other guards in the master bedroom, Ryan pointed the AK forward and flicked on the overhead lights.

Smythe's eyes blinked open, and seeing Ryan, he reached toward his nightstand.

"Don't move or you're dead," the PI said, pointing the rifle at the banker's face. Smythe's hand froze.

Ryan approached the nightstand and opened it. Finding a pistol there, he pocketed it.

Suddenly he heard a piercing scream. The obese woman, now awake, cringed on the bed, pulling the bed sheet up to her neck. She began sobbing, her body shaking.

Ryan pulled out his roll of duct tape and threw it at the banker. "Tie her up with this. And slap a piece of it over her mouth."

The man complied, all while his wife continued to cry.

"What ... do you ... want ...." the banker said haltingly, staring at the barrel of the rifle.

"I want the truth, Smythe. And to quote an old TV show, nothing but the truth."

"Please leave us alone, Ryan. I have cash. Lots of cash ... it's in my safe ... over there, behind that painting...." He pointed to an expensive-looking painting hanging on the wall.

Ryan shook his head. "This isn't a robbery, friend. This is about you telling me everything you know about Nikita Nashamura." He pressed the muzzle of the rifle to the man's forehead. "Start talking!"

Smythe's body trembled. "I can't ... I can't ... tell you ... she's ... she's brutal ... she'll kill me ...."

"You have five seconds to talk or I pull the trigger."

The banker's face blanched. He closed his eyes and shook his head.

Ryan gritted his teeth. *Damn you, Smythe.*

He slapped the man hard across his mouth and blood seeped from his lips, staining his pajamas. But Smythe stayed silent, still shaking his head.

"Okay," Ryan said, "let's try a different approach." He marched around to the other side of the bed and tore the bed sheet off the banker's wife. The obese woman's crying intensified and she cringed away from the PI.

He pointed the rifle at the wife's head. He had no intention of hurting her – in fact one of his core values was to never harm a woman. *But I better do a damn good acting job right now.*

"Talk, Smythe!" Ryan yelled. "Talk now or she dies now!"

The banker's terrified eyes swiveled between his hysterical wife and the PI.

Ryan pressed the muzzle of the weapon to her temple. "Talk, you bastard. I've got an itchy trigger finger!"

"Yes! Yes! ... I'll talk!"

"You sure?"

"Please don't hurt her, Ryan." The man began sobbing also, the tears mingling with the blood seeping from his lips.

Ryan pointed the weapon to the floor and walked around the bed. Sitting on it, he cradled the AK on his lap and waited for the banker to stop crying.

"Tell me about your customer, Nikita Nashamura."

Smythe nodded. "I've known her for years ... she's my best client ... she has many bank accounts ...."

"Okay, that's a start. Tell me more."

"I incorporate businesses in her name."

"What does she do with these companies?"

"They're fronts. To launder money."

"What do you get out of it, Smythe?"

"I get a cut, a per cent of the value."

Ryan waved a hand in the air. "Is that how you can afford this place?"

Smythe nodded. "Like I said, she's my best customer."

"What else does she do with these companies that she operates?"

"Sometimes she buys other companies."

"What kind?"

"Lately, big tech companies. Social media companies."

"Which ones?"

"She purchased Tekk-Sky recently."

Ryan nodded, knowing the man was telling the truth. The info confirmed what he and Kelly had deduced from questioning the Tekk-Sky president. "What other companies?"

Smythe told him. Then he said, "I also think she uses other bankers, people like me in other countries, to buy other companies."

"All right, Smythe. That's very helpful. Where does Nashamura get her money?"

"I don't know."

Ryan slapped the man hard across his face, drawing more blood.

The man yelped and cringed away from him. "Please ... it's the truth ... I don't know where ... she gets her money ...."

"All right. I'll accept that. For now." He glanced toward the guy's wife, who was still sobbing. "But if I think you're lying, I'll kill her and you both."

"I'm telling the truth!"

"Okay." Ryan reached into his windbreaker and took out a 5 x 7 photo and held it for the man to see. It was the picture Ryan had received from the surveillance cameras at Face-Look. It showed a beautiful Asian woman with long black hair and black eyes. Next to her was a big and brawny Asian man with a shaved head. "Is this Nikita Nashamura?"

Smythe nodded. "Yes, that's Nikita."

"And the muscular Asian guy with her. Who is he?"

"Her bodyguard. He's always with her."

"Okay. Last question. Where does this woman live? Here in the Caymans?"

The banker shook his head. "No. She has a private jet. She flies here to do business and leaves."

"Where does she live?"

"I don't know for sure. She uses cut-outs. Post office boxes and dummy addresses all over the world that she's set up."

Ryan nodded. "I figured she'd be cautious and do something like that. But you've known her for years. You must have a clue where she really lives."

"Sometimes," Smythe said, "she and her bodyguard spoke to each other in Japanese. Since she's Asian, my guess is she's from Japan. And one time she mentioned something about Osaka, which I know is a city in Japan."

"That's helpful."

"I've told you everything I know. Will you leave us alone now?"

Ryan nodded. "Yes." Then he raised the AK-47 and pointed the rifle barrel at the man's face. "But our little chat stays secret. You tell Nashamura about me and one thing is going to happen — I'll come back and kill you and your wife. Got it?"

Chapter 37

San Francisco, California

Aki Tanaka stepped out of the SUV, and with her bodyguard in tow, went into the building's private entrance. After going through security, she rode the elevator to the top floor. There she was escorted into the corporate board room. The other directors of Goggles were already there, seated around the large conference table, and they stood when she entered.

Aki smiled at the group and sat at the head of the table, while her bodyguard stood ramrod straight in a corner of the room.

Goggles's company president, a tall, lean man in a three-piece suit was seated next to her. He said, "Thanks everyone for meeting on such short notice. But Nikita Nashamura asked to speak to us about a very important topic." He glanced at her. "Ms Nashamura, would you like to proceed?"

Aki smiled. "Of course." Reaching into a leather satchel she had with her, she removed a stack of papers which she passed out to the twenty directors of the board.

After giving them a moment to read over the document, she said, "As you can see, I'm making you a generous offer to buy your shares in the company. A very, very generous offer. As you know, I'm already the largest shareholder at Goggles. Once a majority of you sell me your shares I'll have total control, something I've always wanted. I want to take Goggles to the next level. It's already the largest search engine on the internet. I and my financial backers intend to make it even more dominant in the U.S. and across the world."

By the enthusiastic reaction she saw on the faces of the board members, it was clear many would sell their shares.

Aki smiled. "May I have a show of hands how many of you will take my offer?"

All of the people in the conference room raised their hands, including the company president.

"That's excellent," Aki said, the smile still on her face. *Viper is happening. No one can stop me now.*

Chapter 38

FBI Field Office
Atlanta, Georgia

"Good work, J.T.," Erin Welch said when Ryan entered her office, "on getting the info about Nashamura."

He grinned. "Did you expect anything else?"

Erin rolled her eyes and he sat at one of the chairs facing her desk.

"Actually I can't take all of the credit," said Ryan. "Kelly was a big help during our trip to the Caymans."

Erin nodded, an amused look on her face. "I'm sure she was. What would men do without women around?"

"Is that humor I detect, Ms Welch? I must be rubbing off on you."

She folded her arms in front of her. "God, I hope not. The Bureau would can me if I pick up any of your bad habits."

Just then Erin's phone buzzed and she stared at the info screen. "It's the general again," she said. "I'll put it on speaker."

Erin pressed a button on the phone.

"This is General Keating," the man said, his voice filling the room.

"Yes, General," Erin replied. "I have John Ryan with me here. You're on speaker."

"Good," Keating said. "I need to talk to you both. Our DIA satellites have picked up chatter. Bits and pieces of conversations. Looks like the criminals we're looking for are ramping up their purchases of social media and other high-tech companies. The sale of Face-Look is complete and we're hearing that Goggles is next."

Erin and Ryan exchanged glances.

"That's not good news, General," Erin said.

"I agree. Not good at all. And with the U.S. elections getting close, I'm extremely concerned about what could happen. We need to solve this case and do it fast."

Erin nodded. "Yes, sir. Ryan and Kelly just got back from the Cayman Islands. They got a good lead and I'd like Ryan to fill you in."

"I could use some positive news," Keating said. "Go ahead, Captain Ryan."

"Yes, General," Ryan replied. "I interrogated Nikita Nashamura's banker. The banker, a man named Smythe, set up several dummy corporations in her name. She did quite a bit of business with him. Using his bank, she set up fake corporations to launder hundreds of millions of dollars and to buy legitimate businesses."

"I see," the general said. "What's the source of all this cash?"

"That's unclear."

"All right. The Asian woman we're looking for – did this banker positively identify her?"

"Yes, sir. I showed him her photo and he was sure it was her."

"Okay, Captain. What else did you learn?"

"Something very important. Nashamura is Japanese. The banker said she and her bodyguard spoke in Japanese to each other. And she mentioned Osaka, which is the second largest city in Japan."

"That's a big break, Captain Ryan. When are you leaving for Japan?"

"I checked the flights out of Atlanta airport. The next flight to Osaka is tomorrow."

"Not good enough, Ryan. I want you over there ASAP."

"But, sir, I just said –"

"Ryan, I'm a Brigadier General at the DIA. That means I have a whole fleet of planes at my disposal. Get your butt over to Dobbins Air Force Base in Marietta, Georgia. I know the commanding officer at that base. He'll arrange a military transport jet to take you to Japan today."

"Yes, General."

"And one other thing, Captain. Take Colonel O'Shea with you."

"But, sir –"

"I don't want any excuses. You'll do it my way, understood?"

"Yes, sir."

"By the way, Captain, do you speak Japanese?"

"I know a little."

"Well, you're in luck. O'Shea is fluent in Japanese along with several other languages."

"That's helpful, sir."

"In the meantime, General," Erin interjected, "now that we know Nashamura is from Japan, I'm hoping I can track her down to an exact address using our FBI database."

"Good thinking, Welch," the general replied. "I'll do the same, using my DIA resources. And one last thing, Captain Ryan. We've got a lot riding on you finding this Japanese woman. If you succeed, you'll end up smelling like roses. In fact, I'd bet you end up getting a promotion to major or if you're really lucky, to colonel."

"General," Ryan said, "when this is all over, I'd rather just be discharged from active duty in the Army. I prefer being private citizen John Ryan."

Keating laughed but there was no humor in it. "I know what you want. But like I've told you before, I don't care what you want." The general paused a moment, then said in an icy tone, "But if you fail in this mission and aren't successful in solving this case, I can always find you a nice, comfy 6 x 6 cell at Leavenworth prison."

Chapter 39

Tokyo, Japan

Aki Tanaka picked up the handset of her desk phone and pressed the encryption button. She dialed a memorized number and waited for the other side to pick up.

"It's me," she said when the man answered it.

"It is great to hear your voice," Karl Strada replied. "You have good news for me, I hope."

"I do, Karl. I just got back from San Francisco. The Goggles deal is complete."

"You purchased it?"

"I did."

"That is excellent, Aki. So we now have Tekk-Sky, Face-Look, and Goggles. All the big players in social media and internet search."

"That's right. And since I already control Tweeter, LikeU, and Inagram, we're very close to running the whole damn show."

"Music to my ears," he said. "We should celebrate. You and me. When are you coming to Vienna? I have something important to discuss with you."

"More important than Viper?"

"Yes, Aki, much more important than that."

Aki swallowed hard, sensing what he wanted to discuss. *Damn you. I don't want that.*

"All right, Karl. I'll come to Vienna. But not right away. I still have several more companies I need to purchase."

"I know, I know, dear. I just want to see you ... so much ...."

"Of course. I want that also. Soon, I promise."

They said their goodbyes and she hung up the call.

Aki nibbled on some peanut butter crackers and took a long swallow from her tumbler of scotch, draining it. She refilled her glass and took another sip, trying to erase from her mind what Karl was implying.

Her desk phone buzzed and she pressed the encryption setting and picked up the handset. "This is Aki."

"Yes, Aki. I have information for you." She recognized the man's voice immediately. He was her best American source.

"Go ahead."

"Aki, do you remember what I told you a while back – that the FBI and DIA were investigating the murders?"

"Yes, of course."

"I have new info on that," he said. "The FBI operation is being run out of the Bureau's Atlanta office. The person in charge of that office is a woman named Erin Welch."

"That's very useful. I need to take care of that problem. I'll call Padilla and tell him."

"Don't bother, Aki. You'll never get a hold of him. He's dead."

"What the hell happened?"

"From what I can piece together, while Padilla was being interrogated by the FBI he had a massive heart attack and died."

"Fuck."

"Not exactly what I said when I heard," he replied, "but, yeah, it's a big setback."

"I agree. Padilla was very efficient at his job."

"I have others I can use, Aki."

"Are they as good?"

"Good enough."

"All right. It's not like we have much of a choice."

"Should I contact my other guy?" the man asked.

"Yes."

"You want Erin Welch eliminated?"

Aki nibbled on a peanut butter cracker as she mulled this over for a moment. "No. I have a better idea."

Then she told him.

Chapter 40

Osaka, Japan

"The general is a real hardass," J.T. Ryan said as he gazed out the window of the military transport plane. The jet was circling the U.S. air base in Osaka, on final approach.

Kelly O'Shea, who was sitting in the seat next to him, nodded. "He's a tough man. I've worked for him long enough to know that. But he's also fair."

Ryan faced Kelly. "I don't mind tough. Hell, I went through Ranger training. Those instructors there are hard as nails. But this is different. I never told you what he said when Erin and I spoke with him."

"What's that, J.T.?"

"He said if I don't solve this case he'll lock me up at Leavenworth."

"At USBD? The penitentiary?"

"That's right."

"I'm sure he was kidding, J.T."

"Bullshit. That bastard meant every word."

She placed a hand on his arm. "Calm down."

Ryan frowned and gazed out the window again as he pushed aside the bitter thoughts.

"So," she said, "what's the plan when we get to Osaka?"

He turned towards her. "The same plan I had when we got to Salt Lake City a while back."

"Which was?"

"Break down doors, kick ass, and take names."

She looked puzzled then flashed a slight smile. "Another one of your jokes?"

He nodded. "You're starting to figure me out."

"Okay, smartass. What's your real plan?"

"So far, we know our suspect is a Japanese woman named Nikita Nashamura and she lives somewhere in Osaka. That's where you come in, Kelly. I need you to use your DIA computer skills and locate this woman."

"I researched her name before, but all I got were women that were squeaky clean. One was a school teacher and the other was a clerk."

"I remember," he said. "But maybe you weren't looking in the right places."

Kelly shook her head. "I used all of the U.S. government and European data bases."

"I think that's the problem. When we get to the hotel I want you to search for her using the dark web."

Just then the big transport plane touched down, its metal fuselage creaking, the jet engines howling as they began to power down.

***

The cab drove them from the American air base to the Kita-Ku district of Osaka and dropped them off at the Granvia, a hotel near the Umeda train station.

After checking in and going to their separate rooms to unpack, Ryan strode down the corridor and knocked on her door.

Kelly opened it and let him inside.

"Ready to work?" he said, pointing to her laptop which was resting on a table.

"How come I'm doing all the work? You're the PI."

Ryan grinned. "You think I brought you along just because you're cute?"

Kelly folded her arms in front of her. "I resent that."

"Just kidding."

She shook her head slowly, the frown on her face dissipating. "All right, buster. But enough with the jokes, okay?"

"Deal."

They pulled chairs up to the table and she powered up her laptop.

"I know you researched Nashamura's name," Ryan said, "using all the official data bases. What I want you to do now is to use the unofficial ones."

"Such as?"

"The dark web. You know what that is?"

Kelly nodded. "Of course. I *am* a computer expert. The dark web is used by criminals using fake internet IP addresses so they can't be traced by law enforcement."

"Okay, then. Now that we're in Japan, go to the dark web here."

Kelly started working on her computer and a few minutes later began scrolling past a multitude of web-pages, stopping at one. "Okay. I'm in. Now what?"

"I want you to look up the name Nikita Nashamura, link it to Osaka, Japan, and cross-reference it to criminal activity."

"Any in particular, J.T.?"

"Put in money laundering, sex trafficking, prostitution, illegal guns, murder for hire, larceny, blackmail. That should be enough."

The DIA woman worked at her laptop for the next ten minutes. Then she said, "Found something." She pointed to a list of names on the screen. "There's a Nikki Nashamura here in this city. I know Nikki is a nickname used for Nikita. Her name links to prostitution."

"Interesting. Can you pull up a photo of her?"

Kelly tapped away and a webpage appeared on the screen. The photo showed an attractive Asian woman with long black hair and black eyes.

"She resembles the woman we're looking for," Ryan said as he studied the picture. "But it's hard to tell from this photo. And I think it's odd that a woman who's buying high-tech companies is also a prostitute. But this is the only lead we have right now." He paused and said, "What kind of website is this?"

"It's a Japanese dating website – but by the crude graphics it uses it's not a high-end dating site."

"All right," he replied, staring at the Japanese letters on the screen. His knowledge of the language was limited and he had trouble reading it. "Is there an address listed?"

"No. Just a phone number." She turned to face him. "So what now?"

He rubbed his jaw, felt the stubble there as he pondered the situation. "There's only one way to do this. We have to call her and set up a 'date'."

"A 'date'?"

Ryan nodded. "Sure. That's how johns meet hookers. They call them up, agree on a price, and they meet."

She tilted her head. "You seem to know a lot about this." She grinned. "Is this how you get girls?"

"I've never used a prostitute in my life. But I've been a PI a long time. I know how this game is played."

"Okay, J.T. Call her then."

"Just one slight problem with that. My Japanese is pretty limited."

"So," she said, "what are you saying ...."

"You'll have to call her and set up the 'date' for yourself."

Kelly's face turned beet red and she covered her mouth with a hand.

"I'm sorry, Kelly. It's the only way."

"Oh, my God! You're really serious about this."

"I'm afraid so. But it's not so bad. Once we get there, I'll take over."

She frowned. "I speak fluent Japanese. But what would I say? I have no clue."

"Calm down. When you call, tell her you want to go around the world and ask her how much that will cost."

Her lips pressed into a thin line. "What does that mean, 'go around the world'?"

"It's not important. This woman will know what it means."

She frowned again. "All right. But when she quotes me a price, do I agree to it?"

"Hell, no. Tell her it's too much. She'll lower the price and you agree."

"Then what, J.T.?"

"Get her location and set up a time to meet. That's all there is to it."

"You make it sound so simple, damn it."

"It's just a phone call. Remember, when we get there I'll take over. You won't have to do a thing."

Kelly let out a long breath. "All right – I'll do it." She stabbed a finger towards him. "But General Keating never finds out about this. It's *so* embarrassing."

Ryan held up three fingers. "I'll never tell. Scout's Honor."

She pulled out her cell phone and turned it on. She took in another long breath and let it out slowly. Then she looked back at her computer screen, read off the phone number, and tapped it on the phone.

Moments later she was conversing in Japanese.

Ryan was able to understand some of the words, enough to know it was going as planned.

Kelly hung up the call. "Okay. It's done."

"When and where?"

"Four p.m. Three hours from now. Nashamura gave me an address. Said it was by the city's port. A warehouse district."

"You did great, Kelly."

She wrapped her arms around herself. "I feel dirty."

He nodded. "The PI business is like that sometimes. You have to deal with sleazy people."

"What do we do now? We've got a few hours to kill."

Ryan glanced at his watch. "Not really. We need to get there early. Check out the location. Make sure it's not a setup. A lot of these 'dates' end up badly. The john gets robbed and beat up, maybe worse."

Her eyes went wide. "By the prostitute?"

"No. By her pimp. The guy who runs her. The guy that keeps most of the money."

"You mean the girls don't keep the money they earn?"

"They get a little of it. Most of it goes to the 'boyfriend', if you can call him that."

"That's pretty shitty," she said.

"Life is like that sometimes." He gave Kelly a long look. "You know, I can go on my own. Now that you set up this meet, I can go by myself. It's safer for you that way."

She shook her head. "No. I've got to see this through. Where you go, I go."

"Okay. Let's gun up and we'll get going."

"Gun up?"

"Yeah, Kelly. Get your pistol from your suitcase. Mine is on me already. My gut tells me we may need it."

***

The cab drove them to the port, which was located on the west side of Osaka. The driver dropped them off at a busy area by the large pier. Several cruise ships were docked there and it was evident the area was a hub for tourists and locals.

They walked north for five blocks and found the address. The building was a red brick warehouse that had been converted to apartments. They found a coffee shop across the street and got a table.

They ordered coffee and Ryan said, "I'll go and check out the place. I want you to stay here and wait for me."

"You don't need me for this?" Kelly said.

"No. I'm just going to check it out, make sure it's not a trap. I want to check the corridor, the elevator, the roof, all of the escape routes, stuff like that."

"Okay."

Their coffee came and Ryan sipped his. Then he turned on his cell phone. "I'll get going. If I need you, I'll call."

"How long will you be gone, J.T.?"

"Probably an hour."

"Why so long?"

Ryan chuckled. "Better to be prepared than dead."

The woman frowned. "Quit kidding around. This is serious."

He gave her a half salute. "You got it, Colonel." He finished his coffee and stood. "Wait here. Feel free to order food."

"All right."

***

Ryan returned to the coffee shop an hour later and sat across from her.

"What did you find?" she asked.

"The place looks safe enough. It's not a dump. In fact the inside of the building is fairly upscale. I spotted a man going into her apartment. He was wearing a business suit and was probably a john."

"What now?"

He glanced at his watch. "Since we've got another hour to kill, we'll hang out here and go up there then."

"Okay. What do I say when we get there?"

Ryan told her and got a refill on his coffee.

At exactly 4 p.m. Kelly knocked on the apartment door.

An Asian woman wearing a shimmering blue kimono opened it and gave Kelly a small bow. Then the woman noticed Ryan standing next to Kelly and grimaced.

"Who is this?" the Asian woman said, her voice irritated.

Kelly turned toward the PI. "This is my husband. He wants to join us." The women were speaking in Japanese but Ryan was able to understand most of what they were saying.

"That was not our deal," the Asian woman spit out.

Kelly nodded. "I understand. We'll pay more."

"In that case, come in. But I need cash. Up front."

"Of course," Kelly said.

The door opened fully and Kelly and Ryan entered the large living room, which was decorated in traditional Japanese style. The woman waved them to a low table set on a tatani mat at one side of the room. "Please sit. I will get us some tea."

The woman left the room as Kelly and Ryan sat on the flat cushions next to the low table.

Nashamura came back a moment later carrying a tray. She placed cups in front of them and poured out tea. Then she sat down across from them.

"You want the same thing for both of you?" Nashamura asked. "Around the world?"

Kelly blushed and Ryan said, "Yes, Ms Nashamura. We both want the same. By the way, do you speak English? My Japanese ... is not so good."

"Yes, I do," Nashamura replied in English. "Since there are two of you, I want double what I quoted you. And I need it now, before we start."

"Of course," he said. He reached into his jacket pocket, took out a wad of Japanese yens and handed it to the woman. While she re-counted the cash thoroughly, Ryan studied the woman's appearance. She looked similar to the criminal they were looking for, but something seemed different.

The prostitute's black hair was pinned up into a bun and Ryan said, "Would you mind letting your hair down?"

The woman gave him a puzzled look, then began unpinning her hair. "You have paid for that privilege."

Once her long black hair cascaded past her shoulders, the PI gazed at her face again. He turned towards Kelly. "It's not her. She's not the woman we're looking for."

Kelly nodded. "You're right."

Nashamura glared. "What are you talking about? What is this?"

"This isn't about sex," Ryan said, pulling out a photo from his jacket and placing it on the table. "We're looking for Nikita Nashamura, the woman in this picture."

"I am Nikita Nashamura. I use Nikki for short."

"You may be, but you're not the woman we're after. But I have a feeling you know who she is."

The prostitute glanced down at the photo and her eyes grew big. She slipped a hand under the table and pressed a button.

A second later a thin, wiry Asian man raced into the room. He was holding a very large handgun and it was pointed at Ryan's face.

The prostitute spoke very fast in Japanese to the man, then turned back to Ryan. "Put your gun on top of the table," she ordered. "And put your hands up. Do it now or he kills you!"

"I'm not armed," Ryan said.

"That's a lie. You have the look of a cop. You sound like a cop."

Ryan shook his head slowly. "God, I am so tired of people telling me that."

"Do it now!" the whore screeched. "Do it now, or he kills you!"

Ryan carefully removed his pistol from his holster and rested it on the table.

Nashamura turned to Kelly. "Now you. Your gun on the table."

Kelly complied, placing the pistol in front of her while Ryan studied the Asian man with the large handgun. "Is he your pimp?" the PI said.

"He's my brother *and* my pimp," the prostitute said with a wicked grin. "Now why are you here?"

"Like I said before," Ryan said, "we're looking for Nikita Nashamura, a Japanese woman who lives in Osaka and has long black hair and black eyes. And she looks a lot like you."

The whore and her pimp exchanged glances.

"All we want is information," the PI said. "Tell us where we can find the woman in the photo."

The prostitute shook her head. "I cannot tell you. I am sorry this has to end badly for you. But I have no choice." She faced her pimp again and spoke rapidly in Japanese.

Ryan grabbed the ceramic tea bowl on the table and hurled it towards the man, hitting him in the head. The bowl shattered, tea flying everywhere. The PI flung up the table towards the prostitute, then he jumped off the floor and raced toward the Asian man, knocking him down with a brutal punch to his gut.

Picking up the pimp's handgun from the floor, he struck the man on the back of his head. The guy's body sagged, the man clearly unconscious.

Turning, he faced the two women.

Kelly was on her feet, her revolver in her hand.

"Are you okay, Kelly?"

"I'm good."

The PI marched over to the overturned table, picked it up, and set it to one side. Then he grabbed his own gun, which had landed in a corner of the room.

The prostitute was on the floor, unmoving, a cut on her forehead. He approached her carefully and checked for a weapon. Finding none, he propped her up into a sitting position, leaning against a wall.

He slapped her face lightly. "Wake up."

Her eyes blinked open and she stared into the muzzle of Ryan's gun. "What ... what do you want?"

"Information. Tell us what we need to know and we'll leave you alone."

The woman frowned. "What ... about the money you paid me ...."

"You can keep it." He noticed the woman's forehead was bleeding. He pulled out a handkerchief and pressed it gingerly to her cut. "Sorry about that. I didn't mean to hurt you."

The whore nodded, took hold of the handkerchief and pressed it to her forehead.

"Find the photo," Ryan told Kelly, "and show it to her again."

The DIA woman located the picture on the floor and held it for the prostitute to see.

"Do you know who this woman is?" Ryan asked.

"Yes, I know. She and her bodyguard came to see me two years ago."

"What's her name?"

"She never told me her real name. She only said she wanted to use my identity, my name."

"For what purpose?"

The prostitute shrugged her shoulders. "Who knows. She paid me a lot of money at the time. And she pays me every month. Cash in the mail. I assumed she picked me because I look a lot like her."

Ryan pressed the muzzle of his pistol to the woman's temple, knowing he would never pull the trigger, but had to act convincingly. "Tell me the truth, damn it!"

Nashamura's face blanched. "I am telling the truth! I don't know who she really is!"

"Do better!" he yelled.

A moment later the whore said, "She called her bodyguard by name. His name is Honshu."

"Okay. That's a start. What else?"

"They are from Tokyo. I heard them talking."

He pressed the gun harder to her temple. "You sure about this?"

"Yes! Yes! They are from Tokyo, Japan."

Chapter 41

Headquarters Building
Defense Intelligence Agency
Washington, D.C.

"Thank you for coming on such short notice," General Keating said as he and Erin Welch shook hands.

"Did I have a choice?" Erin asked.

"No. Not really." He waved to a chair in front of his desk. "Please have a seat."

They both sat down and Erin studied the general as he lit his pipe with a Zippo lighter. He took a puff and exhaled, the sweet aroma filling the office.

"It's starting, Ms Welch."

"What's starting."

"My worst nightmare."

"Explain, General."

Keating rested the pipe on an ashtray. "A while back I told you that part of the reason we at DIA are so concerned about social media was the possibility it could be used by criminals to subvert American elections."

"Yes, sir, I remember that."

"Well, it's beginning to happen."

Erin frowned, wondering if the general was overreacting. "General, we at the FBI are involved in this case because of the multiple murders. I know you have theories about the conspiracy being more than about the killings, but my focus is to catch and bring to justice the murderers involved."

Keating picked up his pipe, relit it with his Zippo, and took several puffs.

"It's more than just a theory," he said, resting the pipe on the ashtray.

"How so?"

"You sound skeptical, Ms. Welch. It's probably better if I show you rather than tell you." Keating turned toward the laptop on his desk, powered it up, and surfed the internet a minute. He tapped his keyboard and the screen displayed the Face-Look social media site. "I'll log on to one of my subordinate's fake accounts at Face-Look," he said, "so you can see what I'm talking about."

The screen now showed Kelly O'Shea's personal page. The auburn-haired woman's photo was on the page, wearing civilian clothes. "You're familiar with Face-Look's news feed, Ms Welch?"

"Of course, General. I have a real account with that social media company."

"Good." He pointed toward the computer screen. "Depending on how you set up your settings, the news feed scrolls down on the right hand side of the page. You get the headlines and the news source it came from – TV news, or newspapers, or an online source. Sometimes videos are part of the feed. If you're interested in a particular story you click on it and it takes you to the original news source."

Erin nodded. "That's right. I've used that feature myself. If I'm interested in a story I'll click on it to find out more."

The general picked up his pipe and puffed on it again, the sickly sweet smell making her a bit nauseous.

Erin waved away the smoke with a hand. "Do you *really* have to do that?"

Keating grimaced and his lips pressed into a thin line. "Fine. I'll stop smoking." Then he stabbed his index finger towards the laptop. "Now, could you please spend the next few minutes studying the news feed?"

She began reading the news headlines that were scrolling down the right hand side of the Face-Look page. A minute later she said, "A lot of the stories have to do with the U.S. election. But that's not surprising, since the election is coming up soon."

"You're right, Ms Welch. Now take a closer look. Are the news articles focused on any particular presidential candidate?"

Erin gazed at the screen again. "Yes, most of the stories have to do with Charles Grant, and how popular and likeable he is."

"You're right again. Did you find any articles about his opponent, Atkinson?"

"There's a few," she said, "but they're all negative stories."

The general nodded. "Do you see a pattern there?"

"It could be a coincidence. I've only spent ten minutes studying this."

"It could be," he said. "But it's not. I've spent hours looking at social media sites recently. And my staff has spent hundreds of hours doing the same thing. And not just Face-Look but others like Tweeter, Inagram, LikeU, and others. They're all pretty much the same."

Erin swallowed hard, the implications of what the general was telling her becoming clear.

"Let me show you another example," he said. Keating typed on his keyboard and the Face-Look page was replaced by the Goggles welcome screen. The general pointed to it. "You're familiar with this, I'm sure?"

"Of course. Goggles is one of the world's largest search engines for obtaining information from the internet. It's now a bigger company than Google."

Keating nodded. "That's correct. I'm going to do a Goggles search for presidential candidate Charles Grant."

"Okay."

He input the man's name on the search box and soon a long list of news articles and photo images filled the screen. Erin noticed that almost all of the articles were positive news stories, and the pictures showed Grant and his family in beautiful settings. All of the photos showed them smiling.

"Now," Keating said, "I'll input his opponent's name, Atkinson, and do the same Goggles search."

Moments later the results appeared. In this case, almost all of the news articles were negative or unflattering in some way. Erin also noticed the photos showed Atkinson with a five-o'clock shadow on his face, dressed in a rumpled suit, his hair unkempt. He was frowning or grimacing in all of the pictures shown.

"I don't follow politics much," Erin said, "but I know about Atkinson. His policies make a lot of sense and I've read many positive articles about him in the last year. And I've seen photos of him where he's smiling and well-dressed, looking clearly presidential. He and his wife are very photogenic. Everything I'm seeing here is negative. How is that possible?"

Keating nodded. "Now you see what we're up against. The conspiracy is trying to influence the upcoming presidential election. And we've seen similar patterns being carried out in several governor and senate races as well."

The enormity of what the general was telling her was now painfully clear. A sick feeling settled in her stomach and her hands formed into fists. *We've got to stop this. And stop it now, before it's too late.*

Chapter 42

Tokyo, Japan

"All right, Kelly," J.T. Ryan said, "it's time for you to work some of your computer magic again."

Kelly O'Shea powered up her laptop, which was resting on the hotel room's desk. After flying from Osaka to Tokyo, the two people had checked into the Wakana Ryokan Hotel, a small inn in the Shinjuku-Ku area of the city, and had gotten adjoining rooms.

Ryan pulled up a chair and sat next to Kelly so he could look over her shoulder. "Get on the Japanese dark web again," he said, "like you did in Osaka. I think that's going to be the best way to find Nashamura's bodyguard."

"Okay," she replied, typing on her keyboard for a few minutes. "All right, I'm in."

"Good. Now put in the bodyguard's name, Honshu."

"Do you think that's his first or last name, J.T.?"

Ryan shook his head. "Don't know. Now cross-reference his name to criminal activity – theft, assault, murder, and anything else you can think of."

"You got it." Several minutes later she said, "Honshu must be a pretty common name here because I got a lot of hits."

"That's too bad. In that case, we'll have to narrow down the list the old-fashioned way."

"Which is?"

From a pocket he removed the photo of the bodyguard, the one that had been taken by the Face-Look security cameras, and placed it on the desk. "We'll have to pull up pictures of each one of the men on your list and narrow the search that way."

Kelly nodded and they spent the next two hours tediously ruling out the wrong guys.

"I never knew PI work could be so boring," Kelly said.

Ryan smiled. "It's not all fun and games is it?"

"Not by a long shot."

Half an hour later the DIA woman pointed to the screen. "I think that's him."

Ryan examined the man's face closely. The Asian man had a shaved head, hooded black eyes, a jagged scar on his cheek, was heavily-muscled, and appeared to be over six and a half feet tall. "That's the right Honshu. I'm sure of it." He tried reading the details about the man but his limited knowledge of Japanese prevented him from learning much. "What's it say about him?"

Kelly translated what was on the dark web. "It says here he was in the Yakuza, the Japanese mafia, for a long time. He spent four years in prison for assault, theft, and illegal gun possession. Recently it looks like he's graduated into body-guarding."

"That's our guy. Any mention of his working for Nikita Nashamura?"

"None."

"Okay, Kelly. Can you find a location for him?"

"His current address is listed here. It's an apartment in a high-rise in Tokyo. I know this city somewhat and that area is exclusive, not the kind of place I figured a hood like him would live."

"Since he's Nashamura's bodyguard," Ryan said, "maybe he lives in the same high-rise she does."

"Good thinking. I'll pull up tenant records for that apartment building and see if she does."

"You can do that?"

Kelly grinned. "In my sleep."

"I'm glad you came along on this trip."

"Not like you had a choice, J.T. The general ordered you to."

Ryan nodded. "Well, this is one time General Keating was right." He smiled. "But you know what they say. Even a broken clock is right twice a day."

Kelly chuckled and went back to working at her computer. Five minutes later she said, "No, there's no Nikita or Nikki Nashamura living in that building."

"Okay. In that case I'll shadow Honshu for however long it takes. He'll lead us to Nashamura."

"Correction, J.T. We'll do it together."

"Fair enough." He glanced at his watch. "It's too late to get started today. Plus, I'm starved. I need to get some dinner."

***

The Wakana Hotel they were staying at was a *ryokan* type of inn and had its own small restaurant. After Ryan and Kelly were seated, she ordered *sake*, a Japanese liquor made of rice, and he ordered a Sapporo beer.

Ryan tried reading the menu and gave up. "Can you order some food for me?"

She grinned. "Of course." She held up two fingers.

"What's that mean, Kelly?"

"That's twice in one day my being fluent in Japanese has come in handy." She grinned again. "Not to mention my wizardry with computers."

He smiled back. "So you want a medal?"

"No. A simple thank you would suffice."

"Thank you, Colonel O'Shea. You've been a big help."

Kelly nodded, then signaled the waitress and the woman approached their table. Kelly spoke to her rapidly in Japanese and the waitress went toward the kitchen.

"What did you order for us?" he asked.

"Lot's of healthy food. For an appetizer, rice and soybean crackers with seaweed, and for our meal, *yokimono* which is grilled eel basted in a sweet sauce. I also ordered squid, ramen noodles, and *tempura*, which is deep-battered vegetables with fish. I also got a side order of sushi."

Ryan made a face.

"Don't worry, J.T. I've had this type of food before. It's delicious."

He shook his head slowly and let out a long sigh. "Yum, yum."

Kelly held up her glass of *sake*. "You'll love it. I promise."

He clinked his beer bottle to her glass and took a long pull of the Sapporo, a savory Japanese beer he'd had before.

While they waited for their meal to come, Ryan said, "Why did you get into the military? From everything I've seen, you would have been a whizz working for some high-tech company and made a fortune."

"I grew up an Army brat. My dad was an officer and he spent his whole career in the military. I admired him and followed his footsteps."

Ryan nodded. "Makes sense."

"How about you? Why'd you get in?"

"When I was going to college at Georgia State, I signed up for Army R.O.T.C. After I graduated I went into the Infantry as a second lieutenant."

"Then you volunteered for the Rangers?"

"Yeah," he said.

"And you got through. Not many people do. The washout rate for Army Rangers is high." She gave him a long look. "I admire you, J.T. A Ranger and then Delta Force, Tier 1. I never worked with a Delta guy before."

Just then their dinner came.

Although the food looked suspicious to Ryan, it smelled great and to his surprise, was delicious.

When he was done he pushed aside the empty plate. "That was good."

"Told you."

The waitress came, took away their empty plates and served them a new round of drinks. Ryan sipped his beer and studied the attractive young woman as she drank her *sake*. Usually her long auburn hair was pulled into a ponytail but tonight it was loose, framing her pretty face.

She caught him staring at her and she blushed.

"I'm sorry about that," he said.

"About what?"

"For staring at you, Kelly."

She glanced away from him, the blush deepening and accentuating the freckles on her face. Then she faced him again and set her glass down on the table.

"I don't mind," she said, reaching out with a hand and covering one of his. "I like it, actually. You're a nice man. More than nice. A lot more. But you know it won't work. I'm your commanding officer. We'd be breaking every rule in the book."

He looked down at the table, saw her dainty hand covering his brawny, oversize paw. Her skin felt soft and tender and warm and sensual. He glanced back up at her. "I know, Kelly."

He could sense the sadness in her hazel eyes and he felt exactly the same way.

Ryan picked up her small hand and kissed it softly.

Then he said, "I don't think we should have any more to drink tonight. In fact, it would probably be best if we call it a night."

Kelly nodded, the sadness still in her eyes.

Chapter 43

Tokyo, Japan

The exclusive high-rise apartment building was located in the Chuo Ku district of central Tokyo. Situated in a complex of many other upscale residential skyscrapers, it overlooked the Sumida river on one side and bordered the famed Hama Rykyu Gardens.

After parking their rented Toyota sedan in the building's guest lot, Ryan shut off the engine. He turned to Kelly. "It's only 6 a.m. now. Since it's a weekday, my guess is Nashamura and her bodyguard will leave the building within a few hours and head to wherever she works. I'll stake out the lobby."

"What about me, J.T.?"

He handed her the keys to the Toyota. "You wait here. I'll call you if I spot them. Then you drive to the front of the building, pick me up, and we'll tail them."

Kelly took the keys. "All right."

He turned on his cell phone. "I'll check in with you every half hour, Kelly. Any questions?"

"What if Honshu or Nashamura don't show up at all?"

"Then we just wasted a day."

She frowned. "PI work isn't very scientific."

"Tell me about it," he said.

Ryan climbed out of the car and walked toward the front of the skyscraper. Going into the impressive lobby, he glanced around the place. The four-story high atrium had onyx floors, stately columns, high-end furnishings, and even an elaborate garden with a koi pond. It all said one thing: Serious money lived there.

There was a cafe by the lobby and he headed there. He bought a coffee and that day's edition of the Yomiuri Shimbun, the city's major newspaper. He found a plushly-upholstered leather chair near the elevator banks and sat down to wait. Placing his coffee cup on a side table, he opened the newspaper and pretended to read it as he observed well-dressed Asians enter and exit the elevators.

He didn't spot Honshu from 6 to 7 a.m., nor from 7 to 8. Walking back to the cafe, he bought another coffee and returned to the leather chair, hoping the day wouldn't be a total bust.

At 9 a.m. the elevator doors slid open and a very striking Asian woman stepped out. She was tall and beautiful, with perfectly straight, long white hair and white eyes. Her almost porcelain white skin accentuated the doll-like features of her sculpted face. She was wearing an obviously expensive dove gray Christian Dior pantsuit and carried herself with a regal air.

Exiting the elevator right behind the woman was a giant, muscular Asian man with a shaved head and hooded black eyes. Ryan recognized Honshu immediately and quickly scanned the other people exiting the elevator. He didn't spot Nikita Nashamura so his gaze went back to Honshu.

Getting up from the bench, Ryan followed the bodyguard as he escorted the white-haired woman out of the lobby and into the street.

There was a pearl white Rolls-Royce idling by the curb with a uniformed driver standing by the back passenger door. The driver opened the door and the white-haired woman stepped into the car as Honshu went around the car and got in as well.

A moment later the Rolls pulled away from the curb and merged with traffic.

Ryan frowned, confused by what he'd witnessed. He marched back to the visitor's parking lot and climbed into the Toyota.

"Something's wrong," Ryan said to Kelly.

"What do you mean?"

"I saw Honshu, but not Nikita Nashamura. The crazy part is, he appeared to be guarding another woman, a woman with white hair."

"Maybe Honshu has more than one client," Kelly said.

"I thought of that. Which means we're no closer to finding our real target, Nashamura."

"What do we do now, J.T.?"

He thought about this moment. "When Honshu comes back to his apartment later today, I could force my way in at gunpoint and make him tell me where Nashamura is. But there's one problem with that."

"What?"

"I don't want to tip off Nashamura. If she learns we're looking for her, she could vanish. We know she's wealthy, which gives her options. She could skip town and we'd be back at square one."

"I see your point, J.T."

Ryan rubbed his jaw. "Which leaves us with one option."

"Which is?"

"We come back tomorrow and repeat what we did today. We may learn a lot more then."

***

Ryan was sitting on the same leather chair in the lobby of the apartment building, once again pretending to read the newspaper.

At 8 a.m. the elevator door slid open and the same beautiful white-haired woman stepped out, closely followed by Honshu. This time the PI was ready, and using his cell phone, discreetly took photos of the two people. He followed them as they exited the lobby and climbed into the waiting pearl white Rolls Royce. Ryan snapped several more photos, making sure he got pictures of the car and the license plate.

Then he walked back to the visitor's parking lot and got in the Toyota.

"Well, it was no coincidence," Ryan said to Kelly. "Honshu was definitely guarding the white-haired woman again today. And now I've got pictures of her and her car."

"So what's next? Do we follow them?"

Ryan grinned. "Now, Miss Computer Expert, you work your magic. Let's find out about this new woman Honshu's guarding. Hopefully she can lead us to Nashamura."

An hour later Ryan and Kelly were back in her hotel room and she had just powered up her laptop.

Ryan pulled up a chair and sat next to her so he could look over her shoulder. He downloaded the photos in his phone to a flash drive and handed the drive to Kelly.

"Here you go," he said, "work your dark magic on this."

She nodded and a minute later the computer screen displayed a picture of the white-haired Asian woman. Honshu was also in the photo, off to one side.

"Wow," Kelly said. "She's stunning. Beautiful like you said, but those white eyes – mesmerizing, almost spooky."

"Yeah. I thought the same thing. She must be an albino. And notice how white her skin is too."

"Amazing. I've never seen an albino person before. It's a very rare human trait."

"Zoom in on her face," Ryan said.

The DIA woman tapped on the keyboard and the screen filled with a close-up of the face.

"She looks familiar," he said. "As if I've seen her before. Maybe she's a relative of Nikita Nashamura."

"Could be, J.T. You want me to run her picture through facial recognition?"

"I do. Is the DIA software the best there is?"

Kelly smiled. "Of course. Your tax dollars at work."

"Then use that one – it may save us time."

"Okay." She logged on the Defense Intelligence Agency's website and after going through several layers of security, she accessed it.

Fifteen minutes later she got a hit.

"This is her," Kelly said excitedly. "Our mysterious white-haired woman." The screen showed her photo on the left and a detailed description on the right with her personal information.

"Her name is Aki Tanaka," Kelly said, reading from the DIA files. "She's the company owner of a high-tech firm here in Tokyo, and also owns several more high-tech firms in different cities of Japan. She's Japanese by birth and her address is listed as the same apartment building where Honshu lives."

"Can you access her company's personnel records? I'd like to see if Honshu is one of her employees."

"Sure, J.T."

Several minutes later she said, "There's a Honshu listed as a 'security consultant' for her company."

"Bingo. He's a bodyguard there. Now, Kelly, see if a Nikita or a Nikki Nashamura is listed as an employee at any of Tanaka's companies."

After a moment, she shook her head. "No, she's not."

"Okay. So maybe Nikki Nashamura is a totally false identity. An alias."

"But Nashamura and Aki Tanaka look totally different, J.T."

Ryan removed Nashamura's photo from his pocket and glanced back up at the screen. "I've got an idea. Can the software in your computer alter someone's appearance?"

"Sure."

"Pull up that software, will you? I want to try something."

"Okay." Kelly worked at her laptop a few moments. "I'm in it now."

"Put Aki Tanaka's photo in your software."

"All right ... done."

"Now change Tanaka's hair color from white to black. Then change her eye color from white to black."

Kelly did what Ryan instructed.

"Oh, my God, J.T. It's the same woman."

Ryan nodded. "Yes, she is. Nikita Nashamura is really Aki Tanaka. Tanaka leads a normal, law-abiding life under her real name and uses the Nashamura identity for her criminal enterprises."

"Now that we know this, what do we do now, J.T.? Arrest her?"

"My normal instinct would be to break down her door and arrest her at gunpoint. But ...."

"You seem hesitant."

"I am, Kelly. What if we're wrong? What if this woman isn't the one we're after. I could end up shooting and possibly killing an innocent woman. In a foreign country, no less. Erin at the FBI has pulled my ass out of the fire more times than I can count, but even she would have a hard time helping me with something like this."

"You're right. We need to be sure before we go in, guns drawn." Kelly rubbed her forehead a moment. "I've got an idea. What if I go see her at her apartment by myself and ask her a few questions. I'll be able to tell pretty fast if she's lying. Once I'm sure, I'll let you know and you can force yourself in and arrest her."

"You go in by yourself? I don't like it."

She grimaced. "Why? Because I'm a woman? Because you don't think I could handle the situation? You're a sexist pig if you think that, and I resent it."

Ryan shook his head. "I think you're a very capable woman. I just ... don't think it's safe. We know Tanaka is dangerous. I don't want to put you in harm's way."

After a moment the grimace on her face disappeared. She reached out with her hand and caressed his cheek. "I think that's sweet, J.T. But you forget I'm an officer in the U.S. Army. I've had much of the same self-defense training you've had. I can handle myself." She unbuttoned her blazer, exposing the revolver holstered at her hip. "And I have this. And I know how to use it."

He looked at her for a long moment. "I'm not going to be able to talk you out of this, am I?"

"No."

He sighed and then shrugged. "All right. But I'll be in the corridor the whole time. We'll have our cell phones on and connected. That way you can yell out if you sense trouble and I'll break down the door to her apartment."

Kelly nodded. "Sounds good. Let's come up with a good cover story and I'll go see her."

Chapter 44

Tokyo, Japan

Aki Tanaka took a sip of scotch as she gazed out the floor-to-ceiling windows of her luxurious penthouse apartment.

Although it was an overcast evening, she could still make out the city's modernistic skyline of high-rises, the bright neon lights a riot of color. Glancing down to street level, the traffic choked streets looked like pinpricks of white and red from vehicle headlamps and taillights.

Aki took a long pull of the Chivas, draining the glass. *A good day. A great day, in fact. Things are going according to plan. Viper is on track.*

She turned away from the windows and was headed toward her liquor cabinet when she heard her front door chime. Setting down her glass, she approached the door and stared at the CCTV display from the corridor's security camera.

A young, non-Asian woman was in the hallway, dressed in tan slacks and a blue blazer. She had auburn hair pulled into a ponytail.

"May I help you?" Aki said in Japanese through the intercom.

"Yes, my name is Sarah Donovan," the young woman replied in Japanese. "I'm with the U.S. State Department. We're conducting a survey of Japanese people that invest in American companies. Our records indicate, Ms Tanaka, that you're planning on investing in U.S. companies in the near future."

Aki scowled and instantly went to press the emergency button on the security panel. The alarm would alert Honshu, who lived in a small apartment next to hers, with an adjoining door. But before she pressed the alarm, she stared at the young woman again. She was short, no more than five feet, slender, and pretty. And she was alone. *She's no threat.* Since Aki was curious what the survey was about, she said, "All right. Give me a moment and I'll open the door."

Aki turned off the alarm system and opened the door and the woman stepped inside. Aki closed the door and locked it and put the alarm back on.

"Follow me," Aki said. "We can sit in my living room."

They crossed the large foyer and sat across from each other on the plushly-upholstered suede couches. "What's all this about?" Aki asked.

"As I said, my name is Sarah Donovan and I work for the U.S. State Department at our office here in Tokyo. We routinely do surveys of Japanese people planning to invest in American companies."

"I see. What makes you think I want to invest in such companies? I am a business owner, but all of my companies are here in Japan."

Kelly nodded. "We're aware of that. But we also routinely track internet searches of people. Yours stood out because you've done so much online research of American high-tech companies. We like to keep track of those kinds of things for security reasons."

Aki frowned. *Fuck. I never thought someone would be able to track and unmask my internet searches. This Donavan woman must be damn savvy to see through my fake online accounts.*

"I have done that type of research," Aki said. "But that was only for long-term planning purposes. My intent was to invest in those types of companies in ten or fifteen years from now."

The young redhead smiled. "That makes sense. I guess that's why you've made visits to several American social media companies – Face-Look and Tekk-Sky."

Aki tensed. "You are mistaken, Ms Donovan. I've never been to those companies."

The smile faded from the young woman's face. "Our records clearly indicate you were there. I can give you the exact dates to help you jar your memory."

Aki stood abruptly. "I've told you the truth. Now leave. This meeting is over."

"You traveled to the U.S. using the alias Nikita Nashamura," Kelly said, her voice curt. "Isn't that right?"

Aki's face drained of color and her head throbbed from a sudden migraine. "I'm done talking to you!" she screeched. Her hand was in the pocket of her pantsuit and she pressed the alarm button of her security device, instantly alerting Honshu.

Chapter 45

Tokyo, Japan

J.T. Ryan was at the far end of the corridor, listening closely on his cell phone as the two women spoke. But they were talking in rapid Japanese and he could only make out some of what was being said.

Suddenly he heard a woman screaming through his phone and instantly knew it was Kelly's voice.

Ryan sprinted toward the apartment door, and reaching it seconds later, kicked it hard with his steel-toed shoe. The ornate, heavy wooden door held firm and he continued kicking it furiously several more times. The wood fractured in places, but the door still refused to open.

With his adrenaline pumping, Ryan drew his pistol and crossed to the opposite side of the hallway. Then he raced toward the apartment door, slamming fiercely into it with his shoulder. The wood cracked down the middle, splinters flew, and he burst through the entrance.

Ryan crouched in the foyer and held his weapon in front of him with both hands, his shoulder throbbing with pain. His heart sank when he looked into the living room.

The huge bodyguard, Honshu, had his giant forearm around Kelly's neck. She looked tiny in contrast to the massive, muscular Asian man. Kelly's face was ashen, her eyes wide, her expression terrified.

Aki Tanaka was next to them holding a Glock pistol pointed at Ryan's head. She yelled something in Japanese, but she spoke so fast he didn't understand her.

Ryan held his own gun tightly. "I don't know what you're saying," he replied in English.

The Asian woman with white hair nodded. "Drop your gun," she said in English, "or the woman dies."

Ryan glanced at Kelly and noticed her body was trembling. Beads of perspiration rolled down her forehead.

"Hell, no!" he shouted. "I'm not dropping my gun! You'll kill me and Kelly both. I think I'll pull this trigger, Tanaka, and then you die."

Tanaka glared, then erupted in a long, humorless laugh. "You won't do it. You know why? Because if you shoot me, Honshu will break the pretty girl's neck. Show him, Honshu!"

The massive bodyguard tightened his hold around Kelly's neck and her face turned beet red and she began gasping for breath.

Ryan's stomach churned as his gaze swiveled between Kelly's terrified eyes and Tanaka's evil grin. *Damn! Damn it all.*

"He'll do it," Tanaka screeched. "He'll break her neck like a twig. She'll be dead before her body hits the floor."

"Please," the PI pleaded, "please don't do it."

Tanaka cackled again. "Looks like a classic Mexican standoff, don't you think? Which is funny, considering we're in Japan."

Ryan gritted his teeth, realizing the Asian woman was making a joke in the middle of a life and death situation. *She's crazy. Crazy enough to kill Kelly. That's for damn sure.*

With his heart jack-hammering in his chest, he looked down the barrel of Tanaka's Glock. His own pistol was pointed at her head, his finger on the trigger.

"Let Kelly go," Ryan said, "and we'll leave."

"I'm not stupid!" Tanaka screamed. "If I let the woman go you'll kill me and Honshu both. I know who you are now. I recognize you from a photo I was sent. You're the PI from Atlanta. I sent men to kill you and they failed. You must be very good with that gun of yours."

Ryan glanced at Kelly again. Her face was bright red, the giant brute's forearm still holding her by the neck tightly. "Please let her go," Ryan pleaded, "and I swear we'll leave. I won't kill you. You have my word."

Tanaka's face showed pure hatred, her menacing and bizarre-looking white eyes boring into his. She said nothing for a long moment, then nodded. "All right. I'll tell Honshu to let go of her, but you lower your pistol first."

Ryan thought furiously and knew he had no choice. "Okay. I'll do it." He lowered his pistol to his side.

The Asian woman motioned to her bodyguard and he removed his forearm from Kelly's neck. Kelly instantly dropped to the floor. She gasped and held a hand to her bright red neck.

"Take her!" Tanaka ordered. "Take her and get out! And don't come back!"

Ryan rushed forward, scooped Kelly off the floor, and still holding the pistol at his side, slowly backed out of the living room toward the front door. His gaze was locked on Tanaka's eyes, trying to ascertain if the Asian woman was going to shoot them during their retreat.

To his amazement, he saw that Tanaka had an amused look on her face. *She is totally insane.*

Slowly, he continued backing out of the room, holding Kelly up with one arm. She was still gasping, her body trembling. He reached the shattered front door, moved past it, and went into the hallway.

Then, still holding Kelly, he raised his gun and continued walking backward away from the apartment and toward the staircase at the far end of the corridor.

Chapter 46

Tokyo, Japan

Aki Tanaka glared at Honshu. "They'll be back," she screeched. "And soon. And this time they'll bring the police with them. Pack up the computers and my files!"

The huge bodyguard nodded.

"Do it now, Honshu!"

The big man raced out of the living room as she slipped her Glock into a pocket of her pantsuit. Then she sprinted into the bedroom, threw some clothes into a overnight bag and went into her home office.

Honshu was there, putting laptops and files into two large suitcases. When he was done a few minutes later she said, "Let's go, Honshu."

The bodyguard nodded, picked up the suitcases, and followed her toward the condo's private elevator. She'd had the special elevator installed years ago, hoping to never have to use it. It would take her down from the top floor of the skyscraper to the building's underground floor. In a private parking area there she kept a Mercedes Benz sedan.

The bodyguard entered the elevator and set down the suitcases.

Aki hesitated before going into it, and instead turned around to look out the floor-to-ceiling windows of her beloved penthouse. She gazed at the spectacular view of the Tokyo skyline, lit up with a riot of neon lights, looking like jewels in the night. Then she looked at her condo's priceless artwork, its marble floors, and top-end furnishings, knowing this would be the last time she'd see them. *God damn those bastards from the FBI. I will get even!*

Turning around, she stepped into the waiting elevator, the doors slid closed, and the cubicle whispered down to the basement.

After she and Honshu exited the elevator, she faced the security panel by the door. On the keypad she input a long series of numbers, numbers she'd hoped to never have to use.

She faced her bodyguard. "Let's go, Honshu."

The man nodded and carried the two big suitcases toward the pearl white Mercedes a few yards away.

Chapter 47

Tokyo, Japan

The massive SWAT truck rumbled over the city streets, its rack lights flashing and its horn blaring, as it moved in and out of traffic toward its destination.

Inside the truck were ten heavily-armed policemen, all wearing black uniforms, Kevlar vests, combat helmets, and tactical boots. At the rear of the vehicle was J.T. Ryan and Kelly O'Shea. Like the SWAT team, they were also wearing Kevlar.

It was hot in the truck from the close quarters and the stifling air smelled of gun oil and body odor.

Ryan glanced at Kelly, who was sitting next to him. She had recovered from the near strangulation an hour ago, the only sign it had happened were the bright red bruises on her neck. He had wanted her to stay back at their hotel during the police raid, but she had refused, saying she needed payback from Tanaka and her bodyguard.

Ryan admired her grit and held his thumb up to her. Kelly responded in kind, flashing a quick smile.

He glanced out one of the truck's windows, thankful Erin Welch had been able to contact the Tokyo police and arrange for the SWAT raid so quickly.

Just then the big truck's brakes squealed and the vehicle screeched to a halt. Its doors clanged open and the ten-man SWAT team piled out of the truck, their assault rifles trained forward. Ryan and Kelly followed them out with their pistols drawn.

The city street in front of the high-rise apartment building was a riot of light and sound.

Ryan counted four fire trucks nearby, their red lights flashing and their horns blaring. Firemen carrying hoses hustled through the front doors of the building, while other firemen and paramedics were helping wounded people as they exited the structure.

Ryan looked up to the top of the skyscraper and spotted it immediately. The penthouse floor was ablaze, the flames lighting up the nighttime sky. Several floors below that one were also on fire.

His heart sank, suspecting what had happened. *She did this. Tanaka started the fire to destroy any evidence she might have left behind. She did this, not caring at all about the innocent people who could die in the resulting inferno.*

Chapter 48

Nagano, Japan

Aki Tanaka paced the living room of her modest, single-story house, furiously trying to sort through her options. Going to her liquor cabinet she poured herself a large tumbler of vodka. She had already gone through an entire bottle of her beloved Chivas and now had to settle for Absolut.

Taking a long pull of her drink, she continued pacing, still enraged she'd had to burn down her beautiful penthouse apartment. *I'll kill those fuckers! Ryan and that red headed bitch, whoever the hell she is.*

Aki glanced around disgustedly at the simple, plebian furniture and worn wood floors of her second home, which was located in Nagano, a city west of Tokyo. *It's a slap in the face to have to hide in this crappy place.* Her fury intensified, knowing her well-crafted plans had been disrupted. *Damn them! Damn the FBI and DIA!*

She grimaced and gritted her teeth as she continued pacing.

Just then her bodyguard came into the room. He bowed slightly. "What do you want me to do now, Ms Tanaka?"

The white-haired Asian woman jabbed her finger toward the door. "Get out! Get out! I'll call you when I want you, damn you!"

The big man bowed his head, turned, and left the living room, closing the door behind him.

Aki finished her drink and slumped down onto the sofa, its worn springs groaning. *Calm down. Calm down and think.* She took in several deep breaths and let them out slowly, sorting out her options. Finally, after another half hour of tortured thoughts she settled on one.

Pulling out her satellite cell phone from her pantsuit pocket, she pressed the encryption button and tapped in a number she had memorized long ago.

Karl Strada answered on the first ring. "Hello, Aki. I am so glad you called. I miss you."

Aki tried to keep the panic out of her voice. "And I you."

"Are you okay?" he said in a sympathetic tone. "You sound ... worried."

"I've had ... a minor setback ... with the operation."

"Setback?"

She gripped the phone tightly. "Nothing that can't be fixed. I just ... have to make a few modifications."

"What is going on? Tell me, dear, and I can help you."

"That's why I'm calling, Karl. My operation in Tokyo ... has been compromised."

"Compromised how?"

"That's not important. The important thing is I need to move the Viper operation out of Japan. And I'm thinking the best place to move to is Austria."

"To here, in Vienna?" he asked.

"Exactly, Karl. You have so much space there, I thought we could consolidate everything and put the Viper team there."

"That means you would relocate here also?"

She ground her teeth, not looking forward to it. "Yes, of course."

"That is excellent news, my dear Aki!" The old man sounded ecstatic. "When will this happen?"

"I'm putting the Viper computer technicians and their equipment on my jet today." She glanced at her Rolex. "They'll fly directly to Vienna. I'll text you their ETA and any other details."

"Very good. I will start making arrangements at my mansion immediately. What about you, Aki? Will you be on the plane also?"

"I'm afraid not. I have a few other things to take care of in Japan. But I'll be leaving soon."

"The sooner the better, dear. When you get here, I want to talk to you about something very important. But it is not something we can go over on the phone."

Aki grimaced, sensing what it was about. She dreaded that 'conversation'. *But now that I'm moving to Austria, I can't avoid it much longer. Damn the old bastard!*

"I'm really looking forward to that, Karl," she said sweetly, lying through her teeth.

Chapter 49

Tokyo, Japan

"I can't believe she got away," Kelly O'Shea said, sitting down on the edge of the bed. "We almost had her."

J.T. Ryan was nearby, leaning against the wall of the room. "Don't worry, we'll catch Tanaka. Just not today." The two people were in her room at the Wakana Ryokan Hotel.

Kelly had a morose expression on her face. "I wish I had your confidence."

Ryan nodded. "I've been doing this awhile. PI work is like this sometimes – you get close and then –" He snapped his fingers. "It's gone. But I'm sure we'll be able to track her down, no matter where she is. Remember, we have an advantage we didn't have before. We know her real identity."

"I guess," she replied, no enthusiasm in her voice.

"You're just exhausted, Kelly. You were almost killed by that thug."

She touched her bruised neck with a hand. "Thank you for saving me."

Ryan grinned. "No thanks necessary. It's all part of the job."

Kelly stood, went to the small fridge in the room and opened its door. "All they have is *sake* and more *sake*."

"Any beer in there?"

"You're out of luck, J.T." She pulled out a miniature bottle of *sake*. "I'm having one of these. You want one?"

"I'll pass. I'm not into rice wine."

"Suit yourself." She unscrewed the top off the small bottle and drank down the contents in one gulp. Reaching into he fridge again, she removed another miniature bottle and drank that as well. Then she went back to the bed and sat on the edge of it. She was still dressed in a blue blazer, tan slacks, and a long-sleeve denim shirt, the same clothes she'd worn in Tanaka's apartment.

Ryan glanced at his watch. "It's 4 a.m. I'm tired and I'm sure you are too. I think I'll head back to my room now."

Kelly looked up at him. "I'm too wired. Please stay a bit."

"You sure?"

"I don't want to be alone right now, J.T." She patted the bed. "Sit over here, will you?"

He rubbed his jaw. "You sure that's a good idea."

"I'm sure."

Ryan walked over and sat next to her on the bed.

She placed a hand on one of his and left it there. Her palm felt warm and delicate. She stared down at the floor. "Thank you for saving my life earlier tonight."

"You told me that already."

She gazed at him, her hazel eyes sparkling with intensity. "I know. I guess I'm just stalling. Trying to work up the courage."

Ryan frowned. "Courage for what?"

She leaned in close and kissed him hard on the mouth. When she broke off the kiss a moment later, she said, "For that."

"Wow," Ryan said, his face lighting up. "I wasn't expecting that."

He caressed her cheek softly, tracing her cute freckles, then ran his hand over her lustrous reddish hair, which was tied back in a ponytail. Leaning over he pressed his lips against hers and held the sensuous kiss for a long moment.

When they pulled apart, both of them were breathing heavy, their eyes shining. He could tell she wanted it as much as he did.

"You sure about this?" he asked.

She nodded, a demure smile on her lips. "I'm sure."

"What about the Army rule book? Remember what you said a while back?"

"Screw the rule book, J.T."

Ryan wrapped his muscular arms around her, pulled her close, and kissed her again.

She was only five feet tall and he was well over six feet and powerfully built. She felt tiny and vulnerable in his arms and he made a conscious effort not to squeeze her too hard.

Kelly pulled away from him, her green eyes sparkling. "Don't worry, J.T. I'm not a china doll. I won't break."

He kissed her again, this time harder and she kissed him back hungrily, their tongues exploring each other's mouths. Their hands roamed each other's bodies over their clothes. Her curves felt soft and desirable and he was so aroused that his breathing was labored.

She reached out with a hand and cupped his hardness. Ryan groaned in pleasure and kissed her more forcefully as he caressed her breasts over her shirt.

Kelly stood up abruptly.

"What's wrong?" Ryan said.

"Nothing," she whispered, a sensuous smile on her face. "Absolutely nothing."

Holding his gaze with her sparkling hazel eyes, she slowly took off her blazer and let it fall to the floor. She reached back with a hand, removed her ponytail scrunchie, and let her long auburn hair cascade to her shoulders, framing her pretty face.

She looked absolutely delicious, Ryan thought.

Then, still holding his gaze, she began to slowly unbutton her blue denim shirt.

Chapter 50

FBI Field Office
Atlanta, Georgia

"Anything else?" Erin Welch asked.

J.T. Ryan leaned forward in the chair. "No. That covers it." He had just spent the last hour filling Erin in on his trip to Japan. The two of them were meeting in her office at the FBI building.

Erin put down her pen and rested her legal pad on the desk in front of her. "All right, J.T. It's crap that Tanaka got away, but at least we now know who she really is."

"Yeah. Kelly and I spent a week in Japan after Tanaka burned down her apartment, trying to locate her with no luck. We went to all of the companies she owns, but she's vanished."

Erin nodded. "You think Tanaka is still in Japan?"

"No way of knowing. The Tokyo police are still looking for her and I'm keeping in close contact with them. There's still a chance they'll catch her and arrest her."

"You don't seem optimistic, J.T."

"I'm not. Aki Tanaka is a master criminal. She used a false identity, a black wig and black contacts to disguise herself. She may have other fake identities. And she obviously has extensive financial resources. My gut tells me she's long gone from Japan. But where she is, is anybody's guess."

Erin picked up her pen and tapped it idly on her desk. "All right. Now that we know who she is and what she really looks like we may be able to track her down on NCIC and other government records."

Ryan nodded. "And Kelly's been using the DIA database — something may pop from that."

"I was going to ask you how that went, J.T."

"How what went?"

"I know you like to work alone," Erin said, "and I remember you didn't want Kelly going with you to Japan. But you worked with her for what, two weeks? How'd it go?"

Ryan's face reddened and he stared at the floor. "Kelly ... was a big help ... she's fluent in Japanese, you know ...."

Erin grinned. "She's cute as a button, too."

"Cut that out, Erin. I know what you're thinking."

Erin's smile widened. "You're blushing, John Taylor Ryan! That tells me one thing — you and Ms O'Shea were burning up the sheets in Japan."

Ryan frowned. "Please. Don't say another word. If General Keating were to find out, Kelly's career would be jeopardized. That's the last thing I want to happen."

"Don't worry, J.T. It'll be our little secret. In fact, I'm glad for you. You've had your share of women problems in the past. It's good to see you involved with a sweet girl like Kelly."

"Can we *please* get back to talking about the case? You know I hate talking about personal stuff like this."

Erin nodded, her face all business now. "No problem." She reached into a desk drawer and pulled out a small leather-bound notebook. "Remember this, J.T.?"

"That looks like Joe Padilla's notebook. He's the assassin Tanaka hired to murder the Face-Look CEO."

"That's right. There were lots of notes in this book, but they were all written in code. Ever since you found this in Padilla's house, I've had my tech guys trying to break the code."

Ryan's pulse quickened, his enthusiasm surging. "You were able to figure it out?"

"Not exactly. But we were able to pick up one word that was repeated many times."

"What was it, Erin?"

"Viper."

Ryan's eyebrows arched. "Like the snake? A Viper snake?"

"It's unclear. But it appears to be the name of the operation the criminals are running."

"Okay. This could be a good lead."

"I agree, J.T."

Erin stood up from her desk and went to a corner of her office. There was a large white board there and she wheeled it closer to her desk so Ryan could read it. Drawn on the white board was a diagram showing the various stages of the investigation.

Erin picked up a magic marker and pointed to the board. "This case started with the murder of Face-Look's president, then the killings of the Tekk-Sky executives, then finding the sniper Joe Padilla, which led us to the social media companies being purchased and the possible corruption of news regarding the upcoming American elections. All this led us to the banker in the Caymans, who then led us to the mysterious black haired Asian woman named Nikita Nashamura, who it turns out was Aki Tanaka, a Japanese woman who we now believe is the mastermind of the criminal conspiracy."

She wrote a new name on the white board and underlined it. "And now we have Viper."

Ryan nodded. "And now we have Viper." He rubbed his jaw. "Kelly's research found out something else. Several of Aki Tanaka's companies in Japan weren't profitable. Kelly studied their financial reports and saw they were in the red. Tanaka was getting an infusion of cash from somewhere."

"So Tanaka is a ringleader in the criminal conspiracy," Erin said. "But she must have co-conspirators, maybe several. We know the Viper operation is well-funded. Very well-funded. Tanaka must be getting money from an extremely wealthy person or a consortium of people."

Ryan mulled this over a minute. "I met Tanaka only once. But she made an incredible impression on me. She's a strikingly beautiful woman, but also incredibly cold and calculating. And her white eyes are ... exotic and sexually powerful. Almost hypnotic. I could easily see her using sex to get her way with men."

Erin folded her arms across her chest. "So you think there's a wealthy man backing her operation? A sugar-daddy?"

"That's exactly what I think, Erin."

Chapter 51

Vienna, Austria

Aki Tanaka's private Gulfstream jet touched down at Schwechat Airport at precisely 10 a.m. Her partner's limousine picked her up there and an hour later she arrived at his massive stone castle, which overlooked the Danube river.

As usual, she marveled at the historic stone structure with its impressive turrets, wide moat, elaborate arches, and ramparts. Karl Strada, she knew, had spent a fortune refurbishing the Hapsburg Era castle to its former Imperial glory, updating it with the latest in modern technology.

After going through the extensive security measures of the walled estate, she was shown to her usual room, a high-ceilinged bedroom outfitted with a four-poster bed and Austrian Empire tapestries on the walls. The room overlooked the Danube river and had its own stone fireplace, as did most of the rooms of the ancient castle, a remnant of the days before central heating.

Aki unpacked, took a quick shower, and changed into a white Dolce & Gabbana pantsuit. She applied makeup, brushed the long white tresses of her hair, and left the room.

Her ever-present bodyguard Honshu was in the corridor, leaning against the wall. Seeing her, he bowed slightly and followed her to the elevators. They took it down to the first floor, and after navigating several corridors lined with priceless suits of armor from the Middle Ages, reached Strada's huge office.

Aki went inside, while Honshu waited by the open doorway, standing ramrod straight, his eyes alert.

She noticed the room was vacant, although the large stone fireplace was blazing. The crackling flames provided a comforting warmth to the drafty room.

Aki glanced at a corner of the room, where Strada kept a life-size ivory chess set. The elaborately carved chess pieces resembled knights and royalty from the Middle Ages. There was a covering of dust on the pieces, indicating the chess set hadn't been touched since her last visit.

There was a large sitting area near Strada's teak-wood desk. She went there and perched on one of the antique, brocade wingback chairs.

She heard a rustling from behind her and turned, and saw her partner enter the room.

The tall, distinguished-looking man approached her, a wide smile on his lips.

"Aki, it is so good to see you," he said effusively. The 82 year old man was wearing an exquisitely-tailored Sevile Row three-piece business suit. It's gray color complimented his graying hair and graying mustache.

She rose from her chair and smiled. "And I you."

The man kissed her on the cheek and affectionately ran a hand over her long white hair. "You look so beautiful, my dear Aki, without your disguise. I never did like that look, with the black hair and black eyes. It hid your natural beauty."

"I don't have much choice," she said. "That cover's blown."

"Please sit. You must tell me all about it."

They sat across from each other and she said, "I don't want to dwell on that. That chapter's behind us now. The important thing is Viper is intact. You told me on the phone you've set up the operation here. Any problems?"

"None whatsoever. The computer engineers you flew over are already hard at work. I retrofitted part of the basement of my castle with all of their tech equipment."

"That's excellent, Karl. I'll go see them after we've had a chance to talk."

Strada nodded. "Yes. Tell me, how did the FBI locate you in Japan? You have always taken incredible precautions to mask your real identity."

"That's true," she said, grimacing. "I'm not sure how it happened. I do know they have an obviously smart agent that runs the FBI's Atlanta office. Her name is Erin Welch." She flashed an icy grin. "But I won't be blindsided by that bitch again. I've already put some things in motion to change that equation."

"What about the man who almost arrested you – what is his name?"

The Asian woman scowled. "Ryan. That's the bastard!" She ground her teeth, the thought of him making her stomach churn with acid.

"I'll make him pay!" she spit out. "I had to *burn down* my beautiful apartment in Tokyo because of him!"

She gripped the armrests of her wingback chair.

"Calm yourself, please," he said sympathetically. "I do not like to see you so distraught. Now that you are here in Austria we can tackle all of our problems together."

"Of course."

"Aki, have dinner with me tonight. I have something important to discuss with you."

"About Viper?"

Strada shook his head and a slight smile formed on his lips. "No. This is a personal matter. A very important one."

A migraine started pounding in her head. *Fuck. I knew this would happen. But now that I'm here in Austria I can't avoid it.* She massaged her temple with a hand.

Aki forced herself to smile. "Of course, Karl, let's have dinner together. We can talk about anything you want."

She stood up. "I'd like to see the Viper operation now, if you don't mind. I want to talk to my employees."

"Yes, yes. The operation is in the basement. The second room on the right. The guard posted at the door will let you in."

"Thank you."

Aki turned and walked out of the office, and with her bodyguard in tow, went down to the basement level. She entered the large room Strada had converted into the Viper operations area, while Honshu waited outside. Unlike the other parts of the castle that dripped in luxury, this room had gray concrete walls and floors, harsh florescent lighting, and was bare of any decoration.

She scanned the ten computer workstations that had been setup in the area and spotted Kobe at the far end. The young man was the operation's supervisory technician and she approached him.

Kobe stopped what he was doing and stood, bowing his head slightly. "Ms Tanaka. They told me you were coming. I am glad you are here."

Aki waved a hand in the air. "Do you have everything you need?"

"Yes, Ms Tanaka. Mr. Strada has been very gracious and generous. All of our equipment was assembled and is functioning well. And he has provided us with comfortable quarters here in the mansion."

"Good. I'll make sure that continues, Kobe. Anything you need, anything at all, just let me know. I'll make sure you get it."

The man bowed his head. "Thank you."

She pointed to the computer screens on his workstation. "What are you working on today?"

Kobe turned and faced the screens. "Mr. Strada instructed us to focus on the upcoming American elections. Right now we're feeding 'news' stories to the social media sites."

Aki rolled her eyes. *Damn. That bullshit again.*

"Is that okay with you, Ms Tanaka?"

"Yes, for now," she replied, her voice steely. "But soon I'll give you new instructions."

"Of course."

Aki turned to go.

"Ms Tanaka, there's something else I need to discuss with you."

"What is it?"

"My family is back in Tokyo."

"Your family?"

"Yes. My wife and my son are still in Japan," he said, a deep frown on his face.

Aki nodded. "Of course. With everything that's happened recently, I forgot all about that. You miss them, don't you?"

"Yes. Very much."

"Don't worry, Kobe. I'll send my jet to bring them here. I'll take care of that today."

His face flooded with relief. "Thank you!"

Aki reached out with a hand and squeezed one of his broad shoulders, felt a thrill from his hard-packed muscles. In a low voice so that the others couldn't hear, she said, "I made you supervisor of the Viper operation because of your excellent computer skills. But there's another reason you're my favorite. You remember what that is?"

The young man nodded and stared at the floor. "Yes, I know."

"You're my favorite, Kobe, because you follow my instructions so, so well. Here in the operations room and in the bedroom."

He said nothing and kept his eyes on the floor.

Aki squeezed his shoulder again. "I pay you extremely well to run Viper. And I'll make sure you and your wife and child live in a very nice home here in Vienna. But I expect payment for my investment. Are we clear on this?"

Kobe nodded his head.

"Say it, Kobe."

"Yes, Ms Tanaka. I am clear on this. I will fulfill my duties to you in all the ways that you want."

Aki smiled. "I know you will. That's why you're my favorite."

She turned and left the room, Honshu shadowing her every move. As she started walking down the corridor to the elevator, she passed a closed door. Approaching the guard posted by it, she asked the man, "What's this room used for?"

"It's Mr. Strada's private room, Ms Tanaka."

Her eyebrows arched. "What does that mean?"

"Only Mr. Strada goes in there."

Curious, she tried the door knob and found it locked. "Unlock it," she ordered.

The guard shook his head. "I am sorry. I am under strict orders. Only Mr. Strada is allowed in this room."

Her white eyes flashed in anger. "Open it, damn you. Or I'll have you fired!"

The guard nodded, pulled out a set of keys and unlocked the door.

Aki, sensing what the room was used for, turned to Honshu. "Wait here," she ordered, then went into the room by herself, closing the door behind her.

The large, luxuriously-appointed room was exactly what she had guessed it would be. Aki counted at least fifteen women lounging in the place, sitting or laying down on couches and sofas. All were scantily clad in see-thru negligees or were topless, wearing only panties. Some of them were Nordic blue-eyed blondes, while others appeared to be Hispanic, Asian, or of African descent. All were attractive.

The smell of opium, marijuana, and hashish was strong in the air and Aki noticed several of the women were smoking from long, thin pipes. Two of the women were huddled over a coffee table, cutting and snorting lines of coke from a large mound of white powder on the table. There was another nude woman sprawled on the floor, passed out.

As Aki strode around the room, the women stared at her wide-eyed. She inspected each one carefully, amazed at what Strada had created for himself. *A fucking harem. I always knew he kept a few whores. But this?*

None of the women spoke to her, and in fact seemed terrified of her. Aki continued walking deeper into the area, following a corridor that led to a full kitchen, a storage area, a laundry room, one large private bedroom, and a dormitory of sorts, with bunk beds along the walls.

At first she thought the dormitory was vacant but then she spotted a very young girl huddled on the floor at the back of the room.

Aki marched over and noticed the teenage girl was sobbing, her head buried in her hands. The pretty girl, who had Asian features, was completely nude. By her tiny breasts and childlike looks, she realized the girl was very young.

Aki crouched across from her. "Are you okay?" she said in a soothing voice.

Obviously startled, the girl shrank back from her and cowered in a corner.

"I won't hurt you," Aki said. "I promise."

The teen girl wiped tears from her eyes.

"I'm Aki. What's your name?"

"Su-Wei."

"That's a pretty name. Where are you from?"

"Vietnam."

"What do you do here, Su-Wei? Do you clean or cook for the women?"

The girl shook her head. "No. Not that. Other things. Bad things."

Aki grimaced, realizing why the young girl was there. *What a bastard Strada is. Damn him. A harem full of coke whores is one thing. But this?*

"How old are you, Su-Wei?"

"Thirteen."

"Oh, my God." Aki reached out with a hand a gently stroked the girl's long black hair. The girl flinched, her eyes wide with fear.

"I won't hurt you," Aki said. "I promise."

The girl appeared to relax a bit. "Okay."

"How did you get here?"

"My parents sold me ... to the man who owns this house."

"Your parents *sold* you?"

Su-Wei nodded. "They are very poor."

"They sold you to Karl Strada? And he brought you here from Vietnam?"

The girl nodded.

"And Strada makes you do things?" Aki said.

"Yes. Bad things. Horrible things. Things I don't want to do." She began sobbing again, tears flowing down her face. She wrapped her thin arms around her body to cover her nakedness.

"Poor baby," Aki said. "I'm sorry this has happened to you. I'm going to help you and get you out of here."

The teen girl continued crying for another minute, then raised her eyes and stared at Aki.

"I'm going to help you," Aki repeated.

"You are?"

"Yes."

"Why?"

Aki placed a hand gently on the girl's shoulder. "Because you don't deserve this. Nobody does."

Aki stood and scanned the dormitory. She noticed a blanket on one of the cots, walked over, picked it up, and came back to where Su-Wei was huddled. She wrapped the blanket around the naked girl's body and took her hand. "Come with me, Su-Wei. I'll make sure you're safe from now on. I'll take you back to my room. You can take a long bath there and I'll get you some proper clothes. Then I'm going to find you a good foster home where you'll be safe and cared for."

The girl gazed up at her, an amazed look on her face. "Really? You'll do all that?"

"Yes I will, honey."

The young girl smiled and squeezed her hand. "Thank you."

Aki felt a wave of compassion run through her, something she hadn't felt in many, many years. It was something she didn't think she was capable of feeling anymore. *Imagine that. Even a cold-hearted bitch like me can do something good.*

Chapter 52

Vienna, Austria

Aki Tanaka strode into the castle's immense dining room and found Karl Strada was already there, seated at the head of the onyx top dining table, which could easily sit forty people. There were no other guests in the room, only several uniformed maids who hovered by him, pouring drinks and setting down dishes.

A roaring fire was burning in the stone fireplace, giving off a warm glow to the drafty, high-ceilinged room. The aroma of scented candles filled the air.

Strada rose from the table and went around it. He approached her and smiled widely, kissing her on the cheek.

"You look so lovely tonight, Aki."

She was wearing a very low-cut, form-fitting dress with a high slit that showed off her hourglass figure. The custom-made dress was made of shimmering white silk, its color perfectly matching her eyes and hair.

Aki smiled but said nothing as they sat down next to each other at the long table.

"I thought we should dine first," Strada said, "then we can talk. I had the chef prepare us a very special dinner."

"I'd like a drink first," she responded.

"Of course. How thoughtless of me." He clapped his hands and one of the maids poured a goblet of scotch for the Asian woman while another maid served coffee to the billionaire.

They made small talk while the meal was served, an elaborate seven-course affair that included Dom Perignon champagne. Aki mostly picked at her food, which as usual was delicious, and downed champagne and Chivas scotch whiskey non-stop, her stomach churning in trepidation and foreboding of the conversation she knew was coming. A sense of dread overcame her, making it almost hard to breathe.

When the two were done eating and the dinner plates were cleared, Strada clapped his hands. "You may leave us now," he said to the maids. "And close the door behind you."

The women nodded and scurried out of the room, the massive wooden door shutting with a loud thud. To Aki it sounded like the closing of a tomb, a tomb she was trapped in.

Strada took a sip of coffee and set the cup down. "Are you all right, Aki? You have been ... rather quiet tonight."

She gave him a wan smile. "I have a lot on my mind right now."

He patted her hand. "Understandable, with everything you have gone through lately ... that horrible situation in Japan ... and having to leave your home so suddenly."

He patted her hand again. "But do not worry, my dear Aki. You will see. Viper is on track." He paused and smiled. "In fact, that evil man, what was his name again? Oh, yes, that horrible man Ryan, he may have done us a big favor."

Aki grimaced. "A favor? I despise that bastard! I want him dead!"

"Now, now, calm yourself." He squeezed her hand and smiled. "Don't you see what he has done? He has brought us together!"

Aki ground her teeth and said nothing.

His grin widened. "You are here, in Vienna, with me. What I always wanted."

She felt her stomach churning and sensed a migraine building in her head. She wanted to slap the billionaire across the face for what he had done to Su-Wei. And not just for that reason, but also because she sensed where this conversation was headed.

Instead of slapping Strada, she forced a smile on her face.

"You're right, Karl," she said, honey in her voice. "Ryan did bring us together. For that I'm grateful."

He patted her hand again. "It is so good to see you smile, dear. Now, I want to ask you an important question. A question I have been hinting at for some time."

She nodded but said nothing.

"Will you marry me, Aki?"

A sense of cold dread ran down her spine. Although she had known it was coming, she didn't really know how she would react when the moment came.

"I ... ," Aki said shakily, her voice a mere whisper. "I ... don't ... know ... what to ... say ...."

"Say yes!" He waved a hand in the air. "You can have all of this. Think of it, Aki. You will be the wife of a billionaire. I am one of Europe's richest men. What woman would pass that up?"

Tears flowed from her eyes and she pushed them away with a hand. They weren't tears of joy but tears of fear, of terror. Of giving up control over her life. *But all that money. More money than I ever dreamed of making on my own. Can I pass that up?*

Suddenly she came to a decision. "Yes. I'll marry you."

Strada beamed, grinning like a kid in a candy store. "You have made me the happiest man in the world!"

"But I have conditions," she said, her voice hard.

His smile dimmed a bit. "What conditions?"

She stabbed her index finger toward his face. "First, that den full of coke whores has to go."

He frowned. "You saw it? I told my people not to let you in there."

"Yes, Karl. I fucking saw your harem full of whores. And I want it gone from this house immediately!"

Strada nodded. "Of course, dear."

"Second, that child you've been fucking. Su-Wei. She's in my room now, safe from you. I'm going to find her a good foster home here in Vienna, far away from her evil parents who sold her to a bastard like you." Aki stabbed her index finger into his chest. "She's only thirteen years old! You're a pig for fucking a child!" She paused. "You disgust me, Karl."

"Are you still going to marry me?" he said, his voice pleading.

She stared at him, her white eyes blazing. "Yes. I will marry you. Because even though you're a bastard, I'm a cold-hearted, greedy bitch."

She paused and jabbed his chest again with her index finger. "But I have more conditions."

"More conditions?"

"Yes, you bastard."

He let out a long breath and then shrugged his shoulders. "All right. What are they?"

"We sleep in separate bedrooms."

He grimaced. "But Aki, we will be husband and wife. Are you saying we will not make love?"

"I didn't say that. We will make love, or fuck, or whatever else you want to call it." Aki smiled, a cold grin that had no humor in it. "But when we do fuck it will be on my terms."

His eyebrows arched. "What do you mean?"

With the icy grin still on her face, she said, "In the bedroom, I'm the boss."

Chapter 53

Buckhead
Atlanta, Georgia

Erin Welch was startled awake by the ringing doorbell.

She sat up on the bed and groggily scanned her dim bedroom, catching the time on the alarm clock: 2:26 a.m. *Christ. Who could it be at this hour?*

She slipped on a robe, picked up her Glock from the bedside table, and still barefoot, padded out of the bedroom toward the condo's front door.

The doorbell ringed again as she glanced at the screen of the security panel by the door. The surveillance camera showed two large men wearing dark suits, white shirts and dark ties in the corridor.

"What do you want?" Erin said into the intercom.

One of the men held up a badge. "Ms Welch, we're with DHS and we need to speak with you. I'm Special Agent Mallory and this is Special Agent Smith."

"Do you know what time it is?" she replied in an aggravated tone.

"Yes, ma'am. We apologize for the late hour. But like I said, it's urgent we speak with you."

"Hold up your badge closer to the camera so I can read it."

"Yes, ma'am." The man raised the badge and she could clearly see he was an agent from the Department of Homeland Security.

"If you'll just open the door, Ms Welch, we'll explain everything."

"All right." Still holding the pistol at her side, she turned off the house alarm, unlocked the deadbolt, and opened the front door partway.

"You've got two minutes, Agent Mallory," she said. "Start talking."

The agent nodded. "Of course, ma'am. Once again, I apologize for the late hour."

Suddenly the other agent barreled forward, pushing the door fully open, almost knocking Erin off her feet.

She stumbled backward, her heart jack-hammering in her chest, as she tried aiming the pistol at the men. One of them swatted the weapon away, the Glock flying in the air.

"Grab her!" one of the men yelled as he slammed the door shut behind him.

Her adrenaline pumping, Erin went into a fighting stance, warily eying the two big men who were edging closer to her in the foyer.

One of them grabbed her arm and she kicked him hard in the balls. He grunted, let go of her arm and clutched his groin.

The other guy rushed her and punched her in the gut. She gasped from the blow and staggered back. Out of the corner of her eye she saw him stab her neck with a large hypodermic. She felt a sharp pain from the needle and started to feel drowsy.

Then the man wrapped his muscular arms around her and wrestled her to the floor.

Erin fought back, kicking him, head butting him, biting his ear, all while trying to pry her arms loose.

But the guy easily outweighed her by a hundred pounds and was much stronger. She also felt herself getting sleepier and weaker by the second.

Moments later she lost consciousness and everything went black.

Chapter 54

Headquarters Building
Defense Intelligence Agency
Washington, D.C.

"So you see, General, we've made some good progress on the case," J.T. Ryan said.

General Keating lit his pipe with a Zippo lighter, took a puff and exhaled, the sweet aroma filling the general's office. Keating rested the pipe on an ashtray on his desk and stared at Ryan and Kelly O'Shea, who was seated next to the PI.

"But not enough progress," the general replied. As usual Keating was wearing his Army Class A blue uniform. "You haven't arrested the conspirators yet."

Ryan glanced at Kelly, then looked at Keating again. "That's true, sir. But at least now we know who the ringleader is. The Japanese woman, Aki Tanaka."

General Keating scowled. "The woman you let get away."

Ryan clenched his jaw. "It's not as simple as you make it sound. True, I was not able to capture Tanaka – but Kelly, I mean Colonel O'Shea's life was at stake. I had no choice, General."

Keating glared at Kelly. "Well, Colonel? What do you have to say for yourself?"

"Sir," Kelly said, "the situation happened exactly as Ryan described. I don't believe he had a choice. And by the time we got back to her condo with the Japanese police, Tanaka was gone."

"All right you two," general said in an irritated tone, "I'm not happy with your results. But I do grudgingly have to admit you have made some progress." He paused, took another puff from his pipe and exhaled.

"When Erin Welch was here recently," Keating continued, "I showed her how this Viper conspiracy was already influencing the upcoming U.S. elections. We're now even closer to them, a key time for voters to be swayed toward one candidate or the other." The man pointed his pipe toward Ryan. "It's imperative that we stop these people now."

Ryan nodded. "I agree, sir."

Just then Ryan's cell phone vibrated in his pocket. He slipped it out and looked at the info screen. Glancing at Keating, he said, "I need to take this. It could be urgent."

"Go ahead," the general said.

"Ryan here," he said into the phone.

"This is Special Agent Puller from the FBI office in Atlanta."

"Yes, Puller. What is it?"

"Assistant Director Welch is missing. We believe she's been kidnapped."

Ryan tensed. "What? Damn! Agent Puller, I'm going to put this call on speaker. There's several other people here who need to hear this." Ryan pressed a button on his phone. "Go ahead, Puller. Tell us what happened."

"Assistant Director Welch didn't show up at work today," Puller said, his voice filling the room, "which is extremely rare for her, especially since she had several important meetings scheduled. We couldn't get a hold of her – her cell and her home phone went to voice mail, so I sent some agents to her condo in Buckhead. They found the front door unlocked and signs of a struggle in the foyer. The agents reviewed the security camera footage and from the looks of it, it appears two men posing as DHS agents broke into her condo and abducted Welch. I wanted to call you right away since I know you're working a big case for her. We at the Bureau think her kidnapping and the case are connected."

"I'm sure it's connected," Ryan said. "It's too coincidental. I'll call you back, Puller, when we figure out our next steps."

The PI hung up the phone and put it away.

The three people stared at each other for a long moment, then Ryan said, "General, I think Kelly, I mean Colonel O'Shea, and I need to work separately for a while on this investigation. The colonel should stay here at the DIA and try to locate Tanaka. You have incredible resources here that will help us track her down. In the meantime, I'll return to Atlanta and try to locate Erin Welch – which may also lead us to the Viper conspirators."

General Keating glared. "I don't like your plan."

"Why not, sir?"

"Because I don't trust you, soldier. You're a cowboy. A loose cannon. You need someone stable like the colonel here to keep you focused."

Ryan balled his fists. "With all due respect, sir, I've been a private investigator for a long time. And I get results. Otherwise the FBI wouldn't keep hiring me, would they?"

Keating frowned and didn't reply. He faced Kelly. "What do think about this, Colonel?"

"Sir," Kelly replied, "I think J.T. is correct. If we split up we have a much better shot at solving this case faster."

The general scowled at her and then at Ryan. Finally he said, "All right. We'll do it your way, Ryan. But if this thing goes sideways, I'm holding you personally responsible. I'll lock you up in Leavenworth and throw away the key."

Chapter 55

Headquarters Building
Defense Intelligence Agency
Washington, D.C.

Ryan and Kelly left the headquarters building, located her car in the huge parking lot, and climbed inside.

Kelly inserted the key in the ignition, but instead of firing up the Chevrolet sedan, she turned toward Ryan. "It's too bad we have to split up."

He gave her a long look. "I agree. We make a good team."

"I was going to ask you ...." she said, her voice low.

"Ask me what?"

She averted her eyes, staring toward the front windshield. "What happened back in Japan. Was that real ...?"

He touched her shoulder with a hand. "It was real."

Kelly faced him again and he could see her eyes glistening. "It wasn't just a one-night fling, J.T.?"

He caressed her face and gently wiped a tear away. "I don't do one-night stands. That's not me."

"I'm glad. I don't either." She gave him a tentative smile, her face flushing pink, accentuating her freckles. "You're the first man I've been with in a very long time ...."

"I could tell. You're a very special woman, Kelly."

"Where does that leave us?"

Ryan let out a long sigh. "I go back to Atlanta. You stay here. We keep working the case."

She reached out and placed a hand on his chest. Her palm felt warm and sensuous. "Will we see each other again, J.T.?"

"I hope so. I really hope so." He leaned over, gently touched his lips to hers. They held the kiss for a long moment.

When they separated her eyes were red-rimmed.

"I don't want you to go," she whispered, "not just yet ...."

Ryan nodded and stroked her hand, his heart racing.

Kelly smiled and rested her head on his shoulder. They sat that way for several minutes, silent, holding each other close.

Finally he said, "I need to go."

"I know. You want me to drive you to the airport?"

"Yes. I need to catch the next plane to Atlanta."

"Call me when you get there?"

"I will."

Kelly turned on the ignition and fired up the Chevrolet. Then she drove out of the parking lot and headed toward Reagan National Airport.

Chapter 56

Vienna, Austria

Aki Tanaka twirled the wedding band on her finger, unaccustomed to the heavy gold ring. Strada had purchased the jewel-encrusted band from an artifacts dealer in Vienna, who claimed the ring dated back to the Hapsburg Empire and had been worn by Empress Maria Theresa in the 1700's. Aki didn't know if that was really true, but did know the jewels were genuine and that Strada had paid a fortune to purchase it.

And I'm worth every penny of it, she mused, admiring the rubies and diamonds adorning the ring. She flashed a cold, hard grin, recalling their torrid lovemaking on their wedding night. She'd finally given herself to him, though grudgingly, and only after having him grovel for it, making sure he knew who was in charge.

All in all, Aki was pleased how it had all turned out. Strada's den of whores had been banished from the castle and she had her own private bedroom suite, where she was now. Also, she'd been able to find a good foster home for Su-Wei, the 13 year old Vietnamese girl. And best of all, Aki was now a billionaire's wife, with access to all his wealth.

"Aki Tanaka Strada," she said out loud, twirling the ring around her finger. "I like the sound of it."

Just then her cell phone buzzed and she took it out of her pocket. "Yes?"

"It's Kobe," she heard the young man say. "I'm in the operations room, Ms Tanaka. There's something important I think you'll want to see."

"I'll be right down." She hung up the call, draped a shimmering white silk jacket over her matching Dolce & Gabbana pantsuit and headed out of the bedroom suite.

Five minutes later she entered the Viper room in the basement, and closing the door behind her, approached Kobe's workstation.

"What do you have for me?" she asked.

The computer programmer bowed his head slightly and pointed to one of the screens on his desk. "Ms Tanaka, we just received new recordings from the Tekk-Sky cloud operation in Salt Lake City. Now that Viper owns that company, we have access to all their data."

"Okay," she replied. "Show me." He was seated at his workstation and she looked over his shoulder.

He pressed a button on his console and she began hearing a bland, innocuous conversation between two people, a man and a woman. The couple were talking to each other and periodically asking questions to what was obviously a computer device in their room.

"I don't understand, Kobe. How is this important? This conversation is boring beyond belief. This couple is talking about some silly television program. Why should I care about this?"

"Are you familiar with Alexa, and Siri, and Echo, and Cortana, and the other artificial intelligence devices people have in their homes and cars now? They use these virtual assistant devices to search for music, or movies, or to do research, or to find out the weather, or a million other reasons."

"Of course," she said. "Theses devices are being used more and more every day, in many countries around the world."

"That's correct, Ms Tanaka. And after the devices are used, they usually go into 'sleep mode.' Well, I've been able to hack into and reprogram the software of these AI programs. Reprogram them in such a way that the AIs continue to listen to whatever is being said, even if they're in 'sleep mode', and even if they're shut off. As long as they're plugged into a power source, I can access everything that is being said, twenty four hours a day, seven days a week."

Aki's jaw dropped. "You mean we can access everything?"

"Yes, Ms Tanaka."

"Damn!" she stated, her white eyes flashing in excitement. "Think of the possibilities. We have access to every conversation, no matter how intimate and personal. Nothing will be private. We'll know every dark secret ...." Her thoughts raced, realizing the vast potential for blackmail. "You've done well, Kobe. Very well. I need to reward you."

He was still sitting at his workstation and she was standing behind him looking over his shoulders.

Placing her hands on his broad shoulders, she squeezed his hard-packed muscles. Her heart pounded and she felt herself getting wet. It was a feeling she knew an old man like Strada could never give her. She leaned over and whispered in Kobe's ear. "I want to see you tonight."

He sat ramrod straight in his chair. "But Ms Tanaka. You're married now. I thought ...."

"That's where you're wrong. I need you now more than ever." She massaged his shoulders. "If you're worried about my husband finding out, don't be. My bedroom is in a separate wing of the castle. He'll never know."

"But —"

"Now, now, Kobe, don't be difficult. You know how generous I can be," she said, continuing to whisper. "You also know what a cold bitch I can be if I don't get my way."

"Yes, Ms Tanaka. I know."

"Good. I'm glad we understand each other. Come to my bedroom at nine tonight. And don't be late."

Then she turned and abruptly left the room.

Chapter 57

Flying at 30,000 feet

Erin Welch was cold, exhausted, and disoriented. She was sitting on a hard metal floor, her hands and legs bound in heavy shackles.

The small room she was in was pitch black, but by the loud engine noise and the vibration coming from the metal floor, she guessed she was in the hold of a plane. *What the hell's going on? Where am I?*

Her neck throbbed and suddenly her memories flooded back. *Her apartment. The phony DHS men. Being stabbed in the neck with a hypodermic.*

Erin remembered nothing after that. She blinked her eyes several times, trying to get a better feel for her surroundings. In the gloom, she could make out large wooden crates and boxes stacked on pallets all around her. She was wearing dark coveralls made of a rough material and she sensed she was naked underneath.

The engine noise changed and she felt the plane descending. *Are we landing?*

Erin struggled with her chains, trying to break loose. The heavy metal shackles were too strong and after several minutes she gave up the effort.

Soon after a loud creaking noise filled the room and instantly she knew the plane's landing gear was extending. Wherever she was headed, she'd be there soon. Desperately she scanned her immediate surroundings, searching for anything she could use as a weapon. With a feeling of dread she realized there was nothing.

Erin swallowed hard, her heart pounding in her chest, as she tried to come up with a plan, any plan, to escape.

Chapter 58

Buckhead
Atlanta, Georgia

FBI Special Agent Puller removed the crime scene tape and unlocked the front door of the condo. He stepped inside, followed by J.T. Ryan.

"We think it all took place right here," Puller said, motioning to the foyer where they stood. "We found blood stains on the tile floor and scuff marks on the walls."

"Have you identified the blood?" Ryan asked.

Puller nodded. "It was Ms Welch's."

"Any shell casings?"

"No. No guns were fired from what we could tell. No trace evidence of gunpowder and her Glock was on the floor, but it hadn't been fired. It appears the two men overpowered her, bound her up, and kidnapped her."

"What about facial rec?" Ryan said. "Were you able to identify the men from the security video?"

Puller shook his head. "Nothing yet. We're still trying to run it down through NCIC."

"I'd like a copy of the camera footage. Can you make me one?"

"I'm ahead of you there," Puller replied, reaching into a pocket and pulling out a flash drive which he handed to the PI. The FBI agent was a tall and lanky black man in his early forties. "I thought you'd want it."

Ryan nodded. "Thanks. Erin always said you were one of her best agents."

"Good to know."

"I'll keep you in the loop as I work the case," Ryan said, pocketing the flash drive. "I'm sure Erin's kidnapping is tied in with the Viper conspiracy."

"I agree, Ryan."

"But when I get a lead, don't ask me how I got it. I don't always go by the book."

"So I've heard," Puller said.

"Especially now, with Erin in danger. She's a good cop. And a good friend. This is personal now."

The PI extended his hand and the other man shook it.

***

Ryan drove to his office in midtown, made a 5 x 7 photo of the two phony DHS men in the surveillance tape and slipped it in his blazer pocket. Then he took out his cell phone and punched in a number.

"It's Ryan," he said when the woman picked up.

"I'm glad you called," Kelly O'Shea replied.

"I just got a lead from Puller, the FBI agent working the case here. I'm going to text you a photo of the guys who abducted Erin. Try running facial recognition on your DIA database. The FBI is doing the same here on their system. Hopefully something will pop from all this."

"You got it, J.T. I'll call you if I get anything. What's next for you?"

"Something a lot less high-tech than facial rec and computer databases."

She chuckled. "Old school tactics?"

"You know me too well, Kelly."

They said their goodbyes and he hung up the call.

***

Ryan pulled into the lot of the Starlight and parked his Ford Explorer. The run-down one-story concrete building looked just as seedy as the last time he'd been there. Its garish neon sign still read *The Starlight – Georgia's Premier Gentlemen's Club* but now some of the letters had gone dark. He also noticed the business next to the club, a massage parlor, had been boarded up.

Ryan climbed out of his SUV, paid the cover charge at the door, and strode into the place. Rock music pounded from overhead speakers and cigarette smoke hung in the air. The whole place stank of sweat, tobacco, vomit, and stale beer. Multi-color strobe lights illuminated the stage at the far end of the room, where three female dancers gyrated listlessly on poles. The women wore tiny G-strings, hooker heels, and tired smiles.

The place was half-empty, the patrons all men, all wearing soiled blue-collar work clothes and heavy boots.

He approached the long bar and sat at a stool. When the overweight bartender came over, the PI said, "Is Ruby around?"

"She's in the back. You want a beer?"

"No. I just want to talk to Ruby."

"Beers are twenty bucks, buddy."

Ryan slid aside his blazer, revealing the large pistol holstered on his hip. "Just go get her, will you?"

The fat bartender held up his palms. "Okay, okay. Don't get your panties in a wad, I'll go get her." The man turned and went into a back room.

A minute later a middle-aged brunette wearing a white robe and flats walked out of the back room and sat next to Ryan at the bar. Ruby had short, curly hair, a haggard look, and from the way she filled out her thin robe, sported 36DDs, a slim waist, and generous hips.

"I remember you," she said with a crooked grin, turning in the stool to face him. "You're the PI guy, Ryan."

"That's me."

"Looking for information again?"

Ryan nodded. "We need to talk, Ruby. But not here."

She glanced at her scuffed Timex. "I go on stage in half hour. I got time now."

"Meet me in the parking lot. I'm driving a Ford Explorer."

She placed a hand on his arm. "I'll throw some clothes on and meet you there."

Five minutes later Ruby got in the passenger seat of his SUV, now wearing yoga pants and a tight zip-up sweater.

Ryan noticed she had applied fresh ruby-red lipstick and had sprayed on a pungent lavender perfume. Although she wasn't pretty, the stripper exuded an animal sexuality that was difficult to ignore.

Ruby flashed a tired grin. "You brought cash?"

He patted his blazer. "Yeah."

"Let's see it, sweetheart. You know what they say, money talks and bullshit walks."

He reached into his jacket, took out two hundred dollars and gave it to her.

Ruby smiled and tucked the cash into her yoga pants. Then, still holding his gaze, she unzipped her sweater, revealing her voluptuous breasts. She was nude under the sweater.

"See something you like, baby," she whispered, reaching out with a hand and cupping his pant's groin area.

Ryan was instantly aroused, his heart racing. "I just want information," he said, his breathing labored.

She continued to sensually stroke his hardness. "Oh, come on, baby, let's have some fun first. I don't get hunky guys like you coming to see me at this dump. I know exactly what you need ...."

It took every ounce of willpower he had to push her hand away.

Ruby frowned. "Well, you're no fun." She zipped up her sweater and folded her arms across her large chest. "All right, Ryan. Ask away."

"Last time we talked, you told me where I could find Joe Padilla, your old boyfriend."

She grimaced. "He wasn't my boyfriend. But I did suck his cock plenty of times. I'm guessing you found him?"

"I did. He's dead now."

Her eyes got big. "Shit. You kill him?"

Ryan shook his head. "No. He died of a heart attack."

She gave him a skeptical look. "Yeah. I bet."

He reached into his jacket and took out the 5 x 7 photo and showed it to her. "Look at this. The guys in the picture may have been friends of Joe Padilla. You know either one of them?"

She studied the photo, then cocked her head to one side. "Maybe I do, maybe I don't. Let's see more green."

Ryan sighed. He took out another two hundred dollars and handed it to her.

She tucked the cash into her yoga pants. "Yeah, Ryan. I know one of those guys. He came to the Starlight a couple of times. I sucked his cock too."

"What's his name?"

"Let's see more green."

"Bullshit. I already gave you four hundred."

Ruby flashed an icy grin. "You got to pay to play, baby."

"I don't have any more cash," he said, his voice hard.

"Then you're fucking out of luck. Come back with more money and then I'll tell you." She turned away from him and reached for the door handle.

Ryan grabbed her arm and roughly jerked her back.

"Ow!" she screeched. "You're hurting me!"

"Bullshit. Now talk! I'm not leaving until you tell me what you know."

"Fuck you."

He squeezed her arm harder. "A good friend of mine was kidnapped. She was kidnapped by those two men in the photo."

Her eyes flashed. "What the fuck do I care?"

"Tell me, or you'll regret it."

"Go to hell, Ryan. Pay up or shut up!"

He pulled out his Desert Eagle pistol and pressed the muzzle of the gun to her forehead. "This gun fires a .50 caliber bullet. It'll blow your head clean off."

Her eyes bulged and her jaw dropped.

"I'm not kidding, Ruby. Now talk, damn it!"
Then she told him.

Chapter 59

Vienna, Austria

Aki Tanaka was in her bedroom suite in the east wing of the castle when she heard a knock at her door.

She closed the lid on her laptop, got up from the leather sofa, and opened the door. Her bodyguard was there.

"What is it, Honshu?"

"The prisoner. She is here."

"Where?"

"I had the men put her in the level below the basement."

"Good. Show me."

They took the elevator and Honshu led her into an area she didn't know existed until a few days ago. It was a dark, damp, cavern-like sub-basement with rocky walls and a concrete floor. The corridor was illuminated by flickering incandescent bulbs hanging from the rocky ceiling. The whole area stank of mold and mildew.

Honshu stopped in front of a padlocked metal door and unlocked it. He and Aki went inside the cavernous room.

The prisoner was sitting on the concrete floor, leaning back against a rocky wall. She was wearing black coveralls and was barefoot. A hood covered her head and her hands were bound behind her back. Her feet were shackled to the floor.

Aki approached her and tore the hood off the woman's head.

The brunette jerked back, her eyes blinking rapidly.

"Do you know who I am?" Aki spat out.

The woman didn't reply. She was an attractive, slender brunette in her mid-thirties and looked just like the photos Aki had seen of her.

"I'm Aki Tanaka. Your worst nightmare. And I know who you are, Erin Welch. Who, according to your impressive bio, is a rising star at the FBI."

Aki kicked her in the gut and Erin groaned. "But I'll tell you this, Welch. You don't look so impressive right now." Aki let out a long, heartless laugh, which echoed in the cave-like room. "You and that bastard Ryan created some big problems for me." She kicked her again in the stomach and Erin screamed and folded over.

"And for that," Aki screeched, "I'm going to make you pay, you bitch."

After a moment Erin raised her head and looked up at the other woman. "Are you going to kill me?"

"Oh, no," Aki said. "You're worth more to me alive than dead. No, sweetheart, you're my insurance policy." Her voice dropped to an acid-tinged whisper. "But I promise you this. Once I'm done with you and I don't need you anymore, I'm going to turn you over to Honshu here. You'll become his own sex slave. He hasn't had a tasty morsel like you in a long time."

Aki looked over at her giant bodyguard. "How does that sound, Honshu?"

The thug nodded and flashed an ugly, dark grin, baring his crooked and stained teeth.

Then Aki turned and left the room. After her bodyguard had closed and relocked the door, she said, "Nobody goes in there but me. No one. Is that understood?"

"Not even Strada?" Honshu asked.

"Especially Strada."

"Yes, Ms Tanaka."

Aki took the elevator and went to the billionaire's office on the first floor. As she had expected, Karl Strada was there, sitting on one of the wingback chairs by the roaring fireplace. She approached him. "I thought you'd want to know," she said. "The FBI woman who's caused us so much grief is now our prisoner."

"Where is she, Aki?"

"In a safe place. A place she'll never escape from."

"Where is that?"

Aki waved a hand in the air. "Don't worry about the operational details. I'll deal with her."

"What are you going to do with her?"

"I'm going to interrogate her, Karl. Get every ounce of information I can from her. Find out what the FBI has learned about our operation."

"How will you do that?"

"I'll cause her pain. As much pain as it takes."

Strada nodded. "All right. Now that this FBI woman is out of the picture, is Viper back on track?"

"Yes, Karl. The Bureau has other agents, but her disappearance will disrupt their investigation. Viper is back on track."

The man smiled. "That is excellent." Strada's grin widened. "Aki, I was hoping ... to see you tonight."

"Of course. Let's have dinner together."

"That's not what I meant."

Yeah. I know what you meant, you old bastard. Aki smiled sweetly. "But we were ... intimate ... three days ago ... wasn't that enough?"

"We *are* married, my dear Aki. I was hoping to be with you much more often."

She let out a long breath and plastered a phony smile on her face. "Yes, we'll spend the night together. But remember, in the bedroom I make the rules."

Strada's grin dimmed a bit. "Of course. I understand." He got up from the wingback chair. "I will go see the chef now. Have him prepare a special dinner for us."

"How sweet of you. You're such a thoughtful husband." *You're a tiresome old man who's lazy in bed, but you are thoughtful.* She placed a hand on his arm and offered her cheek for a kiss.

Strada kissed her cheek, beamed, and left the room.

Aki watched the crackling fire for a long moment, the pleasing aroma of the burning wood filling the large room. She wrapped her arms around herself, trying to get warm in the chilly office.

Then she stared at the life-size chess set in the corner of the room. She approached the elaborately-carved ivory chess pieces, which resembled knights and royalty from the Middle Ages.

On a whim she walked over to the black Queen and with a big shove, toppled over the heavy piece. *You may have had power before, Erin Welch. But now you have nothing.*

Chapter 60

Atlanta, Georgia

The man's name was Bill Wilcox and he was an ex-con with a rap sheet ten pages long. According to his parole officer, Wilcox now worked at an auto-body shop on Buford Highway. Ryan had already been there and found out Wilcox quit the place a month ago.

Ryan had also visited the man's last known – the address listed for him in the FBI's NCIC database. That address had also been a bust – the house turned out to be a vacant, weed-grown lot on Atlanta's south side.

Ryan sat in his Ford Explorer, mulling over the situation. So far, the info he'd gotten from Ruby had been a total waste of four hundred bucks.

He turned on the ignition, took a couple of surface streets, and drove north on I-75 and SR 400. Half an hour later he parked in front of a run-down bungalow with peeling paint and a sagging roof. A rusted-out Chevy pickup was in the driveway.

Ryan checked the load on his pistol, re-holstered it, got out of his SUV and knocked on the bungalow's front door.

There was no answer so he tried the knob. It was locked. The PI took out a lock-pick set, fiddled with the knob and heard a click. He pulled his pistol and slipped inside, closing the door behind him.

The place was dark so he flicked on the overhead lights. Just like last time he'd been there, the place was a shit hole. Empty beer cans, pizza boxes, and trash littered the dilapidated living room. The whole place stank of mildew and piss.

"Stich, you here?" Ryan called out.

He heard a moan from behind the sofa. Tightening the grip on his gun, he edged around the couch.

Stich was on the floor, flat on his back, a hand covering his eyes.

Ryan crouched next to him and holstered his weapon. "It's me, Stich. Ryan."

The man groaned. "Go away. I need to sleep." Stich was a thin, wiry man in his fifties who looked much older. He had bloodshot eyes, an unkempt beard, and long greasy hair. He was wearing dirty jeans and a torn flannel shirt. The man stank of body odor.

"No can do," Ryan said. "We got to talk." He noticed a spent needle on the floor among the litter. "You've been shooting up again."

"No shit, Sherlock."

The PI grabbed one of the man's skinny arms and hoisted him up to his feet. Then he steered him toward the sofa and Stich sagged on it, the worn springs groaning.

Ryan pulled up a chair and sat across from him. "What happened to the rehab program I put you in, Stich?"

The man's eyes blinked rapidly. "It didn't take ...."

"Yeah. I can see that. Listen, I need your help. You awake now?"

"I could use a beer first."

"It's ten in the morning."

"C'mon man," Stich said, rubbing his bloodshot eyes. "Give me a break. My heroin's all gone. But I'll be better if I can get a beer buzz going ...."

Ryan shook his head slowly. Standing, he went into the trash filled kitchen and grabbed a Budweiser from the fridge. He came back into the living room and handed Stich the can.

The man popped it and sucked down the Budweiser in one long pull. He burped and wiped his mouth with a hand. "All right, Ryan. What do you wanna know?"

"I'm looking for a guy. An ex-con by the name of Bill Wilcox. He served at the state pen, just like you. Ryan pulled out a 5 x 7 photo and showed it to the man. "He's one of the guys in this picture. You know him?"

Stich stared at the photo, rubbed his bloodshot eyes again, then looked at the picture a second time. "Yeah. I know him."

"I'm trying to find him. Do you know where he lives?"

"How much is it worth to you?"

"Two hundred."

"Bullshit. I need more than that. Five."

"Too much. I'll give you three hundred. In cash. On one condition."

"What's that?"

"You don't spend the money on drugs. I'll drive you to the rehab place today. I know the director there. He'll make sure it works this time."

Stich looked at him. "You're kidding, right?"

"No."

"What do you care what happens to me?"

Ryan let out a long breath. "You're a good CI. One of my best informants. But more important than that, you're a veteran. You were a good soldier once. Then you made some really bad choices, Stich." Ryan waved a hand around the fetid, trash-filled room. "And now you're flushing your life away." He stared into the man's sunken, red-rimmed eyes. "You'll be dead in a year from shooting up every day."

Stich stared back. In a low voice he mumbled, "Yeah, man, you're right. Okay. I'll go back into rehab."

"Good." The PI took a wad of cash out of his jacket and counted out three hundred dollars and handed it to the man.

"Thank you," the drug addict said. "I don't know where Wilcox lives. But he's an enforcer for my drug dealer. They hang out at a bar called McGinty's. It's south of downtown, not too far from Central Avenue. Wilcox drives a green Jeep Cherokee."

"That's good, Stich."

"Why do you want to find this guy?"

"You remember Erin Welch?"

Stich nodded. "The FBI woman."

"Yeah, that's her. This Wilcox thug kidnapped her."

"Jesus Christ."

"Okay, Stich. Let's go."

"Go where?"

"To the rehab place."

"You weren't kidding."

"No."

"Okay, Ryan. But I better grab another beer first." He stood and began walking toward the kitchen, but his legs were shaky and he turned back and slumped on the sofa.

Ryan pulled him to his feet and helped him to the front door and out of the house.

Chapter 61

Atlanta, Georgia

McGinty's Bar was located exactly where Stich had said, off of Central Avenue a few miles south of downtown. It was in a sleazy, run-down strip mall, nestled between a pawn shop and a tattoo parlor.

Ryan was in the parking lot now, slouched down in the front seat of his Ford Explorer. He'd been watching the bar for over four hours, waiting for Wilcox to show up. He sipped cold coffee as he scanned the parking lot for the thousandth time. By the furtive glances of the people going in and out of McGinty's, it was evident they were mostly there for illicit purposes, most likely to buy drugs. A lot of the clientele were young white guys driving late model BMWs and Audis, looking to score dope.

Ryan poured more coffee from his thermos into a foam cup, trying to remember how many times he'd done similar surveillance in run-down parking lots just like this one.

He took a bite of a stale doughnut and washed it down with cold coffee, losing count of the low-lifes he'd encountered as a private investigator. A lot of PI work was dull and boring hours of watching and waiting. *Not like in the movies or TV*, he mused. Mostly you needed lots of patience and a strong bladder.

Ryan rubbed his jaw, felt the growing stubble there, and sipped more of the cold coffee.

An hour later a green Jeep Cherokee rolled into the lot and Ryan ducked lower into his seat. The Cherokee parked a few rows away, and a heavyset, muscular man climbed out. Ryan recognized him immediately. Wilcox went into the bar and the PI settled back in his seat. He stretched his legs, trying to get comfortable and hoping the wait would not be too long.

By the time Wilcox came out of the bar it was nighttime. The thug climbed back in the Jeep Cherokee and drove out of the lot and into the street.

Ryan followed, keeping his Explorer a few cars behind the Cherokee. Fifteen minutes later the Jeep pulled into the driveway of a one-story, red-brick home with a well-maintained yard and white picket fence. The guy got out of his vehicle and walked into the house.

Ryan drove past it and parked on the street several houses down, scanning the middle-class neighborhood. The PI slipped his pistol out of the holster, checked the load, and racked the slide. Re-holstering the gun, he climbed out of the Explorer and strode on the sidewalk toward the home. He bypassed the front of the house and instead crept toward the back where he hugged the wall by the rear door.

Lights shone from the windows and he heard muted sounds from what was probably a television. Through a window he checked out the interior and viewed a vacant kitchen outfitted with upscale, stainless-steel appliances.

Ryan studied the doorknob, slipped out his lock-pick set, and moments later turned the knob and slid inside, closing the door behind him.

With his heart racing, he pulled his pistol and held it at his side as he crept into a corridor.

Suddenly he felt a blinding pain in his right shoulder as his gun clattered to the floor. In a blur of motion he spotted a baseball bat swinging toward his face and he spun left to avoid the blow.

Wilcox swung the bat again and this time it struck the wall, cracking the plaster board.

Ryan charged the man, head-butting him in the chest. The thug groaned and staggered back, dropping the baseball bat and going to his knees.

With his right arm throbbing in pain, Ryan picked up the bat with his left hand and clubbed the guy hard on his neck. The man's eyes rolled white and he slumped to the floor.

The PI pulled out flex-cuffs and bound the guy's hands behind his back, then tied up his feet. Then he dragged the unconscious man into the living room and propped him up into a sitting position with his back leaning against a wall. A television was on in the room and Ryan went to it and increased the volume.

That done, the PI picked up his pistol and searched the rest of the house. He found no one else there, so he began rummaging through a cabinet in the garage where Wilcox kept tools. Finding several items that looked useful, he put them in a toolbox and went back to the living room.

The thug was still unconscious so Ryan slapped him hard until he awoke.

Wilcox blinked a few times and after a moment snarled, "You a cop? You look like a cop."

"Something like that."

"I want a lawyer," the man spat out. "I know my rights."

His right shoulder still throbbing with pain, Ryan saw red. He punched the guy with his left hand, a hard jab to his jaw.

Blood spurted from Wilcox's lip.

"Listen, Wilcox, you're going to tell me where Erin Welch is. Now!"

At the mention of Erin's name, the guy's eyes bulged. But after a moment he scowled again. "Lawyer. I'm not talking."

Ryan closed his fist and struck him, drawing more blood from his mouth.

"You don't scare me," the thug spit out as red gore dripped on to his shirt front. "I've done time. I've taken worse beatings than you can dish out. I know what'll happen if I talk. Kidnapping an FBI agent is a big fucking deal. I could get twenty years at a federal pen." More blood spurted from his cracked lips. "No way I'm talking."

Ryan pointed his index finger at the man's face. "Then you leave me no choice, friend." He rummaged through the tool box, and finding what he wanted, pulled it out.

He held the nail-gun in the air so Wilcox could see it.

The thug's eyes went wide. "What are you going to do ... with that?"

"You're about to find out."

Ryan aimed the nail-gun so that it pointed at the wall about three inches left of the man's head. The PI pressed the trigger, the nail-gun recoiled, and a large nail sank into the wall with a loud thud.

Wilcox's eyes grew as big as saucers. "You're ... you're crazy!"

"Yeah. I am." Ryan aimed again, this time to a spot only one inch left of the thug's head. The nail-gun recoiled and the sharp projectile whizzed past Wilcox's face, just barely missing his ear.

"Last chance, Wilcox. Talk now or I will literally, nail you to the wall."

The foul odor of excrement filled the room and Ryan knew the man had lost control of his bowels.

"I'll talk! I'll talk!" the thug screamed.

"You sure?"

"Yes! Yes! Please ... put that damn thing down!"

"All right." Ryan rested the nail-gun on the floor. "Start talking."

"I was hired ... me and my buddy were ... to kidnap Welch ... I got 50 large ... $25,000 up front ... and $25,000 at delivery ...."

"Who hired you?"

Wilcox shook his head. "I don't know."

"Wrong answer!" The PI picked up the nail-gun and pressed the muzzle to the man's forehead. "Tell me, damn it!"

Wilcox's face turned beet red. "I swear! It was all done over the phone! I got the money in cash in a package by mail. Along with the phony DHS badges and instructions of what to do. When we delivered the FBI woman we got the last 25K."

"Where did you take her?" He pressed the nail-gun's muzzle deeper into the man's forehead and a trickle of blood dribbled from the spot. "Lie to me and by God I will press the trigger!"

"Don't! Please ... don't ... we took her to a private airport down by Macon. The place is used for transport planes, shipping companies, that kind of thing. I had the tail number of the cargo jet and we drove up to it. Two guys got out of the plane, paid us the 25 large, and they carried her into the hold of the plane."

"Any logos or markings on the jet?"

"No. The plane was painted black ... the only ID was the tail number."

"What was the number?"

Wilcox told him and Ryan lowered the nail-gun to the floor. He then jabbed his index finger into the guy's chest. "If I find out you lied to me I will end your life in a very, very slow and painful way."

The man recoiled from him, his face still beet red, perspiration dripping from his forehead. "No ... I swear ... it's the truth!"

Ryan stood and slipped out his cell phone. He punched in a number and waited for the other side to pick up.

"It's Ryan," he said when the FBI agent answered. "I found the guy that kidnapped Erin. I need you to send some men here to arrest him."

"What about Ms Welch?" Special Agent Puller replied. "Where is she now?"

"I don't know. But I'm getting closer to finding her."

Chapter 62

Headquarters Building
Defense Intelligence Agency
Washington, D.C.

Kelly O'Shea was on her computer working on spreadsheets, when her cell phone buzzed. She slipped the phone out of her uniform's pocket and took the call.

"Hi Kelly," Ryan said. "It's me."

"J.T. It's good to hear your voice. What's going on?"

"I've got a lead. A good one. And I need you to work your computer magic and see where it takes us."

"Of course. Whatever you need."

"I just arrested the guy who kidnapped Welch. He bound her up and put her on a cargo plane. This is the tail number for the jet." He told her and then said, "The plane had no other logos or markings. It flew out of a private airport in Macon, Georgia. I need you to find out the owner of the plane."

"I'll work on it right away, J.T."

"Good. Call me back as soon as you find out something."

"You got it," she replied. In a low voice she added, "I miss you."

"I miss you too, Kelly."

"Listen, I need to tell you something."

"What?"

"We have to be careful, J.T. About us. I think the general suspects something."

"What do you mean?"

In a whisper she said, "I think General Keating suspects ... you and I are ... you know ...."

"Damn."

"That's what I thought too. The general is a good commanding officer and a good boss. But he can be vindictive, too. I just wanted to alert you."

"Glad you did, Kelly."

"Okay. I guess we should say goodbye now ...."

"Yeah. We should ...."

Neither one said anything for a long moment and it was clear neither wanted to disconnect the call.

Finally Kelly said, "I guess we should hang up now, so we can get back to work."

"We should, Kelly. But just so you know, I want to see you again."

She gripped the phone tighter. "I want that too."

Then she disconnected the call quickly, afraid of what she might add.

Chapter 63

Vienna, Austria

Honshu stopped in front of the padlocked metal door, unlocked it, and stepped inside. Aki Tanaka followed him into the subterranean, cavern-like room and switched on the overhead light.

Like the last time she'd seen her, Erin Welch was sitting on the concrete floor, leaning back against the rocky wall, her hands and feet shackled to the floor. The FBI woman was still wearing the same black coveralls, but now the garment was stained with dried blood. A black hood covered her head.

Aki approached her and tore off the hood.

Erin's face was covered in black and blue bruises and both her eyes were puffy. Blood oozed from the cuts on her face. Her lips were cracked, blood dripping from her mouth.

The FBI woman's eyes blinked rapidly. She saw Aki and recoiled away from her.

"You've been a bad girl, Welch," Aki said. "A very bad girl. Honshu told me you've answered none of his questions. You told him nothing of what the FBI knows." Aki leaned down and touched the cuts on the other woman's face. "You left him no choice but to do this to you."

Aki cackled, the mirthless laughter echoing in the cavern-like room. "You were very pretty when you got here. But you're not so pretty now."

She slapped Erin's face hard.

Erin screamed and tried to move away but the heavy shackles prevented her from moving much. More blood dripped from the cuts on her face.

Then the Asian woman said, "But just to show you I don't hold a grudge, I brought you a present, Welch." Aki had brought with her a black neck brace and she held it in front of the FBI woman.

Erin stared at it. "What's that?"

Aki laughed again. "Like I said. A present. From me to you." She opened the metal brace, placed it around Erin's neck, closed it, and locked it with a key. Then she turned around and began walking to the door.

"Wait!" Erin yelled. "What happens now?"

Aki turned back to face her. "I'm going to have a delicious lunch, drink some champagne, and then take a long, relaxing soak in a hot tub."

"What about me? What happens to me?"

Aki cackled and without saying another word left the room.

Chapter 64

Headquarters Building
Defense Intelligence Agency
Washington, D.C.

Kelly O'Shea knocked on the open office door.

"You wanted to see me, General?" she said, stepping into the office. "You said it was urgent."

General Keating nodded. "Yes, Colonel. Take a seat."

Kelly perched on one of the visitor's chairs fronting his desk and Keating pointed to his laptop computer.

"I want you to see this," he said, tapping on his keyboard. A moment later a Face-Look page filled the screen. "Take a close look at the news feed."

Kelly studied the news headlines as they scrolled down the right side of the page. At least three of the stories were about the arrest this morning of Tom Atkinson for embezzlement and money-laundering. Atkinson was one of the two candidates for U.S. president in the upcoming election.

"Oh, my God!" Kelly said. "I never suspected Atkinson was a criminal."

"You never suspected that because it's not true."

"What do you mean, sir?" She pointed to the computer screen. "It's all right there."

"That's why I said it was urgent, Colonel. Those stories on Face-Look are all fake news. I checked with the district attorney's office and the local police. Atkinson was not arrested. In fact, he's not being investigated at all."

Kelly's heart began to race. "So these news stories were planted ... to influence voters in the upcoming election. Which is only a month away. When it becomes clear that these news stories are fake, the news organizations will issue a disclaimer or a retraction, and Face-Look will blame them, and they in turn will blame Face-Look. But in the meantime, the damage has been done. Voters will be confused as to the real truth and will decide to go with the other candidate, Charles Grant."

"That's exactly right, Colonel."

Kelly shook her head slowly. "I never anticipated social media could be such a destructive force."

"Nobody did." Keating leaned forward in his chair. "Tell me what progress you've made on the case."

"Yes, General. Ever since I got the lead from Ryan, I've been trying to track down the owner of the plane used by the kidnappers of Erin Welch. The jet is registered to a company in Macon, Georgia. It turns out that company is a shell, a corporation that exists only on paper, and is owned by another operation based in New York City. That company is also a cut-out with no employees, and is run by an outfit in Paris, France –"

Keating glared at her and held up a hand. "Cut to the chase. You don't have to give me the details."

Kelly nodded. "Yes, sir. Using DIA software and databases, I was finally able to track down the real owner of the plane. It's a company based in Vienna, Austria. The name of the corporation is Strada – Austria Enterprises."

"Who's the owner of that?"

"A billionaire named Karl Strada."

The general shook his head. "Never heard of him."

"Neither did I until I started doing research on him. He's very reclusive. Hardly seen in public. According to what I could piece together, he made his money in hedge funds and precious metals, gold and silver. Strada is the richest man in Austria and probably the wealthiest in all of Europe."

"What else can you tell me about him, Colonel?"

"He's in his eighties and from what I could figure out, he uses his vast wealth to fund political elections in Europe."

Keating nodded. "That makes sense. So he's purchased these social media companies in the U.S. to influence our elections here."

"Yes, sir. That's what I think also."

"So what's the Japanese woman's connection to Strada?"

"That part is unclear, General. I suspect Aki Tanaka and Karl Strada are co-conspirators in the Viper operation."

"Where does Strada live?"

"In a historic castle on the outskirts of Vienna. He's refurbished it into a luxurious mansion and put in high-tech security. Sir, I had our DIA satellites take detailed photos of the estate and I can tell it's heavily-fortified with armed guards and sophisticated weaponry."

Keating nodded. "Do you think Tanaka and Strada are both there?"

"I do. I think that when Tanaka fled Japan she went there."

"What about Erin Welch, Colonel?"

"I suspect she's being held there also."

"All right. It's clear then we need to get in there and shut this damn thing down."

"General, that may not be as easy as it sounds."

"What do you mean?"

"Sir, I've already talked to our State Department who in turn contacted the Austrian government. It appears Strada is a *very* influential man in his country. He's bankrolled a lot of politicians there, including the prime minister and most of the other top leaders."

Keating frowned. "I see. From what you're saying the Austrians would never agree to us going in there and arresting him."

"That's exactly what I'm saying."

The general scowled at her. "Colonel, you're in charge of this investigation. So I'm expecting you to come up with a plan." In a harsh voice he added, "And do it damn fast, because the clock is ticking."

Chapter 65

Vienna, Austria

Aki Tanaka went into her private bedroom suite in the east wing of the castle and locked the door behind her.

Going to the lavish, onyx-walled bathroom, she quickly stripped off her clothes, in a hurry to shower and wash off the stink of the old man. She'd just spent an hour with Strada making love, if you could call it that, and it had felt interminable. *He's become tiresome. The groping, the leering, the wheezing, his old man smell.* She hadn't realized how difficult it would be to maintain the facade of a happy wife.

Weeks ago the sound of it, Aki Tanaka Strada, was exciting and new. *And now?* She grimaced at the prospect of him pawing her for years to come. Even if she made him grovel for it, it still sickened her and made her stomach churn.

She turned on the water tap to scalding hot and stepped in the shower stall. Aki lathered up in the nearly-burning water and scrubbed her body thoroughly. Then she rinsed and got out of the shower. She toweled herself dry and ran a comb through her long, lustrous white hair.

After throwing on a white silk robe, she padded out of the bathroom on bare feet and went to her laptop, which rested on a teak desk in a corner of the bedroom.

Aki powered up the device and logged on to the internet.

She took a deep breath and let it out slowly. Then she twirled the jewel-encrusted gold wedding band around her finger. The genuine diamonds and rubies glinted from the overhead light. The priceless ring dated back to the Hapsburg Empire and had been worn by Empress Maria Theresa in the 1700's. She had loved it when Strada first gave it to her. *But now? The ring feels heavy. Damn heavy.* Pressing down on her like a thousand-pound weight on her shoulders.

She glanced away from her wedding ring and fixed her gaze on the computer screen.

She typed on the keyboard and logged on to her Swiss bank account. Then she opened another screen and accessed one of the bank accounts of Strada – Austria Enterprises. That done, she paused to savor the moment. With her heart pounding in anticipation and excitement, she transferred five billion U.S. dollars from the Strada – Austria Enterprises account to her secret, numbered bank account in Switzerland.

Aki flashed a cold, hard grin. *Five billion dollars. It has a nice ring to it.* For an immensely wealthy man like Strada, that amount was merely a dent in his vast financial resources. But to her it meant eventual freedom. Freedom and security for her own future.

She grinned again. *I may let you fuck me, you old bastard. But now I'll have the satisfaction of knowing you've paid for it.*

Chapter 66

Atlanta, Georgia

J.T. Ryan's cell phone buzzed and he slipped it out of his pocket.

"Hi, J.T.," Kelly O'Shea said when he answered the call. "Did you get the email I sent you?"

Ryan stared at the laptop screen. "I did. I also got the satellite images attached to the email." He was in his office in midtown and had spent the last ten minutes reviewing the information. "Looks like the castle Strada lives in is quite a fortress, Kelly. Walls, a moat, multiple guard stations, and security cameras everywhere."

"I agree."

Ryan pressed the phone tighter to his ear. "What's the situation with the Austrian police? Can we get their help in arresting Strada?"

"No go, J.T. I checked with the State Department and so has General Keating. Karl Strada is very influential with his country's government. He's put his billions to work – he's pretty much funded every top political leader there."

"I get the picture. So whatever we do, it's got to be black ops."

"Exactly." She paused and then said, "Listen, the general is expecting results. ASAP. Especially with the U.S. election looming. The Viper conspiracy has really ramped up the fake news dissemination campaign on social media. So the general is leaning on me hard to shut down Strada's and Tanaka's operation."

"I hear you. Let me think about this and come up with a plan. I'll call you back."

"I'm sorry, J.T., but that's not good enough. When you come up with your plan, General Keating wants to hear about it first hand. You have to come here."

"All right." They said their goodbyes and hung up.

Ryan stared at his laptop, scrolling through the satellite photos of the billionaire's estate. Then he reread the other information Kelly had supplied, furiously trying to find a way into the place without alerting the Austrian authorities.

Chapter 67

Headquarters Building
Defense Intelligence Agency
Washington, D.C.

"I think I've come up with a way in," J.T. Ryan said.

General Keating took a puff from his pipe and exhaled, the sweet aroma filling his office. "Go ahead, Captain," the general replied, resting the pipe on an ashtray on his desk.

Ryan glanced at Kelly O'Shea, who was sitting next to him, then looked back at Keating. "General," he said, "it's clear from the satellite images that if we try to break in the place with a frontal assault it would set off all types of alarms, which is the last thing we want."

"I agree," Keating said. "That option is clearly unacceptable. If the police in Vienna were alerted to what we were doing, it would create an international incident. The State Department told me relations between the U.S. and Austria are already strained. So what's your plan, Ryan?"

"General, I studied the location of the castle thoroughly, taking into consideration the topographical features. The mansion is adjacent to the Danube River. I've come up with a possible way in." Ryan spent the next ten minutes describing his plan.

Keating picked up his pipe, relit it with his Zippo lighter and took a puff. "So, you're suggesting we send a Special Forces team in there in the way you describe. But if we send in a U.S. Army unit and this thing goes sideways, it'll create the international incident we're trying to avoid."

"Actually," Ryan said, "I was thinking of a team of one. Me."

Keating's eyebrows arched. "Sounds like a suicide mission, Captain."

"Sir, it's the only way. I have to go in solo, with no ID, nothing that ties me to the U.S. government."

The general nodded. "It could work. You were in Delta Force. You have the training. But if you get caught, or arrested, or wounded, you'd be on your own. I wouldn't be able to send in the 82nd Airborne to save your ass."

"I understand, sir."

Keating glanced at Kelly. "What do you think of this plan, Colonel?"

"I think it's very risky," she said. "Crazy even. But I can't come up with a better way."

The general nodded. "All right, Ryan. I'll approve your plan. But you'll need logistical help and specialized equipment."

"Yes," Ryan said. "I can get everything I need from Special Operations Command at Fort Bragg. I used to be stationed there and know the people well."

"I'll authorize that," Keating replied. "In fact, you can get started immediately."

"General, I'd like to work out some of the operational details with Colonel O'Shea before I go."

General Keating glared at him. "No, Ryan, you will not. I have a pretty good idea what kind of 'operational details' you have in mind." The general then glared at Kelly and she blushed.

"No, Ryan," the general continued, "I want you to immediately start on this operation. If you need to 'coordinate' with Colonel O'Shea use your SAT phone and call her."

Ryan nodded, disappointed. *Well, it was worth a shot.*

Keating picked up the handset of his desk phone and spoke into it for several minutes. He hung up and said, "Captain, I've authorized your mission. A transport jet will fly you to Fort Bragg. The plane leaves Joint Base Andrews in thirty minutes."

Chapter 68

Delta Force (1st SFOD-D)
Special Operations Command
U.S. Army
Fort Bragg, North Carolina

"Never thought I'd see you here again, sir," Senior Master Sergeant Cord said with a wide grin.

J.T. Ryan smiled back, extended his hand and they shook. "Me neither, Sergeant. Me neither."

Cord waved him to a chair fronting his metal desk and Ryan sat. The PI glanced around the sparsely furnished office and noticed framed photos on the walls. One of the pictures showed a group of armed soldiers standing in front of a Humvee and an M60 Main Battle tank. Ryan was in the photo, along with Sergeant Cord and the rest of Ryan's Delta Force team. He had been Captain Ryan at the time and Cord had been his top NCO.

Ryan pointed to the picture. "That brings back a lot of memories. That was in Kabul, right?"

Cord nodded. "Yes, sir, it was. In fact, I just got back from another deployment in Afghanistan."

"How many does that make?"

"Five, sir."

Ryan frowned and shook his head slowly. "Sorry to hear that. How's your family holding up?"

"They're managing. My wife's a saint."

The PI let out a long breath. "The Army's too small, Sergeant. We're policemen everywhere in the world, with a force smaller than in the 1950s. The endless deployments are bad for troop morale and the families that stay behind."

"Yes, sir. That's a fact. That's why the suicide rate for military is twice that of civilians."

Ryan nodded and said a silent prayer. Then he said, "Do you know why I'm here?"

"Yes, sir. I got a call from my base commander, who had gotten a call from General Keating at the Defense Intelligence Agency. I was told to arrange whatever you needed."

"How is that going?"

"I've got all of the equipment you wanted. And I've arranged for a C-130 to fly you over."

"Good."

"You're going by yourself?"

"I am, Sergeant."

The NCO rubbed his jaw. "Sure you don't want backup? I could get a dozen volunteers with a snap of my fingers." He grinned. "A lot of the guys wish you were still leading our Delta team."

"Yeah, I miss you guys too. We had a hell of a team."

"By the way, sir, I heard you had been reactivated back into the Army. Is that true?"

"Yeah, it is. I'm Captain Ryan. Again."

Cord's eyebrows knitted. "How'd that happen?"

Ryan shook his head slowly. "It's a long story, Sergeant. A long story for another day."

Chapter 69

Vienna, Austria

Erin Welch felt like she was going to suffocate. The metal brace around her neck was so tight that every breath she took was painful.

She was still in the same place she been imprisoned in for weeks: A dark, cavern-like room. She was shackled to the cold, concrete floor, leaning back on a rocky wall. It was almost pitch black in the room, with the only illumination coming from the slit at the bottom of the door nearby.

Her hands were chained tightly behind her back and heavy metal shackles gripped her ankles, chafing her skin.

Erin shifted her body, trying to find a comfortable sitting position, but the movement only caused her more pain. Every part of her ached, a result of the multiple beatings she'd received from the huge Asian man, Honshu. Her face hurt the worse. Her eyes were puffy and bruised, her lips were cracked, and congealed blood covered her cheeks from the numerous cuts on her face.

Erin closed her eyes and tried to recall her FBI training at Quantico years ago. *Focus. Focus. Come up with a plan to escape. But escape how?*

Nothing in her training had prepared her for this.

Her eyes snapped open, the dread of the Asian man returning to deliver more pain crowding her thoughts.

He'll be back. To give me more pain. He'll be back and this time I may not survive.

Chapter 70

Vienna, Austria

J.T. Ryan slowed the cargo van and pulled it off the road and into a wooded area.

Climbing out, he scanned his location. The woods were deserted, as had been the road he had used to get here. He glanced at his watch and the luminous dials read 1:06 a.m.

Pulling out his night-vision binoculars, he focused on the massive structure across the river. Even from a mile away the historic castle loomed large, its black stone turrets and high walls looking menacing against the dark night sky.

He spotted several guards carrying rifles along the ramparts, and a few more guarding the entrance gate. The castle was nestled by the Danube River, one of its stone walls adjacent to the waterway.

Ryan put away the binoculars and strode toward the back of the van. Opening the cargo doors, he took out the wetsuit and put it on over his black fatigues, which had no identifying marks. After zipping up the wetsuit, he grabbed the air tank, slipped it over his shoulders and strapped it on. That done, he took the Heckler & Koch MP-5 assault rifle out of the van, capped the muzzle of the weapon, and slung it over his chest. Then he strapped on several more tools and weapons, grabbed a face mask and swim fins and closed the van doors.

He made his way around the trees toward the water's edge. Crouching by the river, he slipped the mask over his face, pulled on the swim fins, and placed the regulator into his mouth. He breathed in some of the tank's stale air, adjusted the volume, and slid into the dark, icy river. Although he was wearing a wetsuit, his hands and face were exposed to the cold water, and his whole body shivered.

Using the fins to propel himself to the bottom of the river, he reached it a few minutes later. Then he began swimming forward, using the luminous compass on his watch to guide him through the almost pitch black water.

The current was strong and fast and he fought against it, kicking hard with his fins. He sucked in stale air while periodically glancing at the compass.

The mile-long crossing took much longer than he had anticipated and when he reached the other side he was exhausted. He took a moment to rest and then swam forward until he was able to reach out and touch the black stones of the castle wall.

Ryan looked up toward the surface of the river. The water color was lighter there, shimmering from the moonlight. He recalled what Kelly had told him from her research of the mansion. Luckily, she'd been able to find the building blueprints that Strada had used when refurbishing the structure. Water and sewage exhausts fed out into the Danube River. They were located somewhere along this wall.

He swam slowly along the wall, his left hand tracing the rough stone surface.

Some time later he felt a metal grate and stopped swimming.

Squinting through the cloudy water he could just make out the heavy-mesh grate in front of him. He felt water rushing out of the grate and hoped the sewage had been treated before being expelled into he river.

Suddenly a new burst of exhaust water rushed out. The water stank and he tried not to think about what it contained, and instead focused on the task at hand.

Unclipping a stainless-steel saw from his wetsuit, he began cutting through the grate. The mesh was constructed of heavy-gauge metal and it was laborious work slicing through it. He cut a hole big enough for him to crawl through and he swam into the tube.

Ryan kicked forward with his fins, reaching the end a few minutes later. Taking out a penlight he shined it forward. In front of him was a large propeller blade, probably the back end of the sewage treatment motor. Shining the light above him, he spotted a closed panel at the top of the tube. He guessed it was an access panel for workers to use in case repairs were needed.

He swam up to the panel and felt the latches that held it in place.

Just then he noticed a red light flashing on the regulator he was breathing into. Checking the gauge, he realized his air supply tank was almost empty.

Reaching with his hands, he tried pushing open the latches that held the access panel in place. They were jammed shut, probably from lack of use.

He sucked in air as he worked, trying to pry off the thick metal latches.

Suddenly he tried breathing in more air but none came out of his regulator. Fighting off a sense of panic, he struggled with the latches, pushing with all his strength.

One latch slid open partway and he slammed the heel of his hand into it. He grimaced from the pain as the metal latch opened fully. Holding his breath furiously, he struggled with the second latch, which gave way seconds later.

The access panel lifted and he slid it aside.

Ryan hoisted himself out of the tube and dropped to the floor. He tore off his swim mask and regulator and gulped in lungfuls of fresh air. Still gasping, he looked around the area he was in, which appeared to be a boiler room. It was illuminated with overhead fluorescents and thankfully no one was around.

He quickly took off his wetsuit and empty air tank. Then he removed the waterproof cap from the muzzle of his assault rifle and slung the weapon across his back.

Noticing water gushing out of the sewage tube into the room, he slid the access panel back in place and locked the latches. That done, he scanned the boiler room for a way out, recalling the labyrinth of corridors Kelly had told him about.

There was a door at the far end and he headed there. It was unlocked so he opened it partway and peered around the doorjamb.

The corridor was vacant so he slipped into it, closing the door behind him.

Ryan checked the load on his assault rifle, made sure its suppressor was screwed on tightly, and took the safety off the weapon. Then he advanced down the corridor, once again recalling what Kelly had learned. The level he was in was a basement and the living quarters were on the upper floors of the mansion. The closed door at the end of this hallway, he guessed, led to a stairway.

Just then he heard metal creaking and he froze. His heart pounding, he pointed the MP-5 in that direction.

The closed door opened and a big guy with a rifle slung over his shoulder stepped through. The man's eyes went wide and he reached for his rifle just as Ryan pulled the trigger.

The MP-5 coughed three times and the guy staggered back and dropped to the floor. The PI raced forward, checked the man's pulse and finding none, searched the dead guy's pockets. He found a loop of keys and a keycard, which he took. Clipped to the man's belt was a walkie-talkie and he took that also.

Then he went through the open doorway and crouched at the base of the stairway, which led both up and down. He began climbing toward the upper floor, his adrenaline flowing, his finger near the trigger of his weapon.

Ryan reached the landing a moment later and there he found a closed door.

Suddenly the walkie-talkie he'd taken from the dead man crackled to life. He listened closely to the rapid talking, which sounded like German. He understood enough to know it was a radio check from one of the other security guards. *Damn. I didn't plan for this.*

He squelched the walkie-talkie and tried the door knob, which was locked. Pulling out the loop of keys he tried several until the lock clicked and he stepped through the doorway, closing it behind him.

Ryan crouched, his weapon at the ready. He was in a wide, marble-floor corridor. Historic-looking tapestries and gilt-edged paintings hung from the walls. He also spotted several Medieval suits of armor lining the sides of the hallway. *This is the living area of the castle. Most likely the first floor.* Once again he recalled what Kelly had told him about the floor plan of the castle.

Still crouching, he turned the walkie-talkie back on and set the volume to low. He heard more Germans talking, but now the tone was urgent. Obviously the guy he'd killed had missed his radio check and the security team was on high alert.

What the hell do I do now? The element of surprise he was counting on was slipping away.

With his stomach churning, he advanced slowly down the wide corridor, glancing into several vacant rooms. Hearing footsteps behind him, he whirled around.

There was a rifle pointed at him and Ryan pulled the trigger and threw himself to the floor.

The guard clutched his heart and dropped his rifle, staggering to his knees.

A second guard appeared behind the wounded guard and Ryan fired again, his rounds slamming into the man. The guard dropped to the floor, but not before firing off several wild shots of his own, the unsuppressed rounds echoing loudly through the first floor of the estate.

Ryan hid behind a suit of armor, his MP-5 at the ready.

Then he heard it.

The high-low wail of a piercing house alarm, the sound so loud it must have reached every part of the castle.

Chapter 71

Vienna, Austria

Aki Tanaka was in her bedroom suite working at her computer when she heard the alarm. Slamming the lid shut on her laptop, she raced through the room and flung open the door.

Honshu was in the corridor, a grimace on his face.

"What's going on?" she demanded. "Why is the alarm on?"

"An intruder. That must be the reason, Ms Tanaka."

"Fuck! How can you let this happen?"

"I ... I am sorry, Ms Tanaka ... I am not in charge of security here ... Mr. Strada ... he has his own people for that ... I protect you ...."

"I know that, damn it! Still, you've let me down, Honshu!"

The huge bodyguard stared down at the floor, his massive shoulders hunched. "Yes, Ms Tanaka." He looked back up at her. "Should I go see ... what is going on?"

"Fuck that. Come with me!"

Aki raced down the wide hallway, with her bodyguard close behind. She took several more corridors until she reached the other residential wing of the castle. At the far end of this corridor was a closed double door. Two armed guards were posted there and she approached them.

"Open this door!" Aki ordered.

"I am sorry," one of the guards replied. "The house alarm has sounded. We are under strict orders from Mr. Strada. No one is allowed in here once that has happened."

"Fuck you!" she yelled. "Open it now or I'll have Honshu tear you apart, limb by limb. You fucking hear me?"

The guard stared at Honshu, then back at Aki. "Yes, Ms Tanaka." Taking a loop of keys from his belt he unlocked the double door and let Aki and her bodyguard enter.

They were in the spacious sitting area of Strada's bedroom suite. Turning toward Honshu, she said, "Wait here."

Honshu bowed his head slightly. "As you wish."

Aki marched to the door at the far end of the room, put her keycard in the slot, and opened the door. Slipping inside, she closed the door behind her.

The massive bedroom was dim and she heard snoring coming from the king-size bed.

The piercing house alarm was clearly audible in the room. *Jesus Christ. The old bastard is still asleep. Fucking unbelievable.* She shook her head slowly, once again disgusted with her pathetic husband.

Aki flicked on the overhead lights and went to the bed to wake him up.

Chapter 72

Vienna, Austria

J.T Ryan reached the foot of the wide, marble-step staircase and crouched by the gilt-edged banister.

His mind raced as he looked up toward the second floor, the wailing alarm making it hard for him to focus. *I've killed three guards. But there's more.*

He'd counted six guards through his binoculars a few hours ago. Which meant there were at least three, and probably more, up there in the upper floors, guarding the bedrooms of the mansion.

Training his assault rifle forward, he climbed the stairs one step at a time, his finger on the trigger. He reached the second floor and crouched by the wall. Peering around the banister he looked both ways. The marble floor hallway was vacant, but he did notice more Medieval-era suits of armor lining the walls.

Ryan stepped into the corridor and advanced cautiously.

A split-second later he heard the crackle of a walkie-talkie and the boom of gunfire. He fired blindly just as he felt something smash into his chest. Ryan gasped and stumbled backward, the pain in his chest blinding.

A guard rushed out from behind one of the suits of armor and the PI fired again, the MP-5 coughing three times. The guard sank to his knees and toppled forward.

Ryan crawled to the man, and after making sure he was dead, gasped for breath as he felt his own chest with a hand. Luckily the body-armor Kevlar he was wearing under his fatigues had saved his life, although he'd be sore as hell for weeks.

He crouched there for several minutes, expecting more guards to appear.

When none didn't, he advanced slowly and searched the rest of the second floor. There were no other guards there, although he found five women huddled in a large kitchen. They told him they were maids. He used plasticuffs to bind their hands, although by their panic-stricken faces it was clear they were no threat.

That done, he slowly made his way to the staircase again and glanced up to the third floor. *They're up there. I'm sure of it. Strada and Tanaka. And more guards. What about Erin? Where is she?*

Ryan crouched by the banister for several more minutes, waiting for the sharp pain in his chest to abate.

Then he began climbing the wide staircase, his adrenaline pumping, his MP-5 at the ready. He reached the third floor and squatted a few rungs below the corridor. The house alarm was still wailing, still loud even on this floor.

He peered around the wall and spotted a closed double door at the far end. A large wooden credenza had been moved in front of the doors and he noticed several rifle barrels poking out from behind the furniture piece. *Guards. At least two. Probably more.*

His thoughts raced.

Making a decision, he ejected the nearly empty clip of his MP-5, inserted a full one, and put the weapon on full-auto. Next, he unclipped one of the flash-bang grenades from his belt.

Peering around the wall again, he pulled the pin on the grenade and lobbed it toward the far end of the corridor.

Chapter 73

Vienna, Austria

Aki Tanaka crouched on the floor, hiding behind the king-size bed, gripping the SIG Sauer pistol.

Karl Strada was huddled next to her, a terrified look on his face. "What ... do you think ... is happening ...." he whispered, his voice breaking.

Aki glared at him. "Grow some balls, Karl. And shut up and let me think!"

The old man nodded, huddling even closer to her.

Suddenly Aki heard a loud boom, the explosion echoing for a long moment. Then gunfire erupted from nearby, probably the corridor outside the bedroom suite.

Aki took the safety off the gun and waited.

Chapter 74

Vienna, Austria

Ryan pressed the trigger, the MP-5 firing non-stop, spitting out all thirty rounds in seconds. He pulled back the weapon and used the wall for cover. He was still crouching by the stairway banister.

Return fire boomed, the bullets whizzing past him, tearing up walls on the other side of the corridor and ricocheting off the marble floor. He reloaded his assault rifle, then unclipped another grenade from his belt. This one was not a flash-bang, but the real thing.

He pulled the pin and rolled the grenade down the hallway toward the now bullet-riddled credenza and pock-marked double doors.

A second later he felt the concussion from the grenade at the same time that he heard the deafening blast.

Peering around the wall he waited for the haze of smoke from the explosion to dissipate. He spotted four bloodied bodies sprawling among the jagged pieces of furniture. He also noticed that the wailing house alarm had been silenced by the blast.

With his ears still ringing from the detonated grenade, he advanced into the hallway. When he reached the end he squatted and inspected the bloody body parts, knowing those four guards were no longer a threat.

He turned his attention to what was left of the double doors, which had been seriously damaged by the explosion. He peered through the large hole at the room inside. It appeared to be a sitting area, which probably led to a bedroom. He spotted no one inside and he crept closer, with his MP-5 leading the way.

Going past what was left of the shattered double doors, he entered the sitting area.

Suddenly he felt a blinding pain in his jaw, dropped his assault rifle, and staggered back.

In a blur of motion he saw a huge Asian man rush toward him, his giant fist swinging at his face a second time.

Ryan ducked and the man's punch hit the wall, cracking a large hole on the surface. Ignoring the intense ache in his jaw, the PI spun his body around 360 degrees and delivered a martial arts roundhouse kick to Honshu's gut.

The massive bodyguard grunted but stood his ground, the blow barely affecting him.

Honshu spread his huge arms and rushed forward, obviously trying to bear hug Ryan to the ground. The PI side-stepped him and punched Honshu in the kidney.

The bodyguard grunted again and went to one knee, while Ryan grabbed his MP-5 from the floor.

But Honshu got up in a split-second, backhanding the weapon out of Ryan's hands, sending the rifle flying in the air.

Gasping for breath, Ryan pulled his Desert Eagle from his holster, only to have the gun knocked away.

The bodyguard, his coal black eyes full of hate, charged him again and this time grabbed Ryan and literally threw him to the floor.

Honshu was on top of him in a second, both of his massive hands clutching his throat. The PI tried to punch the giant man off of him, but it was like hitting a granite boulder.

The man's enormous hands kept squeezing Ryan's throat, cutting off his breathing. He felt himself losing consciousness.

Willing himself past the pain, the PI kneed the giant thug in the groin.

Honshu grunted, his eyes closed for a second, and for a brief moment relaxed his death grip on Ryan's throat.

Ryan kneed him again in the groin and rolled out from underneath the man. He spotted his Desert Eagle on the floor, picked up the gun and turned back to Honshu.

The huge Asian was already on his feet, rushing towards him, his eyes blazing.

Ryan pulled the trigger twice, the powerful weapon recoiling in his hands.

Honshu clutched his heart as the .50 caliber booms echoed in the room. The man staggered and collapsed to the marble floor.

Chapter 75

Vienna, Austria

Aki Tanaka heard the loud shots from the other room and gripped her gun tighter.

Her husband, his face beet red and his eyes wide, cowered behind her. The two people were hiding, using the king-size bed for cover. Aki was pointing her SIG Sauer at the closed door of the bedroom.

"Those shots ...," Strada whispered, "...came from ... the sitting room ...."

Aki ground her teeth. "No shit, Karl! Tell me something I don't know!"

"I don't ... want to die ...." the man said, his voice cracking.

"Grow some balls," she spit out. "You disgust me!"

"What ... do we do ... now?"

"Let me think, damn it."

"Yes, Aki."

"The door to the bedroom. You said it's reinforced?"

"Yes ... yes ... solid steel."

"Good. That'll buy us some time."

"Do you think ... the guards ... will come ... and save us?"

"You're a fucking moron, Karl! You know that? You may be rich, but you're an idiot. They're dead! I'm sure the guards are dead."

"Please Aki ... get us ... out of here ...."

Then Aki heard it. The bedroom doorknob being rattled. And then muffled thuds, indicating the door was being pounded.

She aimed the gun at the door, ready to pull the trigger.

Chapter 76

Vienna, Austria

Using the assault rifle like a club, Ryan struck the door with the butt of the weapon repeatedly. But the blows only glanced off.

Damn. It must be made of reinforced metal.

Ryan moved several feet away and kneeled behind a bookcase. Then he aimed his rifle at the door and fired off a three-round burst. The bullets ricocheted off.

Shaking his head, he weighed his options. *Only one option left to gain access. But what if Erin Welch is in there with Strada and Tanaka? I could end up killing Erin also.*

Ryan let out a long breath, knowing he had no choice. He had to get to the criminals. Slinging his rifle over his shoulder, he walked to the middle of the sitting room and took cover behind one of the leather couches. Unclipping his last grenade from his belt, he pulled the pin.

He lobbed the grenade toward the bedroom door and pressed his hands to cover his ears.

A second later he felt the concussion from the blast at the same time he heard the deafening roar, which echoed in the room.

With his ears ringing from the explosion, he peered over the sofa through the haze of smoke. The metal door had been blown to shreds, with only a few jagged pieces of metal clinging to the hinges. Parts of the wall around the door had also been damaged.

He waited a moment for the smoke to clear and gazed into the interior of the other room. He saw a large bed at the far end of the area and several other pieces of furniture.

After pulling his pistol from his holster, Ryan crept closer to the doorway. When he was next to it he peered around the jam and looked inside.

He heard whispering from behind the bed and spotted the muzzle of a gun pointing to the doorway. *They're there. And they're armed.*

"Come out!" Ryan ordered. "It's all over! Come out and put your guns down."

"Hell, no!"

It was a woman's voice, harsh and cold. He thought he recognized it. Tanaka.

"Come out with your hands up," Ryan yelled again. "And I won't shoot you. Do it. Do it now!"

"Fuck you!"

Ryan was sure of the voice now. It was Aki Tanaka.

"I have a Desert Eagle," Ryan said. "That's the most powerful handgun in the world. It fires .50 caliber rounds. Which means it'll blow a huge hole through the bed you're hiding behind. If I pull the trigger you'll be dead in a second."

He heard more whispering, this time sounding panicked. He could tell it was a man and a woman.

"All right, don't shoot!" Aki said. "We'll come out."

The woman rose from behind the bed, holding a pistol at her side. Her long white hair was tousled and she was wearing white pajamas. Her white eyes shimmered in defiance and Ryan recalled their almost hypnotic affect.

Ryan held the Desert Eagle with both hands, pointing the weapon at her head.

A man stood up next to her and the PI recognized the elderly guy immediately from the photos Kelly had found. It was Karl Strada, the billionaire. Like her, the man was in sleepwear. But unlike her, he was terrified, holding his hands high in the air. His body was trembling and he began to hyperventilate.

"Where's Erin Welch?" Ryan demanded.

Aki flashed a wicked grin. "In a safe place."

"Where?"

"You'll find out soon enough, Ryan."

"Drop the gun."

Aki placed her pistol on the bed. Then she fingered a black pendant that hung from her neck on a gold chain. "You know what this pendant is, Ryan?"

The PI stared at it. It looked like a large piece of jewelry. "I don't have time for games, Tanaka. Now get on your knees and I'll handcuff you both."

"Look at it closely, Ryan. This pendant is my insurance policy."

"I don't care how expensive your jewelry is," Ryan spat out. "You can't buy me off, bitch!"

Aki laughed a cold, mirthless chortle. "It's not a piece of jewelry. It's something much more valuable. It's a kill switch. It's a radio frequency detonation device. When I press it, a bomb goes off."

"You're insane, Tanaka. But you're not crazy enough to kill yourself and the rest of us. You're too greedy for that."

The Japanese woman laughed again. "That's true. I won't kill myself. Now listen closely, Ryan. I'm going to reach into my pocket. There's a photo there I want you to see. It'll show you what I'm talking about."

Ryan gripped the butt of his gun, his finger on the trigger. "All right. But one false move and you die."

The woman reached into a pocket and slowly removed a 5 x 7 photo and tossed it across the bed toward the PI. He glanced at the picture and his heart sank.

The photo showed Erin Welch shackled to the floor. There was a black metal brace secured around her throat. He recognized what it was immediately. A bomb had been built into the neck brace. The kill switch was in Tanaka's hand.

"Drop the kill switch," Ryan ordered, "and I'll let you and Strada live. That's the deal."

"Bullshit," she yelled, her white eyes blazing. "That's a shit deal!"

Ryan aimed his pistol at a spot right between her eyes. "Take it or leave it."

"Fuck you, Ryan! Here's the deal. You let me and my husband leave and I won't kill the FBI woman."

"Hell no!"

"Hell, yes!" she shouted back. Her hand was still clutching the kill switch.

"How can I trust you, bitch? If I let you go, you'll set off the bomb anyway and kill Erin."

"You're highly trained, Ryan. If you weren't, you wouldn't have been able to break into this mansion. So you know how kill switches work. They use radio frequencies with a limited range. My husband has a helicopter on the property. Once we've flown away, the kill switch won't work."

She's right. But still. Can I trust her?

"Once I let you out of this room," he said, "how do I know you won't press the button?"

Tanaka's white eyes shimmered. "Because I have nothing to gain. Yes, I could kill your precious FBI agent, but you'd come after me and kill me before we boarded the helicopter."

Tanaka's right. She has nothing to gain.

"Anyway, Ryan, you really don't have a choice. You can shoot me, but I'm not going to prison. Not now. Not ever!" Her hand was still clutching the kill switch tightly, with one finger touching the black button.

"I don't ...want to die ...." Strada whimpered.

Tanaka's hypnotic white eyes blazed in anger. "Shut up, Karl!"

Ryan grit his teeth, his adrenaline pumping, his thoughts racing.

Finally he said, "I'll take my finger off the trigger and you take your finger off the kill switch."

"We have a deal?" she spat out.

"Yes, bitch, we have a deal."

Ryan noticed her finger slide off the black button and he lowered his gun.

Chapter 77

Vienna, Austria

Ryan, with his pistol trained in front of him, raced through the labyrinth of rooms on the third floor of the castle, looking for Erin.

Not finding her anywhere, he went down a floor to search for her there. When he got to the corridor he heard the loud whine of an engine and the spooling of a rotor blade. Sprinting to a window, he spotted a large helicopter lift off from the grounds and fly away.

He resumed his search, looking throughout the estate. Besides the maids, a gardener, and a few other house workers, he located no one else on the upper floors.

He continued further, searching the basement where he found a group of men huddled in a room full of computers and electronics. None of them were armed and all appeared terrified by the gunfire noise and explosions. After handcuffing them, he questioned a young Asian man who said he was the supervisor of the group. His name was Kobe and he appeared as frightened as his co-workers.

"What's this room used for?" Ryan asked, pressing the muzzle of his gun to the man's head.

Kobe's body trembled. "It is the Viper operations room." He spoke English with a Japanese accent.

Ryan nodded. He had already guessed as much, but wanted to see if the man would lie to him. "All right. I'm looking for a woman who's being held prisoner here. An American woman. Her name is Erin Welch. Where is she?"

"I have heard she is here," the man replied, his voice shaky with fear. "But I do not know where she is kept –"

"Tell me now! Or die now!"

"I swear! I do not know! I am telling the truth. But I do know there is a sub-basement, a floor below this one. She could be there ...."

"How do I find this sub-basement?"

Kobe told him and Ryan sprinted out of the room.

A few minutes later he located the cavern-like area. Along the rock-walled corridor he spotted a padlocked metal door.

He fired his Desert Eagle, blowing apart the lock, and he kicked open the door. It was dark and dank inside. He cautiously stepped into the room, sweeping it with his pistol.

Then he flicked on the overhead light and saw a hooded figure shackled to the floor. It was a woman wearing black coveralls.

Ryan crouched next to her and removed the black hood. He clenched his teeth at the sight.

Erin Welch had been badly beaten. Her body was inert. Both her eyes were black and blue and puffed up. Her lips were split in several places and congealed blood covered the cuts on her face.

He felt for a pulse – it was weak. *She's alive! Thank God, she's alive!*

Attached to her neck was the black metal brace Tanaka had shown him on the photo. On the side of the brace was a blinking red light and next to that was an on-off switch. He pressed the button and the blinking red light turned green, disabling the bomb.

Ryan used a knife to pry open the lock on the brace and he removed it from her neck. That done, he pried open the shackles and carried her limp body out of the dungeon-like room.

He made his way to the upper floors. Going into one of the vacant bedrooms, he stretched her out on the large bed. She was still unconscious, but she seemed to be breathing easier now, probably because the metal brace was off her neck. He covered her with a blanket. Finding a first-aid kit in the bathroom, he tried as best he could to clean and bandage the cuts on her face and neck.

Then he took out his satellite phone and pressed one of the preset numbers.

General Keating picked up on the first ring.

"Sir," Ryan said, "I'm here. Inside Strada's mansion. I was able to overpower the guards. I've arrested the computer technicians that run the Viper operation. I've shut it down."

"Good work, Captain."

"But I need an airvac. ASAP. I found Erin Welch but she's badly hurt. Needs to get to a hospital right away."

"I'll arrange it," Keating said. "I'll send a chopper to pick her up. We'll put her on a plane and fly her to Walter Reed Hospital."

"Thank you, General."

"What about Strada and Tanaka?"

"They escaped, sir."

"Damn! Any idea where they went?"

"No. Not yet. I'm going to search the mansion thoroughly, see if I can find a lead."

"Do that, Ryan. Anything else you need?"

"The technicians I arrested. They need to be transported back to the States and interrogated."

"I'll arrange for that also."

"Thank you, sir."

They spoke for several more minutes, going over the logistical details of the incoming support operation and Ryan hung up.

Then he began searching every room of the labyrinth-like castle, looking for any clues that would lead him to the fleeing Viper ringleaders.

Chapter 78

Vienna, Austria

Aki Tanaka tapped the helicopter pilot on the shoulder. "We need to make one stop," she yelled, trying to be heard over the roar of the chopper's engines.

The pilot nodded and Aki handed him a slip of paper.

Karl Strada, who was sitting next to her in the back seat, said, "What are you doing, Aki? We need to get to the airfield as soon as possible. My jet is waiting."

She turned toward him. "I have to do this."

Strada frowned but after a moment shrugged his shoulders.

Several minutes later the Bell helicopter yawned left and descended. It landed in the back yard of a modest home in the suburbs of Vienna.

The roar of the engines mellowed to a whine and Aki waited until the rotor blades stopped spinning. She climbed out and marched across the yard toward the house. The home's occupants, obviously shocked a helicopter had landed on their property, were already on the back porch, their faces showing alarm. Three people were there, a man, a woman, and a teenage girl.

The girl must have recognized Aki because she grinned widely and ran towards her.

Aki crouched so that she was eye level with Su-Wei, the 13 year old Vietnamese girl. "I came to say goodbye," Aki said, placing a hand on the girl's cheek.

Su-Wei's happy expression turned somber. "Where are you going, Aki?"

"To a place far away."

Su-Wei frowned. "But why?"

"Some bad people are after me," Aki said. "Karl and I have to leave Vienna."

"Don't go, please. You're the only real friend I have."

"You'll make other friends." Aki motioned toward the couple on the porch. "And you have your foster parents now. They'll take good care of you. I've paid them well."

Su-Wei grimaced. "I don't like them."

"Please, honey. Please try to make this work."

Tears formed on the girl's eyes. "I hate them. I want to be with you."

Aki caressed her cheek gently. "I know. I'd like that too. But I have to go away."

"Take me with you, Aki."

"That's impossible, honey. It's going to be dangerous. I told you, very bad people want to hurt me."

Tears rolled down Su-Wei's face. "I don't care if it's dangerous. You're ... more my mother than my real mother ever was. Please ... please take me with you ...."

She stared into the girl's almond shaped eyes, saw the anguish there.

Aki's heart pounded and her eyes watered. *God, this is hard.*

Making a split-second decision, she held out her hand to the teenage girl. "All right, Su-Wei. I'll take you with me."

The girl's face brightened immediately, a wide smile on her lips. She clutched Aki's hand.

Then Aki led the Vietnamese girl toward the helicopter and they climbed inside. The engines roared and the rotor blades whirred and the chopper lifted off a minute later.

Chapter 79

Headquarters Building
Defense Intelligence Agency
Washington, D.C.

General Keating scowled. "So you found no clues to Strada's whereabouts?"

"That's correct, sir," J.T. Ryan said. "I searched every square inch of that castle. He and Tanaka took their computers and files with them."

The general rested his pipe on the desk in front of him, the glare still on his face. "You let me down, Captain."

Kelly O'Shea, who was sitting next to Ryan, said, "General, in J.T.'s defense, he did manage to shut down the Viper operation."

Keating glanced at her. "I am aware of that." His lips pressed into a thin line. "But Strada is a billionaire. He can set up shop anywhere in the world. He has the money to fund a new operation." He snapped his fingers. "Like that."

Ryan nodded. He had already thought the same thing. "Sir," he said, waving his hand in the air, "I believe that if we focus the resources of the Defense Intelligence Agency, we can track him down. You have satellites photographing every country on earth. You have very sophisticated databases. And Colonel O'Shea is adept with computer technology."

"Yes, she is," Keating replied, his voice hard. "Colonel, I'm assigning you to this task immediately." He glowered at her and pointed an index finger at her face. "You are to work on this exclusively." He glanced at Ryan, then stared at Kelly again. "And you will not be distracted by *anything*. Am I making myself clear, Colonel?"

"Crystal clear," Kelly replied.

Chapter 80

Geneva, Switzerland

Aki Tanaka loved her new home.

In fact, she liked the sprawling, secluded estate adjacent to Lake Geneva much more than Strada's castle, with it's chilly labyrinth of rooms. The Geneva mansion was constructed in the mid-century style made famous by Frank Lloyd Wright. In fact, this particular home was designed by the renowned architect himself.

Lounging in one of the suede leather sofas of the huge den, she sipped Chivas and munched on her beloved peanut butter crackers. The smooth scotch burned slightly as it went down her throat, the liquor giving her that familiar buzz she craved.

The room overlooked Lake Geneva, and through the floor-to-ceiling windows she saw its sparkling water reflecting light from the brilliant sunshine. In the distance she could make out the snow-covered peaks of the Alps mountains. *A perfect day. A beautiful day.*

She toyed with her jewel-encrusted wedding band, the ring bringing her back to reality.

Aki frowned, recalling she and her husband's recent 'lovemaking', if you could call it that. *It's getting harder to fake a smile.* The wheezing old man disgusted her. His arthritic hands pawing her breasts, his pathetic groveling for sex, all of it making her almost physically ill.

She glanced around the beautifully furnished room with its priceless artwork, rich deep-pile carpeting, and exclusive architectural details. *At least I'm rich. Rich beyond my wildest dreams.* A smile played across her lips. *Put up with Karl. He's already in his eighties. How much longer can he live?*

Suddenly Su-Wei raced into the room, a wide grin on her face.

"How was class today?" Aki said.

"It was very, very good! I like my tutor."

"What did you learn about today, honey?"

"Lot's of things! About history, and math, and science."

Aki placed a hand on the teen girl's shoulder. "That's great. So you like it here?"

"I love it!" Su-Wei squealed. "I absolutely love it here!"

"I'm glad, honey."

"Thank you for bringing me with you."

Aki nodded. "I'm glad I did. Now run along. I'm sure you have homework to do."

The 13 year old girl grinned. "I do. And I can't wait to do it! I want to make you very proud of me!"

Aki nodded again, her heart swelling in an unfamiliar way. A feeling she'd never experienced before she'd met the young Vietnamese girl. *She's like the daughter I never had.* Aki's eyes watered a bit and she gulped down the rest of her drink, trying to push away the motherly instincts she was feeling. "Go do your homework now, okay?"

"Yes, Aki! I'll see you later!"

Then Su-Wei hugged Aki tightly and raced out of the den and toward her bedroom.

Chapter 81

Washington, D.C.

Kelly O'Shea yawned and rubbed her bloodshot eyes, totally drained. She was exhausted, having spent the last four days working non-stop, trying to locate the Viper criminals. The lack of sleep was catching up to her, no matter how much coffee she consumed.

Kelly forced her eyes to stay open as she flicked her gaze between the two computer screens. One of her laptops displayed satellite images of locations around the world, while the second one showed a very long list of properties and businesses owned by Strada – Austria Enterprises. She had been trying to pin down the billionaire's current location based on the activity at the properties.

On the desk in front of her was a yellow legal pad on which she was checking off each location, after she reviewed the satellite photos. She made a note on the pad and crossed off another property, then yawned and reached for her coffee cup. Draining it, she stood and stretched her arms, and then padded out of her small home office toward her kitchen. There, she refilled her coffee cup and began to brew another pot.

She rummaged through her refrigerator for something to eat. Finding leftover chili, she pulled out the bowl and placed it in the microwave. After turning it on, she went to her bedroom and put a sweater over her short sleeve polo shirt and jeans.

Just then her front door chimed. Tensing, she glanced at her watch: 11:35 p.m. Going to her nightstand, she took out her handgun and tucked it into the waistband of her jeans.

Kelly went to her apartment's front door and squinted through the spyhole.

She unlocked the deadbolt and opened the door. "You're a sight for sore eyes, J.T. Come in."

Ryan grinned and stepped inside and she closed the door behind him.

"Hope I didn't wake you," he said. "I got the red-eye out of Atlanta and went to DIA headquarters. They told me you had left the office at nine and were probably home sleeping."

Kelly yawned. "I wish. I brought my computers home – I'm still working."

He reached out with a hand and touched her cheek. His hand felt warm and comforting.

"You look tired, Kelly."

"Nothing another pot of coffee won't solve. Can I get you some? In fact, I was just warming up some leftover chili. I'll share."

Ryan nodded. "Thanks. I'd like that."

He followed her into the kitchen and she poured out two coffees and set them on the dinette table. That done, she spooned out the chili into two bowls, carried them to the table, and sat across from Ryan.

"How's Erin doing?" she asked.

"I got her transferred from Grady over to Emory Hospital. They've got a top-notch medical staff there. The doctor told me she'd be there for at least a week."

"Strada's people really hurt her."

Ryan nodded, a grimace etched on his rugged, handsome face. "They did. Erin's lucky to be alive. Those bastards beat her up badly. She lost a lot of blood." His hands formed into fists.

Kelly reached over and covered his hand with her palm. "I'm sorry, J.T. I know you and Erin have worked together for years."

"We have. She's the best FBI agent I've ever known. A true professional."

"Don't worry. We'll catch Strada and Tanaka."

Ryan spooned some of the chili and swallowed. "How's the search going?"

She sipped coffee. "Not as fast as I'd hoped. Strada owns lots of properties around the world. It's slow going."

"Can I help?"

Kelly grinned. "Are you a computer expert?"

"No."

"Are you good at analyzing DIA satellite photos for minute changes in topography?"

"No."

Kelly grinned again. "Then you can't help me, caveman."

"All right, smarty-pants," he replied with a chuckle, "you've made your point."

He spooned more of the chili and took a sip of coffee. "This is good food. I didn't know you were a gourmet cook."

"I'm not. But I do have a lot of takeout menus."

Ryan nodded. "Me too."

They finished eating and he said, "I guess I'll get going. I'm staying at the Sheraton Hotel by DIA headquarters."

"Don't go," Kelly replied. "Not yet."

"You said I couldn't help you with the search."

"I did." She reached out and covered one of his hands with her palm. "What happened back in Japan. Between you and me. Was that just sex? Or was it more ...."

He locked his eyes with hers. "It was more. A lot more. And we both know it."

"Don't go, then. Stay here. For a little while longer. Please ...."

Ryan shook his head. "The general said no distractions, remember?"

She grit her teeth. "I'm so sick of that man."

"That's insubordination, Colonel," he said in a playful tone.

She stood. "I don't care anymore. I know what I want."

Ryan got up from his chair, put his powerful arms around her and held her tight. She felt safe, and needed, and aroused all at the same time. She looked at his eyes, went up on her tiptoes, and kissed him hard on the mouth. He kissed her back hungrily, their tongues exploring each other's mouth.

Ryan hugged her tighter still, pressing his muscular body against hers.

With her heart pounding in her chest, she broke off the kiss, reached down with her hand and touched the hard bulge in his pants.

He groaned and kissed her again, locking his lips to hers.

Kelly was breathing heavy now and could feel herself getting wet. She broke off the kiss and whispered, "Let's go to the bedroom ...."

He said nothing, simply took her hand and led her in that direction.

***

Kelly lay on her back staring at the ceiling fan as it revolved slowly. She glanced over at Ryan who was next to her, asleep. Both of them were nude. The room was dim, but she could still make out his rugged features.

She traced her fingers lightly over his broad chest, not wanting to wake him up. *God, it was good. The best sex I've ever had. And more than that. A hell of a lot more.*

Even though he was 6'4" and muscular, and she was 5' tall and tiny in comparison, she had never felt more safe than today while engulfed in his powerful arms.

She stared back up at the ceiling, the exhaustion of four days without sleep now gone. She felt energized and refreshed.

Kelly rose from the bed and sorted through the pile of clothes on the floor. Locating her jeans and polo shirt, she slipped them on. Finding her scrunchie, she pulled her hair into a ponytail and put the scrunchie on. Then she padded out of the room on bare feet and closed the door behind her.

Going to her small home office, she powered up her two laptops and sat at her desk, her legal pad in front of her.

Minutes later she was hard at it, flicking her gaze between the screen showing the satellite photos and the one listing Strada's numerous businesses and residences.

It was tedious, eye-straining work, and after two hours of fruitless searching, she got up from the desk, stretched her arms, and went to the kitchen where she made a fresh pot of coffee. Then she peeked into the bedroom, heard Ryan snoring lightly, and went back to her work, now carrying a large, steaming mug of coffee.

Kelly found nothing unusual for the next hour, then spotted something interesting. Strada Enterprises owned many homes around the world besides the castle in Austria. One of his houses was a large estate next to a lake in Geneva, Switzerland.

She had noticed nothing unusual about it when she'd first checked out the property two days ago. The satellite images had shown a dim property with no lights on in the evening. That was from a satellite photo taken by the DIA a few weeks ago. She compared that photo to one that had been taken last night.

The change was dramatic. In the photo taken last night, lights shone from many of the windows.

Her heart raced at the find. Typing furiously on her laptop she brought up more images taken by the satellite today during daylight hours. Vehicles and people were evident on the grounds of the property where there had been no activity a few weeks ago. What was even more interesting was that no other surge of activity had happened at any other of Strada's homes from around the world, only this one.

Wanting to make sure this was indeed the right location, she spent the next thirty minutes hacking into the power company records of the city of Geneva, Switzerland. She compared electricity usage in this home now, versus weeks before. She grinned when she read the numbers. Usage was almost zero before but had spiked dramatically recently.

Still grinning, she raced out of the room, eager to wake Ryan and tell him what she'd found.

Chapter 82

Geneva, Switzerland

Aki Tanaka nodded to the armed guard standing by the door, used her keycard to unlock the knob, and stepped inside.

The operations room was a hub of activity as workmen erected workstations on the left side of the large space. The right part of the room was also busy. There, computer technicians were already hard at work at their fully assembled workstations, staring at computers screens while tapping away at their keyboards.

The new Viper room would be fully operational soon, once all of the equipment was set up. Even though Aki's technicians in the Vienna operations room had been arrested, she had flown in new technicians to Geneva who were more than willing to do the work because of the extremely generous salaries she paid.

Satisfied by the progress being made, Aki turned and left the Viper room and took the elevator up to the first floor.

She headed toward Su-Wei's bedroom on the west wing of the sprawling estate, eager to see how the teen girl was progressing with today's homework.

Reaching the closed door, she heard muffled sobs from inside. Aki's pulse quickened and she opened the door and went in.

Su-Wei was sitting on the bed, holding her head in her hands, crying.

Racing over, Aki sat next to her on the bed and put an arm around her shoulders. "What's wrong, Su-Wei?"

The teenager continued sobbing, her head downcast to the floor. Aki noticed the girl's clothes were torn and her arms were bruised.

Her heart breaking, Aki said, "Please ... please tell me what's wrong."

Su-Wei finally looked up at her, the girl's red-rimmed eyes continuing to water. "He came ... to my room ... and did this ...."

"What? Who?"

"He forced me to do it, Aki! I tried to push him away! But he's too strong ...."

"Who did this? Tell me!"

"Mr. ... Mr. Strada ...."

Aki saw red. Her face flushed and her heart jack hammered in her chest. She gripped the teen girl by the shoulders. "Karl raped you? Is that what happened?"

Su-Wei nodded, her expression terrified as more tears flowed down her face. Her body trembled.

Aki hugged her, trying to calm her down.

After a few moments Su-Wei stopped shaking. While still holding the girl close, Aki said in a soothing voice, "I promise you, this will never happen to you again. I'll protect you, Su-Wei. I swear to you."

The girl's almond shaped eyes looked up at her. "Really? I'm afraid of him. That he'll come back. And hurt me again ...."

"I won't let that happen. I swear, honey."

Su-Wei's terrified expression relaxed a bit.

"I have to go now, Su-Wei. But just for a little bit. I'll be back soon. When I leave the room, I want you to lock the door. Then I want you to shower and put on your pajamas and go to bed and try to sleep. Okay? I'll come back in a little bit to check on you and make sure everything is all right."

"You'll come back?"

"Of course, honey."

"Okay." Su-Wei hugged Aki tightly. "I love you, mommy."

"I love you too."

Aki stood up from the bed. "Now remember, lock the door. I have a key. And try to get some rest. I'll be back soon, I promise."

Su-Wei nodded and Aki left the room, closing the door behind her.

Aki's mind raced, her thoughts tortured, as she tried to process what her husband had done. *Damn that man! Damn him!*

She sprinted down the corridor, past her own bedroom and followed the hardwood floor hallway toward the east wing of the mansion.

When she reached Strada's bedroom, she noticed the door was closed. She turned the knob and barged inside, finding Strada by the floor-to-ceiling windows, staring outside.

"I can't believe you did it, you bastard!" she yelled, storming toward him.

Strada turned around and faced her, holding his palms in front of him. "I am sorry, Aki. I apologize."

"You're sorry?" she screeched, her white eyes flashing with hate. "You're sorry?"

"I do not know what came over me," he pleaded. "I was weak ... it will never happen again ...."

She raised her hand and slapped him hard across his face.

Strada flinched and rubbed the bright red mark on his cheek. He then stared at the floor.

"You raped a 13 year old girl! How could you, Karl?"

He shook his head slowly, still staring at the floor. "I was weak ... I could not ... stop myself ... please, Aki ... please forgive me ... I swear ... I swear! ... I will never do that again ...."

Aki's thoughts raced, her mind replaying the images of Su-Wei's terrified face, torn clothes, and bruised arms. Aki gulped in several lungfuls of air and let them out slowly, trying to calm her rage.

In a measured voice, she said, "How can I be certain you won't rape her again, Karl? Tell me that."

Strada looked up from the floor and fixed his gaze on her. "I swear to you! On my mother's grave! I will never do that again."

She placed a hand on his cheek and stared into his eyes, looking for truth, looking for something, looking for anything. *I admired you once. I used to look up to you. For all that you had accomplished. For being one of the richest men in the world. And now. Now you disgust me, Karl.*

"Please, Aki. I swear to you. It will never, ever happen again."

Aki saw red as the thoughts of a trembling Su-Wei with her terrified eyes crowded back in her mind.

She smiled. "You're right, Karl. It will never happen again."

Relief flooded on Strada's face. "Thank you, Aki! Thank you for believing me!"

She reached into a pocket of her flowing white pantsuit and removed the stiletto. Then using both hands she plunged the long knife into Strada's gut.

His eyes went wide and he staggered back. Blood spurted from the wound. He screamed as his knees began to buckle.

Aki stabbed him again several more times as blood splattered on his clothes.

He fell to his knees and collapsed forward on the deep-pile carpeting. His body twitched for another minute then he was still.

Aki looked down at the corpse and spit on it. "You will never rape her again, Karl. Of that, I am sure."

Chapter 83

Geneva, Switzerland

Aki Tanaka, her heart pounding in her chest, turned away from the corpse and went into the room's bathroom. She thoroughly washed her bloody hands in the basin, then rinsed her face, trying to wipe away the dark thoughts of Karl and what he had done to Su-Wei.

She glanced at the mirror at her appearance. Her white clothes had been stained by Strada's blood, so she cleaned them as much as possible with a wet towel. After hand combing her long, flowing white hair she left Strada's bedroom, closing the door behind her. Next she headed to her own bedroom, where she changed into clean clothes.

She left her room and found one of the guards she trusted implicitly. In a low voice, she said, "Go to Strada's bedroom. My husband has had a tragic accident."

The guard's eyebrows shot up.

"Strada is dead," she continued. "Dispose of the body and clean up the mess."

He stared at her for a long moment.

"You will get a large bonus," she said, "along with your regular paycheck this week. I'm also giving you a promotion — you will now be in charge of the security team."

The man nodded. "I will do what you want. I will follow your instructions."

"Excellent."

Aki turned and headed toward Su-Wei's bedroom to check on the young girl and make sure she was okay. But as Aki crossed the large den of the estate, she spotted the life-size chess set in a corner of the room. The stainless-steel chess pieces in this set were modernistic in design, keeping with the contemporary decor of the mansion.

She began toppling over all of the chess pieces, including the white King.

When she was done, the only chess piece that remained standing was the white Queen. A diabolical grin settled on her face.

Chapter 84

Geneva, Switzerland

J.T. Ryan steered the inflatable Zodiac boat over the lapping waves of Lake Geneva. There was no moon tonight and he squinted through his night-vision goggles at the sprawling, ultra-modern estate on the other side of the lake. The Zodiac's electric motor hummed, the low sound camouflaged by the action of the waves.

Kelly's DIA satellite photos had shown that the mansion was not as highly fortified as Strada's castle, but still had numerous armed guards that patrolled the grounds on a regular basis. Like in Vienna, making an assault from the water side appeared to be the safest way.

When Ryan was a hundred feet from shore he shut off the motor and began paddling the rest of the way. His head was on a swivel, trying to spot any guards that were in the vicinity. Seeing none, he continued paddling forward.

By his feet was his suppressed MP-5 and holstered on his hip was his Desert Eagle. He was wearing a Kevlar vest, a black camo uniform, a black watch cap, and black combat boots.

Moments later the Zodiac hit the private beach. He slung his rifle over his shoulder and climbed out of the boat. Then he dragged the craft ashore and hid it behind a sand dune.

Crouching, he gazed toward the single-story estate. Through his night-vision optics, the scene appeared a hazy gray-green and he zoomed in for a closer look.

Spotting a large man carrying an AK-47, he waited until the man made his circuit of the lavishly-landscaped back yard.

Propping his MP-5 on the sand dune in front of him, he tracked the guard's movement. He held his breath and when the man was ten yards away, he slowly squeezed the trigger.

The rifle coughed once and the guard crumpled to the ground.

Ryan's head swiveled again, trying to spot any movement in the back yard. Seeing none, he scampered forward and checked to make sure the guard was dead. Then he took cover behind a large, decorative fountain. He gazed in all directions and waited. This area was fairly well-lit from the home's floodlights so he removed his night-vision optics.

A second guard moved out of the shadows on the left side of the house and strode toward the back entrance. He input a code into the keypad and went into the home through the large patio doors. *A house alarm. Controlled by the keypad.*

Ryan mulled this over, wanting to maintain the element of surprise as long as possible. Coming to a decision, he propped his MP-5 on top of the fountain's side wall and crouched behind it.

He waited a full ten minutes and almost gave up the wait, when he saw the patio door open. The same guard that had gone in now came out. Ryan aimed his rifle, his finger on the trigger.

When the guard approached the door's keypad to reset the alarm, Ryan squeezed.

Thud. Thud.

The guard dropped to the ground.

The PI sprinted forward and hugged the back wall next to the patio doors. He crouched by the inert body and felt for a pulse. Finding none he dragged the body behind some nearby bushes.

Ryan peered inside the home through the patio doors' glass panes. There was no one in sight in the well-lit interior, a sitting area from what he could tell. He noticed the upscale furniture and paintings were very modern in design, totally different from Strada's Austrian castle. He slipped inside and closed the door behind him. With his adrenaline pumping he swept the room with his rifle.

Ryan moved deeper into the home along a wide corridor. He passed a den, a kitchen and a dining room, all of which were enormous in size. And all of them were dim and vacant as he had expected. It was well-past midnight and he guessed Strada and Tanaka were asleep.

Suddenly he saw movement out of the corner of his eye. He whirled toward it and pulled the trigger. His rifle coughed twice and the tall, wiry man carrying a submachine gun crumpled to the floor. With his heart racing, Ryan sprinted forward and using the furniture for cover, replaced the clip in his rifle with a full one. But when he tried to rack the slide he realized the weapon had jammed.

Resting the MP-5 on the floor, he unholstered his pistol and took off the safety. Advancing deeper into the mansion, he came to a circular open space.

Multiple corridors led off from this area and he peered around the wall at each of the hallways. There was no one visible in three of the corridors, simply closed doors.

But in the fourth hallway he spotted a Nordic-looking, muscular man sitting in a chair by a closed door. The guard was cradling a submachine gun. By the way the guy's head was resting on his chest it appeared the man was sleepy. No doubt the result of many boring hours doing sentry duty. *This is it. I'm sure of it. Strada's and Tanaka's bedroom.*

Ryan reached into a pocket and removed a SIG Sauer suppressor, which he screwed into the muzzle of his pistol. Then he dropped to the floor in a prone position.

Peering around the wall again he focused on the seated guard, who was about twenty feet away.

Aiming, he squeezed off a round.

Thud.

The man toppled forward, his submachine gun clattering to the hardwood floor. The man groaned and clutched his side. Ryan fired again and the man jerked and then lay still.

The PI scrambled to his feet and raced down the corridor while sweeping the gun in front of him. When he reached the closed door he pressed his ear to it and heard no sounds from inside.

Hoping to maintain the element of surprise, he took out his lock-pick set and fiddled with the knob. The mechanism clicked and he opened the door and slipped inside the dim bedroom.

One person appeared to be under the covers. Otherwise the room was vacant.

Training his weapon toward the king-size bed, he flicked on the overhead lights.

The bed sheets rustled and a beautiful Asian woman with long white hair bolted up to a sitting position.

Ryan recognized her immediately.

Tanaka's white eyes got big, then blazed in defiance.

"You!" she screamed. "You again!" Her shimmering white eyes bore into his and he recalled their almost hypnotic effect.

"Get up!" he ordered. "Now!"

"Fuck you, Ryan!"

He aimed at her forehead. "Get up. Do it now."

The Asian woman glared, but a moment later got up from the bed. She was wearing white silk pajamas, identical in color to her long, flowing hair and eyes.

"Where's Strada?" he asked.

"Dead." She let out a cold laugh. "I killed the old bastard."

"Bullshit. Where is he?"

She pointed toward the floor-to-ceiling windows of the bedroom. "I had him buried in the back yard. That's where he is."

Ryan motioned with his pistol. "Lay on the floor. Face down. And put your hands behind your back."

"What are you going to do, arrest me?"

"That's right. Although I should kill you for what you did to Erin."

An icy grin crossed the woman's face. "She's dead, I hope."

"Sorry to disappoint you but she's alive."

"Too bad. I hated that bitch for disrupting my operation. She deserved everything she got."

Ryan gripped the gun tightly, barely able to contain his rage. "Don't push it, lady. My finger's on the trigger."

"Go ahead! Shoot. I don't think you have the balls to do it."

"You're going back to the U.S.," he said. "Where you'll be tried and convicted. For multiple murders, kidnapping, blackmail, money-laundering, and twenty other crimes. You're going away for life at a Supermax prison. Unless you get the needle first."

"I told you last time we met," she spit out, her voice dripping with acid. "I'm not going to prison. Not now. Not ever. I won't be caged like an animal."

"You have no choice. Now lay down on the floor, hands behind your back."

She didn't move, just stared at him with her hypnotic white eyes. A cold smile settled on her face. "I'll give you a billion dollars if you let me go."

"Forget it, lady."

"Five billion! I'm not lying. I have it. I have much more than that, now that Strada is dead."

"I said no."

"Name your price, Ryan. Everyone has a price."

He motioned with the gun. "On the floor. Now!"

She grinned a seductive smile, her hypnotic gaze boring into his eyes. "I'll give you five billion dollars and me." She began unbuttoning her pajama top, revealing voluptuous, milky white breasts.

In spite of the tenseness of the situation, he stared intently at her delicious-looking body. For a fleeting second he almost lowered the gun.

"I said forget it, Tanaka. On the floor! Do it now!"

Suddenly she pulled out a long knife from a pocket and held it in front of her with both hands. "Hell, no! I told you before, Ryan. I'm not going to prison. Not now. Not ever!"

"Drop the knife, bitch."

"Fuck you."

"I said drop it."

"Come and take it! If you think you're man enough."

He aimed his pistol at her head. "Drop it. You can't outrun a bullet."

A grimace settled on her face. A moment later the defiant look in her white eyes dissipated, changing to resignation.

"I don't plan on out-running a bullet," she said in a calm voice.

Then she charged towards him, holding the knife with both hands. A split-second before she reached him, Ryan pulled the trigger.

The heavy gun recoiled in his hand at the same time that her head exploded.

Bloody pieces of skull and brain matter splattered on the wall behind her. Her headless corpse collapsed to the floor.

Blood began to pool around the body, staining the perfectly white deep-pile carpeting.

Chapter 85

Headquarters Building
Defense Intelligence Agency
Washington, D.C.

General Keating took a puff from his pipe and exhaled, the sweet aroma filling his office. He rested the pipe on an ashtray on his desk. "Shame you weren't able to arrest Tanaka."

"I agree, General," J.T. Ryan said. "But she chose death-by-cop over going to prison."

Keating nodded. "Well, it doesn't really matter. The important thing is Tanaka is dead. And so is Karl Strada. Do you really think she killed him?"

"I do. Aki Tanaka was a brutal, evil woman. I think she was capable of anything."

"But apparently she had an ounce of humanity inside of her," Keating said. "We questioned the teenage Vietnamese girl you found in Geneva. She's heartbroken over Tanaka's death. I think she saw Aki Tanaka as a mother figure."

"What's going to happen to her, General?"

"Su-Wei will be put into foster care, here in the Washington D.C. area. We'll make sure she's placed with a good family."

"Yes, sir."

"You did good, Captain Ryan. You shut down the Viper conspiracy. All of their computer technicians are in custody. Strada and Tanaka are dead. And we were able to obtain enough evidence from the Viper paper trail to arrest top executives in the social media industry who had become complicit in the conspiracy. Some key people are looking at very long prison sentences."

Ryan grinned. "That's great news."

Keating picked up his pipe, puffed on it and exhaled.

"And I've got even better news for you, Ryan. Something you've been looking forward to for quite some time."

"What's that, General?"

Keating opened a desk drawer, took out an envelope, and slid it across his desk.

Ryan picked up the envelope and removed the document that was inside. He scanned the papers quickly. When he finished reading them, a broad smile lit up his face.

"My Army discharge papers," Ryan said.

"That's right. You're no longer Captain Ryan. You're now private citizen Ryan."

"Thank you, sir."

"No thanks needed. You earned it."

Ryan nodded. "Sir, before I return to Atlanta, I want to see Colonel O'Shea. I looked for her earlier and couldn't find her in the building."

General Keating rested his pipe on the ashtray. "There's a reason you couldn't find her. It's because she's no longer here."

Perplexed, Ryan said, "What do you mean, sir?"

"I've reassigned her to a new duty station. Colonel O'Shea is now in charge of our DIA office in Anchorage."

"Anchorage? Anchorage, Alaska?"

"That's correct."

"But, why General? Why? Kelly should be promoted, not banished to the frozen north. I couldn't have solved this case without her."

Keating nodded. "I'm sure that's true. But as you know, life isn't always fair."

"Please, General. Don't do this to her."

The general gave Ryan an icy glare. "It's done. She's gone."

Ryan's hands balled into fists. "Sir, this looks to me like retribution. Because you suspect she and I ... well ...."

General Keating stood up. "I don't care what you think this looks like, Ryan." He pointed to the office door. "Now get out of here before I tear up your discharge papers and lock you up in Leavenworth!"

Ryan grimaced and almost slugged the general. He gulped in a lungful of air and let it out slowly. Then he got up from the chair, turned and left the room, slamming the door shut on his way out.

Chapter 86

FBI Field Office
Atlanta, Georgia

"Welcome back," J.T. Ryan said as he stepped into Erin Welch's office.

"Thanks, J.T.," Erin replied, closing the lid on her laptop. "It's good to be back."

He sat on one of the visitor's chairs facing her desk. "You got cleared by the docs at Emory, I take it."

"I did," she said. "This is my second day back at work. Good thing too – being cooped up in the hospital was driving me nuts."

Ryan studied the FBI Assistant Director. Her attractive face still showed signs of her injuries – one of her eyes was black and blue and there were strips of bandages on her forehead and cheeks. He also noticed a pair of crutches leaning against her desk.

"Well, I'm glad you're back at the helm, Erin."

"Me too. Thanks for getting me out of that hellhole. And thanks for killing Aki Tanaka."

Ryan shrugged. "I tried to take her alive, but ...."

"Tanaka deserved everything she got," Erin said. "That bitch caused me a lot of pain."

"I just got back from DIA headquarters," he said. "I want to fill you in."

Erin gingerly rubbed one of the bandages on her face and flinched. "Go ahead."

"First, the good news," he said. "The Viper operation has been completely shut down. Tanaka and Strada are both dead. And their computer technicians are in custody, awaiting trial. General Keating also said they've arrested several key executives in the social media companies who were complicit with the conspiracy." He paused and grinned. "And to put the icing on the cake, I got my discharge from the Army. Don't get me wrong, I love the U.S. military, but I like being independent even more."

Erin nodded. "Congratulations. Is there any bad news?"

"Yeah," he replied, his smile fading. "Kelly O'Shea has been 'reassigned' to Alaska."

"Why?"

"Mostly because General Keating is a first class son-of-a-bitch."

"Well, I agree with that statement. I never could warm up to that guy. So, I guess this means you and Kelly ...."

Ryan frowned. "We won't be seeing each other much."

"Sorry to hear that, J.T. You two were good together."

The PI let out a long breath and stared out her office window. In the distance he spotted a plane making its final approach over Atlanta's Hartsfield airport. Then he faced Erin again. "Yeah. Kelly and I clicked." He shook his head slowly. "I don't seem to have much luck with women, do I?"

"Cheer up. Look at the bright side. If you don't get tied down by a long-term relationship, you can keep drinking beer and eating pizza and doughnuts, and all that other junk food you like, anytime you want."

"There is that." He paused a moment, remembering something. He slid aside his blue blazer and unholstered his Desert Eagle. He ejected the clip and placed the pistol on her desk.

"I almost forgot," he said. "This is the gun you loaned me when the case started."

Erin stared at the weapon, then looked at Ryan. "Keep it. You did a great job putting the Viper conspiracy out of business. And you saved my life. Consider it a bonus for solving the case."

"Really? I can keep it? That's a $ 2,000 gun."

Erin nodded. "It's all yours."

"Thanks. I appreciate it."

She opened a desk drawer and took out a manila folder which she handed to him. "I just got a big new case, J.T. Thought you might be interested in working it."

Ryan scanned the file quickly and realized the far-reaching implications of the murder investigation. It implicated some of the most important leaders in the U.S. and around the world.

"Sounds dangerous," he said.

"Does that mean you don't want to work it?" Erin asked.

Ryan grinned. "Just the opposite. I want in. When can I start?"

END

***

About the author

Lee Gimenez is the award-winning author of 15 novels, including his highly-acclaimed J.T. Ryan series. His novel FIREBALL, a J.T. Ryan Thriller, was nominated for the 2019 Author Academy Award. Many of his books were Featured Novels of the International Thriller Writers Association, among them FIREBALL, The MEDIA MURDERS, FBI CODE RED, SKYFLASH, KILLING WEST, and The WASHINGTON ULTIMATUM. Lee is a multi-year was nominee for the Georgia Author of the Year Award, and was a Finalist in the prestigious Terry Kay Prize for Fiction. Lee's books are available at Amazon and many other bookstores in the U.S. and Internationally. For more information about him, please visit his website at: www.LeeGimenez.com. There you can sign up for his free newsletter. You can contact Lee at his email address: LG727@MSN.com. You can also join him on Facebook, Twitter, LinkedIn, and Goodreads.

***

Other Novels by Lee Gimenez

Fireball
FBI Code Red
The Media Murders
Skyflash
Killing West
The Washington Ultimatum
Blacksnow Zero
The Sigma Conspiracy
The Nanotech Murders
Death on Zanath
Virtual Thoughtstream
Azul 7
Terralus 4
The Tomorrow Solution

FIREBALL, a J.T. Ryan Thriller
is available at Amazon and many other bookstores in the
U.S. and Internationally.
In paperback, Kindle, and all other ebook versions.

FBI CODE RED, a J.T. Ryan Thriller
is available at Amazon and many other bookstores in the
U.S. and Internationally.
In paperback, Kindle, and all other ebook versions.

THE MEDIA MURDERS, a J.T. Ryan Thriller is available at Amazon and many other bookstores in the U.S. and Internationally.
In paperback, Kindle, and all other ebook versions.

SKYFLASH, a **J.T.** Ryan Thriller
is available at Amazon and many other bookstores in the
U.S. and Internationally.
In paperback, Kindle, and all other ebook versions.

KILLING WEST, a Rachel West Thriller
is available at Amazon and many other bookstores in the
U.S. and Internationally.
In paperback, Kindle, and all other ebook versions.

THE WASHINGTON ULTIMATUM,
a J.T. Ryan Thriller
is available at Amazon and many other bookstores in the
U.S. and Internationally. In paperback, Kindle, and all other
ebook versions.

Lee Gimenez's other novels, including
- Blacksnow Zero
- The Sigma Conspiracy
- The Nanotech Murders
- Death on Zanath
- Virtual Thoughtstream
- Azul 7
- Terralus 4
- The Tomorrow Solution

are all available at Amazon and many other bookstores in the U.S. and Internationally.
In paperback, Kindle, and all other ebook versions.

www.ingramcontent.com/pod-product-compliance
Lightning Source LLC
Chambersburg PA
CBHW021452240626
47154CB00002B/334